Blood for Breakfast

Sydney Newbern Book 1

Helen Bell

Copyright © 2020 Helen Bell
All rights reserved.
Email: Me@helenbel.com
Reproduction of this book and/or any portion thereof, in any media, whether written, electronic, oral, visual or tangible for without written permission of the publisher or author is strictly prohibited. No derivative works may be created without the author's explicit written consent.
This book is a work of fiction. No factual claims and/or statements are made. All character names are fictional, and any similarity to actual events is coincidental.
ISBN: 978-965-599-119-2

Table of Contents

Chapter 1

The first time I heard the wail from the other side of the wall, shock spiraled through me. Not because it sounded strange, unearthly, but because it meant I wasn't alone. The sobbing had occurred every single night at five past two a.m. on the dot.

Tonight was no different. As the wail erupted from the cell next to mine, I pulled the rough blanket over my head to drown out the din. Closing my eyes, I tried to go back to sleep but couldn't. The noise was not the problem; my thoughts were. They bounced like Ping-Pong balls being tossed around in a box. When they finally settled, they decided to replay that day, that awful day my nightmare had begun, three weeks ago...

Laurel, my college roommate, had invited me and some of our friends to her hometown. Her parents were going to be out of town for the weekend.

"Perfect timing to throw a party," she'd said with excitement. To me, she'd also suggested going hiking the day before the party, as both of us loved outdoor activities.

"I don't know. I'll think about it," I'd told her, getting ready for bed.

"Okay, but let me know by tomorrow night," she'd said.

The next day, my alarm hadn't gone off. It was nine a.m. Late for class, I jumped out of bed. Laurel was still asleep, snoring loudly, as I brushed my teeth and got dressed. After I was all set, I shouldered my backpack and dashed out of my dorm, skipping breakfast. Dark gray clouds hovered overhead. I zipped up my coat. It was about to rain, and I wished it were sunny. I needed a break from the constant rain.

"Hey, Syd, wait up." I heard June's voice behind me as I hurried to the philosophy building. I'd met June at freshman orientation, and we'd become close friends.

I turned, walking backward. "Sorry, June, I'm seriously late for class. Talk to you later."

She stopped moving toward me and waved a hand in the air. "Yeah, no prob. I'll see you."

A few minutes later, I reached the lecture hall. So did Professor Reed. I rushed to my seat and sat down.

"Morning, sunshine. Glad you made it. Hot date last night?" Ethan whispered from the seat next to me as Professor Reed started his lecture.

My eyes moved to Ethan. He looked at me through his mess of brown hair. His hazel eyes projected a bit of sadness.

"I wish, but no. Just overslept. Even Laurel's snoring didn't wake me up, and my stupid alarm decided not to work this morning. Where were you yesterday? Laurel waited for you." Laurel and Ethan had dated last year for a short period before they realized they liked each other more as friends.

"Yeah, sorry. 'Bout that. Kimberly called..." He didn't need to say more. The last two words explained everything. His ex-girlfriend had broken his heart when she'd transferred to another college, somewhere in Michigan. Preferring not to do a long-distance relationship, she'd ended their relationship, and now every time he heard her voice, he was a mess.

"Talking to exes you still have feelings for is a big no-no. You gotta meet someone new. Heal your heart. Oh, by the way, Josie—you know, my neighbor across the hall—has a major crush on you. She thinks you're cute. You should totally ask her out." I meant to cheer him up, but instead, he looked offended.

"Cute? What am I, a puppy? Thanks, but it's gonna be a hard pass for me. Besides, I'm kinda dating Cheryl now."

My lips parted with surprise. "Cheryl? Really?" I thought she wasn't his type. Guess I was wrong.

A guy in the row ahead of us turned. At his be-quiet stare, I pulled out my notebook, opened it, and wrote down: *are you coming to Laurel's this weekend? If you are, bring Cheryl with you.*

"I haven't decided yet," he whispered, and the guy who had silenced me shot him a glare. We kept quiet, and our focus went to Professor Reed's lecture.

When it was over, Ethan walked me to the entrance of the philosophy building. It was pouring rain outside. As we waited it out inside the building, Ethan spoke with Cheryl on the phone, and I texted Zoey. I told her about my possible hiking plans with Laurel and asked if she'd like me to stop by her college on my way to Laurel's.

My sister texted right back: *You betcha. You still owe me a drink, and don't think I've forgotten about it.*

I chuckled softly and typed: *see you Friday.*

After I sent the message and put my phone back in my jeans pocket, I decided I'd say yes to Laurel. And why not, actually? I loved hiking. I'd spent a great deal of time in the outdoors with my father when Zoey and I were little. It'd always been fun. Also, saying yes meant I'd get to see Zoey and catch up with her.

When Friday came, I got to Laurel's home, after I'd visited my sister. It was late, and we went right to bed. I slept in one of the many rooms at her parents' house. In the morning, the alarm woke me up. I was bone-tired but forced myself out of bed. I got dressed in a sports bra, pants, a long-sleeved shirt, a jacket, and hiking shoes, then went downstairs to the rustic living room to wait for Laurel to get ready.

I yawned as I looked through the window, which made up the entire wall. I took in the astonishing views of high mountains and green trees everywhere. The sun just peeked over the horizon, casting beautiful colors of red and purple throughout the sky.

"Top of the mornin' to you," Laurel called in a cheerful voice.

Her red hair was tied up in a high ponytail and, like me, she wore hiking clothes.

"Come on, let's fix some breakfast, then move our asses outta here. I wanna be there before the parking lot gets full," she said, and we moved to the kitchen. After we finished eating, I hoisted my bag over my shoulder, and we left the house.

Forty minutes later, Laurel parked at the empty trailhead of Bemis Ledge. I climbed out of the car and rubbed my hands together against the morning cold. The sky was bright and cloudless.

"Great day for hiking," I said.

"I know, right?" she responded as we headed to the wooden sign that marked the beginning of the trail. We climbed over loose stones until we reached an undulating trail that ascended through tall trees. I stopped to take out a bottle of water from my bag. Standing in front of me, Laurel followed suit. We drank and caught our breath for a bit. The chirping of the birds was all that punctuated the silence—until Laurel's scream pierced the air. Her bottle fell from her hand and hit the ground. She stared at something over my shoulder, horror painting her features. I whirled around to see what—or who—terrified her. A man, donning a coat, jeans, and a wool hat, was pointing a gun at us.

"P-please, we have no money." Laurel's voice shook.

"But take whatever you want." With a wobbly hand, I handed him my hiking bag, my heart thundering in my chest.

An annoyed expression on his face, he threw it to the ground and lunged at me, striking the back of my head with the gun handle. I slumped to the ground, and everything went black. When I opened my eyes, I was lying on a cold floor, alone, in a room big enough for a cot, a sink, and not much else. I slowly rose and touched the spot where the man had hit me, hissing with pain.

Where was I? I studied my surroundings. The windowless room was lit by a weak bulb overhead and had a heavy metal door at one end. The walls, ceiling, and floor were gray concrete. In a corner to my left sat a metal toilet/sink combination and a tiny shower with no doors. To my right, a narrow, wooden pallet covered with a nylon pad served as a bed.

I only just recognized that I wore different clothes: loose blue pants, a black T-shirt, and white socks, no shoes.

Cold fear slithered through me. How long had I been out? I looked down at my watch. Jesus, it was six fifteen p.m. I'd been unconscious for eleven hours. Feeling a mild burning sensation in my hand, I turned my palm up. What the hell? There was a number tattooed on it. 777. The skin around the black ink was red and puffy. Panic settled into my system.

I stepped to the metal door and pounded on it with the side of my fist. "Hello? Is anyone out there? I received no answer. I kept banging, but no one responded, so I eventually gave up.

After a few hours, during which I'd been racking my brain for ways to escape, the man who had threatened Laurel and me with the gun entered the room, clad in the same clothes as before but sans the wool hat and coat. His short, dark hair was ruffled. He was tall and around forty-five. His brown eyes were fixed on me, his expression grave. He was holding a glass of water.

I backed away from him. "Why'd you ink me? What do you want with me? Listen, you really don't want to keep me here. My father is a detective with the New York City Police Department. If anything happens to me, you'll be sorry."

"Shut up, Sydney." His voice was sharp with anger.

I frowned. "H-how do you know my name?" Had he forced Laurel to tell him? Oh my God, Laurel! "Where's my friend? What did you do to her?"

He moved toward me. I stepped backward until my back hit the wall. He closed the distance between us and extended his hand to show me a small red pill.

"Swallow it."

I inspected the capsule. What the hell was it? Poison? Drugs? Taking it was out of the question. I craned my neck to the side and saw an opportunity to escape; the metal door behind him was ajar. I ran toward it, but the door shut by itself. I scrunched my face with confusion. Was he controlling it electronically? I turned to face him, frustrated.

Lips pursed with anger, he came to stand in front of me, the pill in one hand, the glass of water in the other.

"Take it."

Petrified, I smacked the capsule out of his hand. "No. I won't swallow anything! Let me go!"

He gritted his teeth in rage and whacked me across the face with the back of his hand. The force of the blow knocked me to the floor, and I hit my head. Dizziness assailed me, and I sank into blackness.

When I regained consciousness, I found myself on my back, bound to the bed by leather straps around my wrists, ankles, and across my waist. I couldn't move.

"Don't you think this is a tad too much?" I said and hissed as pain exploded across my face when he hit me.

He stood by the bed and looked down at me. "I imagine you don't want to end up dead with a bullet in your head, like your friend. So I suggest you take the pill."

Dead? Laurel was dead? Oh God, no, no, no, no. This was not happening. He moved the capsule, which was between his fingers, closer to my mouth. I stared at it.

Angry, sad, and scared all at the same time, I blurted out, "Go to hell!" The side of my face hurt as I moved my jaw, but I continued talking. "It's not going in my mouth. You want to kill me? Do it now. Go ahead! Just do it already!"

He sighed. "Perhaps you don't value your life, but what about Zoey's? What about your parents'? Do you care about their lives?"

How did he know my sister's name? "You're crazy. The police—"

"The police—or your cop father—can't help you." He bent down, put the pill and the glass of water on the floor, and then walked out of the room.

He bent down, put the pill and the glass of water on the floor, and left the room. A short time later, he came back, holding a tablet. He approached the bed.

"Your entire house is wired with tiny cameras. Your parents and sister are being watched by my men twenty-four seven, inside and outside your house. Here's a live video feed from your living room, in case you don't believe me." He flipped the tablet around to show me the screen, which displayed my mother sitting on the couch while reading a book, unaware that she was being watched.

Shocked, I shook my head. "Jesus, you're sick. You need help, you son of a bitch."

He appeared unaffected by my insult. His cold gaze was on me. "One word from me, and my men will kill them. It's up to you whether they live or die. Do as you're told and nothing bad will happen to them."

Despair fell over me. "Why are you doing this? Why? Why me?" Overwhelming helplessness engulfed me.

He ignored my questions and repeated, "Do as you're told every day, and nothing bad will happen to them."

"Every day? No, you can't keep me here. You can't. Please let me go. I won't say anything. I won't call the police. I swear, just let me go, please."

He barked a cruel laugh and sat down on the bed. I wrenched my stare away from him in disgust, and he grabbed my hair, pulling it back and forcing me to look at his face.

"How stupid do you think I am, huh?" he said. "You're not going anywhere, so you better get used to the fact that this room is your new home."

"I won't stay here for long. I'll find a way to escape," I told him, sneering, and then immediately regretted my outburst. Provoking him was a bad idea; he had people—killers—watching my family. One word from him…

He tightened his grip on my hair until I squealed in pain. "Listen to me, you insignificant bitch. Escaping from this room is impossible." A few seconds of silence passed before he let go of my hair and stood up. "But," he went on, "let's entertain the idea that somehow, by some miracle, you manage to do the impossible and break out. What do you think will happen? Huh?"

"You'll murder my family," I said, feeling defeated.

"No. Your punishment for escaping will be worse."

Worse? Was there a punishment worse than killing my family?

"If you succeed in getting out of here alive," he said, "you'll find yourself all alone out there, without friends, without family. You know why? Because I will not allow you to return to your home, to talk to your family, to talk to your friends. I know who they are. You can't go to the police either. Remember, I'm watching your family's every move. One word to the cops and I'll order my men to off your sister and your parents. The same goes if you go back home.

"So you'd be free, but it'd be torture. Your family would be alive, but you could never be with them." A cold smile spread across his face, sending a shiver of fear down my spine. "But enough about that." He picked up the capsule from the floor. "Are you going to keep your family safe? Are you going to behave and do as I say?"

I bit back a nasty reply and answered, "Yes."

"Good. I'll unstrap you, but if you try to run for the door or fight me, you'll be tied up again. Understood?"

"Yes."

He untied me and said, "You'll be taking a pill like the one in my hand every morning instead of breakfast." He pointed at a security camera in a ceiling corner. "Then you'll look up at that, open your mouth, and lift your tongue."

My eyes went up to the small dome in the corner and then to the toilet and shower. So much for privacy.

"Pervert," I murmured as he handed me the pill. I downed it with a glass of water, and I'd been doing it every morning for the past three weeks.

The red capsule hadn't affected my body in any way, at least as far as I could tell, and I wondered what exactly it contained. Why did he want me to take it? What was he planning to do with me?

Since that day, I hadn't seen him, or anyone else, again, and I had a routine. Three times a day, the slot in the metal door opened—my only contact with the outside—and a food tray and other stuff slid in. Everything passed through the aperture: the pills, lunch, dinner, dirty and clean clothes, which were always blue pants, black T-shirts, white socks, bras, and underwear. Also, dishes and things I requested, like tampons. The soft light in the room was always on. Having no choice, I learned to sleep with it. Time dragged by as I languished in the dank room, cut off from human contact. When I wasn't contemplating methods of escape, I thought about my family, especially after I'd woken up from the loud cries.

Tonight, though, my brain decided to relive that day I'd been kidnapped, and it made me restless; I couldn't go back to sleep. When the sobbing stopped, I pulled the blanket from my face and looked at the tattoo on my hand. The black ink showed the number 756.

When I'd first noticed the ink had changed, I freaked out, then pulled some all-nighters to watch it. I'd learned that the number decreased by one every twenty-four hours. I'd come up with two possible logical explanations for the phenomenon: either I was going insane, or I was swallowing a pill that caused the ink to alter. Yeah, the second option sounded crazy. Which led me to conclude that maybe the first explanation was the only explanation. As if to confirm it, a male voice called my name in my head.

Get up and open the door. Push it, the voice said.

What the hell?

I leaped out of bed and spun in a circle to scan the room. No one was there.

Open the door, it said again.

Confused and hesitant, I slowly stepped toward the door. Okay, I had officially lost it. I shoved at the metal door with both hands, and it opened outward without resistance. Expecting it to be locked—as it always had been—I gasped in shock. How was this possible?

My initial impulse was to escape, to pass through and sprint out of here. My body, however, wouldn't listen to me. It was as though someone else controlled it, and I moved out of the room without urgency, no matter how much I willed my feet to run. When I stepped outside the room, excitement trilled through me. Was this really happening?

Uncertainty rolled over me as my hands trembled. I glanced around me. I was in a long, all-white hallway with clean walls, a polished tile floor, and bright lights overhead. Unlike the room I'd spent three weeks in, here it looked sterile. Along the hallway, many closed doors, also metal, occupied both sides of it. But the room adjacent to mine, where the cries came from, had no door.

I was able to stop my feet at the entrance to that room. Inside, everything was the same as in my room: toilet and sink in one corner, a bed against a wall on the other side. In blue pants and a white T-shirt, a barefoot girl around my age inched closer and stood before the entrance. She was pale as a ghost, a bit taller than me, with a delicate frame. She had long, wavy brown hair and... golden tears?

My face twisted at the sight of what must have been an optical illusion. I leaned closer to her. No, it was not an optical illusion. My mind was not playing tricks on me. Shiny liquid slid from her blue eyes, leaving two trails of gold as it rolled down her cheeks.

"Your tears, they..." My voice faded away while I observed them.

Her face contorted with discomfort. "Something powerful is coming our way. Must be a royal."

A royal? Who was she talking about? What was going on? As I struggled to make sense of it all, I also tried to figure out why she hadn't escaped.

"Nothing is stopping you from leaving the room, so why aren't you getting out?" I asked.

"I can't. Magic is sealing me inside."

I knitted my brow. "Magic? You mean magic as in abracadabra magic?"

"As in witch magic."

I blinked at her. Twice. I was not sure if she was serious. "I have no idea what's going on, or why you have golden tears, but—"

A sudden flood of something pleasant enveloped my body, and I felt a strong presence behind me.

Her eyes flitted over my shoulder. Shock appeared on her face. "Oberon," she whispered in astonishment. My first instinct was to flip around, but she stopped me. "No! Don't look back! Your human eyes... He's the king of the fae. You'll die."

The king of the fae? My human eyes? Magic? Clearly, she'd slipped over the line between reality and fantasy, so I turned around anyway. Or tried. In mid-movement, I lost control over my body again, and it stopped moving.

Close your eyes, the voice I'd heard in my head earlier said.

"No," I said, yet on their own volition, my eyes shut. When I attempted to open them, it was impossible.

A hand touched my shoulder, and the next thing I knew, cold air hit me, and the sound of wind moving through tree branches reached my ears.

"I've teleported you far away from your captor. He cannot find you here. I must leave now," the voice said outside my head, and then the pleasant sensation I felt vanished. I tried to open my eyes again, and this time, I succeeded. My body was connected to my brain again.

With my mouth open in disbelief, I scanned my new surroundings, the moonlight casting a soft light. In my hiking clothes again, I was in the middle of nowhere, standing alongside a long, narrow, deserted road. Bare tree trunks loomed on both sides of it. I pinched myself hard. Nope, I was not dreaming. Scared yet calm, worried but excited, I took a deep breath while digesting the fact that I was out of that room. I might be going insane—or already there—but I didn't care. I was free! And right now, it didn't matter how it'd happened—getting help was the priority.

At two in the morning, my chances were slim. Still, I didn't lose hope as I walked down the road, praying for a car to pass by. I'd been hiking for a while when a vehicle appeared in the distance.

I jumped up and down, waving my arms. "Help! Help! Please, help me!" The white sedan stopped near me. Its headlights illuminated the road ahead. The driver's door opened, and I did some more praying. *Please, please, please, don't let it be another psychopath, maniac, or lunatic.*

Chapter 2

A girl stepped out of the car, and I sagged in relief, although women could be dangerous too.

"Are you okay?" she asked, a cell phone in her hand. "Do you need medical attention? Should I call 911?"

The tension drained out of me. Offering to involve the authorities was not something serial killers tended to do before murdering their victims, right?

"Yes, someone ki—" I clamped my mouth shut. I couldn't reveal the truth; my family would be in danger. That man had warned me not to contact the cops if I ever escaped. Plus, I had no clue how I'd managed to break out. *What would I say? The king of the fae—or so I was told by someone with golden tears—rescued me?*

Right. The whole thing was probably just a hallucination. A silly hallucination I did not feel like sharing.

I forced a smile. "I mean, thank you, but no. I'm fine. Just got stuck out here without a ride home."

She stepped closer, and I got a better look at her. On her trim figure, she wore a skintight dress and black heels. She was in her mid-twenties with dark brown skin, straight, honey-colored hair falling over her shoulders, and dark eyes. Her arms were crossed against the cold as her gaze roamed over me. Then she glanced right and left, as if looking for something, like a broken-down car on the side of the road.

"How did you end up here? Are you alone?" she asked. Her tone suggested that wandering alone on deserted roads wasn't smart. *Yeah, totally with you on that.*

"I was with my boyfriend," I lied. "We got into a huge fight while he was driving, and he stopped the car, demanding that I get out. And now, I just really need a ride."

She gave me a what-an-asshole look. "He seriously left you out here all alone and drove off? Wow, way to treat your lady. Boyfriend of the year."

"Tell me about it. He's a complete ass, and I'm so done with him."

"I say good riddance, hon." A cold puff of wind disturbed her hair, and she rubbed her arms. "Look, I'm heading to New Haven. You can tag along if it helps you out, or you can use my cell and call someone to pick you up."

New Haven? Okay, now I had a general idea of where I was.

"I think I'll tag along," I said. "I have some friends in New Haven." I didn't, but it was better than the alternative: being alone on a deserted road.

I climbed into her warm car, and we took off. As we drove down the dark road, my teeth worked my bottom lip while I pulled a strand of hair out from behind my ear, fumbling nervously with it. What was I going to do when we arrived in New Haven? I had no money on me and nowhere to go. My sister went to college there, but since I didn't want to risk her life, I couldn't reach out to her, or my parents for that matter.

"—you with me? Helloooo?" A voice pulled me out of my thoughts.

"Sorry, what was that again?"

"I said you're lucky. On my way home from my friend's birthday party, I suddenly decided to change my regular route and took this one instead. Super strange, huh?"

"I don't know what I'd have done if you hadn't. Thanks for the ride, by the way."

She gave me an appraising glance before returning her eyes to the road. "You seem worried, scared. The boyfriend story was all bullshit, wasn't it? How old are you? Eighteen? Nineteen? Are you running away from someone? Don't be afraid to tell me, hon. Maybe I can help." I pondered what to say until she broke the long silence. "Or maybe the cops can. I think we should call—"

"No!" I panicked. "Don't call them!"

At my reaction, a surprised expression appeared on her face. She glanced sidelong at me before returning her eyes to the road. "Why not?" Her voice held an edge of suspicion, and it was clear she thought I had done something bad and illegal. I couldn't blame her. In her place, I would assume the worst too—*and then call the cops.*

Afraid she'd involve them, I decided to reveal what had really happened, praying she'd understand how important it was not to call the police. For the next fifty minutes, I recounted almost everything: the hiking, my dead roommate, my abduction, the hidden cameras in my house, my abductor's threats, the red pills, even the tattoo on my palm. I left out the countdown, the faerie king, and the girl with the golden tears. After spending three weeks in solitary, it felt good to talk to someone. I hadn't realized how much I craved human interaction until that moment.

I finished my story, and she shook her head slowly. "Wow, that's really messed up. So your bat-shit crazy stalker, why did he give you the pills? Are you sick?"

"No. I have no idea what the capsules were for, but I was forced to take them every day," I replied. "Now do you see why I can't involve the police?"

"Yeah, of course, but what about distant relatives? Friends?" The car came to a halt at a red light. "Can't you call and tell them what happened?"

"I prefer not to. I don't know what that man is capable of. I don't want to risk their lives," I said and noticed we'd entered an urban area.

She stepped on the gas, and the car lurched forward. "So you have nowhere to go."

"No, not at the moment, but I'll manage." I had to.

"You know what? Stay at my place for tonight. I'm just gonna make a quick call to my boyfriend, letting him know we have a guest. Don't worry about your family's safety, he won't involve the police either." With one hand on the steering wheel, she pulled her phone out of her purse and tapped the screen, then pressed it to her ear.

"Thank you, really, but it's"—I checked my wristwatch—"five to three in the morning. I don't want to impose myself on you."

"Nonsense. You are not sleeping on the streets. It's dangerous and cold—Oh, hey babe... Yeah, it was okay... No, no, everything's fine, just calling 'cause I need you to make up the guest room... I'll explain when I get home. See you in a bit. Love you too." She hung up and put the phone in her lap. Her attention returned to me. "I bet you're tired after all that crazy shit you've been through. Get a good night's sleep and you can figure out what to do tomorrow."

Her generous offer instilled a deep sense of relief in me. Yeah, she was a stranger, but spending the night with a bunch of homeless people sounded even less safe.

"I really appreciate what you're doing. You don't even know me," I said.

"That's right, so let's start with your name. What do I call you?"

"I'm Sydney."

She flicked on the turn signal and made a right onto a side road. "I'm Tess. We'll be at my place in a few minutes."

"Great."

After a few sets of traffic lights and some more turns, she slowed down and parked in front of an apartment complex. Tess's apartment was on the sixth floor. She unlocked the front door, and we stepped into a medium-sized living room with three large windows, all the blinds closed.

"Daryl, babe? I'm home," Tess called out, closing the door behind us and kicking her heels off.

Someone, Daryl I presumed, walked into the living room. Tall and muscular, he sported pajama pants and a long-sleeved shirt. His skin was bronze and visibly flawless—smooth, clear, and unbroken. He took a few steps toward us before jolting to a stop.

He scrunched up his face, his hand flying to his nose. "God, Tess, she reeks."

Tess seemed embarrassed by her boyfriend's rude behavior. "Babe, she went through a great ordeal; she was kept in a dirty room—"

He fanned a hand in front of his face as if I hadn't had a shower in a year. "It's not that. She... God, it stinks. Oh, wow, it's awful."

Okay, dude, we get it. I stink. Next time a psychopath kidnaps me, I'll be sure to demand a five-star dungeon with a hot tub and expensive toiletries. I sniffed myself. I didn't smell like roses, but I didn't reek either. What was his problem?

After a short moment, Tess's expression lit with dawning realization. "Oh, *that* kind of stink." Her gaze moved to me. "You'd better sit down for this." Judging by the way both of them looked at me, it sounded serious.

Bewildered, I took a seat on the couch. "What's going on?"

Tess sat next to me, and her boyfriend dropped the bomb. "You have cancer, final stage. The BFB in your blood is wearing off. That's why I can smell the disease, but quite frankly, at this advanced stage of cancer, even a Newborn vampire would be able to smell it."

Tess's eyes grew wide, and her mouth opened in an unexpressed gasp as if he had just let a big secret slip. "Daryl! What did you do? I was about to break the bad news to her and then tell her not to ask us how we know she's sick. She has no idea about the existence of vampires. Or that you are one!"

"She doesn't? Then how did she obtain BFB?"

I stared at them while Tess filled him in on everything I'd endured. As I watched them, a burst of humorless laughter bubbled up my throat. Unbelievable! I had the worst luck ever. I broke free from one psychopath only to end up with two lunatics.

Tess threw her arms in the air. "See what you've done? Now she thinks we're nutcases." She sighed. "Show her we're not."

To her request, Daryl opened his mouth, and fangs flicked into sight. Two gleaming, actual fangs! I shrank back, my stomach flipping over. Sweet Baby Jesus!

"Vampires are real," she told me.

The logical part of my brain refused to accept what was in front of my eyes. It just flew in the face of logic. Unlike my sister Zoey, who was a year younger than me, I'd never believed in the supernatural. In fact, when we were little, I used to make of her fertile imagination. I remembered how one day, when she was twelve, she came into my room before bedtime with excitement in her blue eyes. I placed aside the book I'd been reading in bed.

"What's up?" I'd asked her.

"At school today, I think I saw—don't laugh, okay?" she'd warned. Intrigued, I nodded, and she continued, "I saw a fae. Sydney, she was so beautiful, standing in the courtyard with a white dress and purple gossamer wings, invisible to everyone but me." She tied her chocolate-brown hair into a ponytail.

I couldn't help but titter at her active imagination. "Ooh, was the boogeyman with her?"

Her hands balled into fists at her sides, and her face flushed as she clenched her teeth together. "You promised!" She stomped toward the door, and before leaving, she tossed over her shoulder, "That's the last time I share my secrets with you."

It wasn't, though. Up until her senior year in high school, she'd kept telling me stories about the fae she had seen. Zoey had even claimed that the new girl in her class was a vampire. I'd always thought Zoey made things up because she loved to live in her own magical world. I, on the other hand, preferred to stick to the real world, where fae and vampires didn't exist.

Until now.

Chapter 3

How could I argue with my own eyes? Although it defied any logical thought, I had to accept the truth. In that all-white hallway, I hadn't been dreaming, and I hadn't been hallucinating. And in that moment, I wasn't looking at a human being. Daryl was—in actual fact—a vampire.

I swallowed hard as my eyes flitted to the front door.

"Don't be scared. I'm human, and Daryl won't rip your throat out or anything." Tess tried to calm me down while her boyfriend's knife-sharp fangs drove back up into his gums. He walked to the recliner in front of Tess and me and sank into it, pinching his nostrils. The room fell quiet. He was a freaking vampire, but if he wanted to hurt me, wouldn't he have done so already?

My muscles eased as I leaned against the back of the couch. "You're wrong; I can't have cancer. For one, I don't feel sick. Tired? Yes. Starving? Yes. Creeped out? Definitely. But sick? No. Secondly, my mother is a nurse. I think she would've noticed if I was dying from cancer. And what is BFB?"

"The thing that keeps you alive right now, and the reason you don't have symptoms," he answered.

At my questioning look, Tess explained, "Do you remember you said your stalker forced you to take red pills?" I nodded. "They could have been BFB."

"They most likely were, and the smell of your decaying body is a good indicator that it's wearing off," Daryl said.

Tess's eyes shifted from him to me. "When was the last time you took it?"

"Yesterday morning, at seven." My voice wobbled. Was I really dying? No, it was impossible. They were mistaken. "I know I was healthy before he kidnapped me. So what, suddenly I have final stage cancer? And what kind of medicine is BFB, anyway?"

"BFB is an initialism for Blood for Breakfast," Tess replied.

My stomach heaved. "Whoa, blood? Are you telling me that for the past three weeks I've been consuming blood?"

Tess nodded. "BFB pills contain the blood of vampires in the third stage of their existence."

"Third stage of their existence?" I repeated, feeling like barfing.

Daryl rose to his feet and stepped to a love seat situated farther away from me. Seeming to breathe more comfortably, he moved his hand from his nose.

"When my kind is born," he began, "we're basically humans with the same anatomy and characteristics. In this phase, we're referred to as Daywalkers. The sun doesn't hurt us, and we eat, sleep, breathe, and look just like humans. Then, somewhere between the ages of sixteen and thirty-five, something called the Change occurs. There are no physical signs prior to an impending Change. Or known triggers that would cause it to happen. A Daywalker between sixteen and thirty-five can wake up one morning, and all of his or her human functions stop. It's a process that takes about twelve hours, turning the Daywalker into an immortal who doesn't need oxygen or a beating heart to exist. A vampire."

"You don't breathe, yet you speak. Doesn't air have to pass over your vocal cords to talk?"

He became quiet, seeming to debate with himself whether to share more information about his kind with me.

"Daryl, she already knows vampires are real, so what's the harm in telling her more?" Tess asked.

"Yes," he agreed. "And she'll be dead from cancer soon, anyway." Ignoring the look she shot him, he answered me, "We do breathe, but it's out of habit, not out of necessity. And of course in order to speak." He rested his elbow on the arm of his couch and went on, "Vampires go through three stages in their existence: Newborn, Adult, and Ancient.

"During the first five years after the Change, vampires are babies. They're at the Newborn stage. Our laws state that an official guardian, an Adult or Ancient vampire, must be assigned to them. They guide and teach them everything there is to know about being a vampire. Newborns don't have the power to control the minds of humans. Their senses and physical strength are almost equal to your kind, and they have difficulty restraining their bloodlust.

"The second stage is called Adult for a vampire, like me, who is between the ages of three and one thousand in vampire years. We can control our bloodthirst if fed properly, and we have superior senses, speed, and physical strength compared to humans. Adult vampires have rapid healing capabilities, and our saliva heals human wounds, but not grave diseases or injuries. Like Newborns, any part of our body that has been cut off can grow back—except the head. And we can't control human minds, which we refer to as compulsion.

"The third stage is Ancient and refers to a vampire who is over a thousand years old. My kind's power grows with age, and Ancients are very strong. When we reach this stage, our fangs become larger and wider, and we can use mental compulsion on humans. Much stronger than an Adult's saliva, an Ancient's blood has healing properties that can save humans from life-threatening injuries and terminal diseases—permanently. But it has to be taken directly from the Ancient's vein for a human to be cured." He relaxed in his seat and crossed his legs. "Another thing about Ancients is that some develop unique powers like flying or empathy."

"Yeah, it's crazy. My boss, an Ancient, can smell how old a vampire is. So weird," Tess said.

"Why does the blood have to be taken from the vein if a human wants to be cured for good?" I asked.

"Because an Ancient's blood quickly loses its healing benefit when exposed to air," he answered. "BFB was invented by vampires for financial purposes. The pill contains dried Ancient blood coated with a special substance that preserves fifty percent of the healing properties. That's why in severe cases of diseases and injuries, the healing is temporary." He stopped and looked at Tess, wrinkling his nose. "It's getting worse, the smell. Are there any BFB pills left from when your brother was sick?"

"She can't take one, not until four hours from now," Tess reminded him, then pushed to her feet. "And yeah, we have five pills, I think. Hold on a sec." She disappeared into the kitchen. When she returned, she held a medicine bottle in her hand. She sat back on the couch, unscrewed the top, and spilled the contents onto her palm. "There are three." She looked up at me. "It's not a permanent solution for your sickness, so you have to drink one of these every twenty-four hours on an empty stomach. You have to fast for at least six hours before taking it, hence the name Blood for Breakfast. And you can't eat for three hours afterward." She dropped the pills back into the bottle. "Another downside to them is the price. One hundred bucks for a capsule. It's quite expensive."

My eyebrows dipped. "One hundred bucks for a pill? Yeah, I'd say so. Look, I appreciate your help and all, but I don't have cancer. It's ridiculous. Like I already said, I felt more than fine before that maniac kidnapped me, and I also felt fine, at least physically, during the time I was kept captive. If I was in the final stage of cancer, I think I'd feel some kind of pain, even with BFB, or whatever it's called, in my system."

"You don't have pain since BFB is temporarily healing you. And if you were healthy before, then your kidnapper did something that caused your body to get *that* sick," Daryl said.

Could he be right? Did I really have cancer? And was it even possible that someone had *given* it to me? Then again, was that any crazier than everything else I'd learned tonight? But if he had given it to me, how—

Tess gasped. "The tattoo!"

"What about it?" I asked her.

"Maybe that's what gave you cancer." She gestured to my hand. "It's there, right? Let him see the number."

I turned my left hand up, showing him the ink, then told them about it counting down.

Daryl's mouth opened in shock at the sight of the tattoo. "Dear God," he whispered and got to his feet, stepping to me, his eyes not leaving my palm. He sat between Tess and me.

Too captivated by the tattoo, he didn't seem bothered by my scent while examining my palm. "My knowledge of magic is rather sketchy, yet I can tell that what you have on your hand is extremely powerful dark magic. Something I have never seen before. And I'm one hundred and five years old." His fingers traveled over the black digits. "Your kidnapper is certainly not human. Even in our world, there are few who can cast such a strong, dark spell."

And apparently, I'd happened to stumble upon one. *Yay me*. I pulled my hand back and looked at the tattoo. "Are you sure it's dark magic? Can vampires sense it?"

"Vampires don't have witch powers. We can't perform magic, but we can recognize it, dark or regular, when we see it," he replied.

"Why is the magic on my hand counting down? What will happen when it reaches zero?" A subtle note of fear tainted my voice.

He stood up and walked back to his chair. "I'm sorry. I don't hold the answers to those questions, but I'm certain the cause of your cancer is the ink on your skin. The human body is not suited to withstand this kind of power. To be honest, I'm amazed it did not end your life right away."

Yeah, it only gave me a tiny annoyance called cancer. I had a terminal disease. To say I was shocked would be the understatement of the century.

"I'm dying," I mumbled, feeling like a truck had just hit me.

"You are. The dark magic is weakening your body and your immune system," he said.

It was a lot to take in. I pinched the bridge of my nose and squeezed my eyes shut. My head shook slowly from side to side. Why me? Why had my kidnapper done this to me? Why had he kept me alive with vampire blood? Tears clogged my throat when a comforting hand landed on my shoulder.

"There's an Ancient who may be willing to cure you permanently," Tess said beside me.

I opened my eyes and glanced up. "Really?"

"Don't get her hopes up. Asgard won't heal her. He's the cruelest among the Rulers of the United States," Daryl told her.

"Rulers of the United States?" I said.

"Vampires have a social hierarchy with the Ruler, an Ancient male, at the top," Tess explained. "The States have four Rulers. Each controls a vast area in the US. The Southeast and Northeast belong to Asgard. The West, to Djar. The Midwest and Southwest now have new Rulers, Ivar and Seth. The Ruler has the ultimate authority over all the vampires living within his area, and they owe fealty to him."

"Okay, vampires have an organized society, and the Ruler is like a king. So how does one set up a meeting with a Ruler?" I asked her.

"I work at a nightclub called The Dark Night, as a Donor, a human who volunteers to be a blood source for a vampire. Asgard is my boss. He owns The Dark Night. Lately he has been spending lots of time at the club, heavily guarded."

"Why is he heavily guarded?" I interrupted.

"Someone is targeting the Rulers of the US. Two of them have been murdered, Maximus and Ferdinand," Daryl answered.

I raised a questioning brow. "Two murdered? Aren't Ancients supposed to be like super-strong vampires? Undefeatable?"

"Which is why the Rulers speculate that the killings were committed by another Ancient vampire, perhaps even more than one," Daryl said.

Tess added, "But they don't have any suspects, and until they catch the perpetrator, Djar, the West Ruler, keeps his location secret, while Asgard is surrounded by bodyguards."

I looked at Tess. "Let's say Asgard agrees to help me. What good will his blood do if the reason for my sickness is still on my hand afterward? I'll get sick all over again."

"You won't," Daryl said. "The Ancient blood will destroy your cancerous cells. It won't eliminate the powerful magic on your hand, true. But as long as it's there, the Ancient blood will remain in your body and preclude your cancer from recurring. It'll protect you from other serious diseases too. You should know, though, that for Ancient blood to be able to fend off diseases constantly, it must be pure, clean from substances like high cholesterol and triglycerides. Asgard must be willing to stop feeding on humans who are at risk for a heart attack. Their blood tastes the best."

"I think Asgard will give her his blood, provided she'll agree to work for him," Tess told Daryl.

"Work for him?" My voice rose. "As what?"

She leaned against the back of the couch. "As a Donor. Face it: you can't go back to your home, at least not at the moment, or contact your friends, or call the police to report your kidnapping. The way I see it, hon, you need a cure and money. Asgard will provide both. I know for a fact that he's been looking for new Donors, which are not easy to come by these days. It's a win-win."

She had a point. If I rejected working at The Dark Night, how would I come up with the money to buy BFB pills? And after I was cured, I'd have to support myself financially while looking for a way to get rid of the damn tattoo and contact my family without risking their lives. I sighed. The thought of being a human blood bag in a club full of creatures with fangs sent a trickle of horror down my spine.

But it beat dying.

"The pay is really good," she continued. "You work four days a week, like me, give two, maybe three pints of blood every shift, and that's it."

My eyes grew bigger. "Two or three pints of blood four times a week? How are you still alive? Not allowing your body enough time to recover can lead to serious complications. Or death."

"True," Daryl said. "While not quite as strong as Ancient blood, an Adult vampire's saliva has healing qualities too. Once inside the body—in large amounts—it heals it by producing the same quantity of blood, up to three pints, that the Donor has lost after being fed upon."

I cleared my throat. "Um... how does the Donor consume the saliva?" I bit back a sound of disgust. Did I really want to know? No. Was I going to? Yes.

"There's another pill called S. It contains dried vampire saliva—much cheaper than BFB. Before every shift, a Donor is provided with S, free of charge," Tess said.

"And I'll be needing to take only one S?" I asked.

"For humans, the limit is one S pill every 48 hours. Taking more than that will cause damage to your body," she said. Okay, three pills a week didn't sound so bad. My thoughts drifted to another subject, and she lifted an eyebrow. "You look worried. Why? Other than that, the S pills are completely safe."

"It's not that," I answered. "If everything works out with Asgard, and I drink his blood, would there be a risk I'd turn into a vampire?"

Daryl dismissed my concern. "Humans can't be turned into vampires. You're either born one or you're not."

"Can vampires breed?" I asked.

"No, but Daywalkers can. Though, only with other Daywalkers," Tess answered as she leaned over to her purse on the coffee table and pulled out her cell. "Great, so it's all settled, then. I just need to talk with Mike, the vampire who runs The Dark Night for Asgard, and tell him that I'm bringing a human with me to my shift tomorrow night." Phone attached to her ear, she directed her next words to whoever answered her call. "Hey, hon, it's Tess. Mike with you?" Ten seconds of silence filled the room before she spoke again. "Mike? Listen, I have a friend who knows about the existence of vampires, and she's currently looking for a job. Wants to be a Donor... What's she look like?" Her gaze slid to me. "Straight brown hair reaching the middle of her neck, almond-shaped brown eyes. About five feet, three inches—"

"Five foot six," I corrected.

"No, sorry. Five feet, six inches. Gorgeous body. Mike, she's hot. The vampires in The Dark Night would love her." Tess was still for a short moment, and then a look of concern showed on her face. "Why does he want to see us? Is there something wrong?"

Daryl moved to his feet, tensing at Tess's questions.

After she listened to whatever Mike had said and hung up, Daryl asked her, "Does he know?"

Worry wrinkled her brow. "I don't think so." When she faced me, a forced grin touched her mouth. "Good news, Mike allowed me to bring you to the part of the club where the vampires are. Humans who hang out at The Dark Night, by the way, have no idea that there is a separate section for vampires. Anyway, Asgard will see you when we get there, and you can talk to him."

"I, uh, don't mean to pry or anything, but is everything all right?" I asked.

"Yeah, yeah, it's nothing," she replied.

Daryl stepped to her. "Tess, dear, I think it's time you went to bed. It's three thirty in the morning. You must be tired, and I'm certain your friend needs her rest too. Show her to the guest room."

She nodded and led me to a small bedroom with modern decor and a twin-sized bed. God, it'd been ages since I'd slept on something comfortable.

"Tess, I'm so grateful for what you and Daryl are doing for me. Really. Thank you."

She waved me off. "Don't mention it. There are some clean clothes in the closet. We're around the same size, so it shouldn't be a problem. The bathroom is across the hallway. Oh, and here are the BFB pills. You need to take one in three and a half hours. Don't forget." She handed me the medicine bottle, and I promised to pay her back for the pills once I got the job.

After I showered and changed into Tess's sweatpants and T-shirt, I set the alarm on the nightstand for seven a.m. and fell asleep. When the alarm went off, I took the BFB and returned to sleep. The next time I woke up, it was six p.m. Sitting up in the bed, I let my new reality sink in. Magic, fae, and girls with golden tears existed; vampires and magical tattoos, too. And I was dying of cancer. I was dying of cancer. I was dying of cancer. No matter how many times I repeated it in my head, I had a hard time accepting it. I glanced down at the reason I had a terminal disease and touched the number, 755. I wished I could get my life back, when my main concern had been keeping my GPA up. Self-pity crept its way into my emotions, and I pushed it away. There was no time for that; the clock was ticking on my life.

I slid off the bed and padded into the dark living room. The blinds were closed, and the sole source of light came from the kitchen.

Tess was sitting there alone, eating. "Hey, you slept well?" she said.

I smiled at her. "I did, thanks. Where's Daryl?"

"Still sleeping, and no, not in a coffin. Vampires don't really do that. And in case you were wondering, they do have a reflection." She grinned and motioned to the fridge. "There are some bacon strips, eggs, milk. Make yourself something to eat."

Starving, I fixed myself a sandwich and went to sit at the kitchen table with her. Tess talked about The Dark Night and warned me not to say anything about vampires to the human clubgoers in there. It was forbidden. I also learned that the first floor was for humans only, who were oblivious to the vampires in the underground cave beneath them. I shared my concern about being in a club full of bloodsuckers, and she assured me that humans, employees or not, were safe there. Though, right before we finished eating, she advised me not to wander off when we got inside the club.

After Daryl woke up, Tess took me to her closet and dragged out dresses: short, long, classic, sexy. I tried them all on. They were about a size larger, but the next piece of clothing she pulled out fit perfectly.

"It's my sister's," she said. "And it looks hot on you."

I stared at myself in the mirror. "Wouldn't she mind a stranger borrowing it?"

The navy-blue, long-sleeved dress ended halfway down my thighs and managed to give my small breasts a cleavage. My hair was pulled into a low ponytail. Everything looked perfect, except for the color of my skin. After three weeks without sunlight, it was as pale as fresh cream.

"I know my sister; she wouldn't mind," Tess replied and picked a black spaghetti-strap dress for herself, then showed me her shoe collection. "I never borrow other people's shoes. If you're like me, I have something for you." She lifted ugly neon-green heels. "They're hideous, I know, but this is the only new pair I've got. Daryl bought them for me when I started working at The Dark Night. Ugh, he has no sense of fashion."

I waved a hand in the air. "No worries. I'm sure the fashion police will give me a pass for tonight, given the circumstances."

I slipped into the heels and did a spin in front of the long wall-mounted mirror. Her face twisted in horror at the sight of the shoes.

"Well, the upside is that they're my size," I told her.

In the living room, we met Daryl, and Tess handed me a black jacket. Then we were on our way to The Dark Night.

Chapter 4

A long line of people stretched from the entrance of the club, down the road, and around the corner, waiting patiently to get inside. I followed Tess and Daryl past the line and right up to the bouncer guarding the front door. With folded arms and sunglasses atop his head, he acknowledged Tess with a nod and let us in.

Inside, strobe lights pulsed, changing colors around the packed room as pumping music filled the smoky air. The Dark Night looked like a typical nightclub, nothing hinting that vampires were nearby, feasting on blood.

I trailed after Tess and Daryl, weaving through swaying bodies. The crowd became thinner after we crossed the main hall. We passed the bathroom and turned left. A black curtain faced us. Tess drew it back, and we moved inside a vacant, shadowy hallway with black walls. We continued until we reached a door tucked away.

Tess laid her palm flat beside it, and a bald man in a black suit opened the door a second later. Light spilled into the hallway. His eyes met mine and stayed on me while we entered the room, his expression stony. Tess closed the door behind us, and the loud music stopped at once. Besides him, no other men occupied the windowless space.

"Jack, this is Sydney," Tess told him. "She's here for the Donor job."

He scanned the length of me, head to toe, then said, "Okay, she can go in."

Tess tossed him a smile, and we crossed to an arched passageway on the opposite side of the room. Passing through, I rubbed my arms, feeling the temperature dropping. Our shoes echoed across the stone floor as we moved toward a long stairwell. As we descended the steps, fear sent a shiver up my spine. What if something went wrong? What if I did something that pissed off a vampire and he ripped my throat out? I pushed the disturbing thoughts aside. *Everything will be fine.*

When we reached the bottom of the stairs, the scent of vanilla swirled around me. A row of scented candles lit the underground tunnel, along each side. The passage was paved, and the ceiling, limestone rock, was about nine feet high. With each step I took down the narrow tunnel, the stony walls felt as if they were closing in on me more and more, sucking the oxygen out of my lungs. Sweat gathered on my brow, my heart galloping loudly in my ears.

"God, I feel like I can't breathe. The air circulation is too slow," I said.

"Are you claustrophobic?" Tess asked.

"No, the tunnel is just a bit too narrow."

"Don't panic; you won't suffocate. Vampires don't need to breathe, but for the humans who work down here, they made sure there would be oxygen."

"I hope so," I told her as we kept striding forward. My heart still beat fast. A flashback of the small room I'd been kept in for three weeks popped into my mind, and I felt as if the tight space of the tunnel became even narrower as we continued moving. Then, a rocky wall stopped us.

"Guys, um, we kinda reached a dead end here," I said. "Maybe Asgard moved the vampire's section to another place?"

Tess put her hand in the middle of the wall, and it melted away. Music poured into the tunnel.

"The magic flowing through the stone recognized my hand as a Donor," she said at my surprised look.

I stepped into a spacious cave with Tess and Daryl, and the wall reappeared behind us, sealing me in. The metallic smell of blood hovered in the stuffy air. With my jaw slack, I stared around me. Soft light lit the sandstone cave, which had ornate vaulted ceilings and pillars. There were wooden tables, with candles in wrought-iron holders, scattered around the middle of a dance floor. A long bar was tucked against the stony wall, two bartenders attending to customers. On the opposite side, girls gyrated on an elevated stage with dancing poles. The cave was full, but not packed like the club upstairs. People were dancing, drinking at the tables, and feeding on humans. My skin prickled with discomfort.

As we traveled farther into the cave, Tess told me, "Stay close to us." Oh, she didn't have to tell me twice; no way was I leaving her side.

We passed by a table where a woman with a deep cleavage was wedged between two female vampires, one drinking from her neck, the other from the upper swell of her breast. Nearby there was another group of bloodsuckers. In only underwear, a poor man was sitting on the floor, his wrists and ankles cuffed with chains fixed to the wall. Three vampires, two males and one female, fed on him. Each drank from a different part of his body: neck, stomach, and arms.

Appalled, my steps faltered, and I grabbed Tess's arm. "I-I c-can't do this. I can't work as a Donor."

"What? Why?" she asked over the music and followed my stare. "Sydney, he's not suffering. The opposite is more like it. Look at his face."

I did. Oddly enough, pleasure—not pain—covered his features.

"If you don't work as a Donor," she went on, "Asgard won't heal you, and you'll die from a terrible disease."

I pulled in a deep breath. She was right. *I'll just close my eyes when the time comes, reminding myself how much I love living and having money.*

"Okay, where's Asgard?" I said.

She opened her mouth when a waitress carrying a tray of red drinks walked up behind her and tapped her shoulder. She had a blue pixie cut and a lip ring and was clad in a tight-fitting tank top with a low-cut neckline and a pair of black jeans.

"Tess, what are you doing here? Your shift doesn't start until one."

Tess turned to her. "Need to talk with the boss. You seen him?"

The waitress looked surprised. "Asgard? He's in his room, but I don't think

anyone is allowed to interrupt. He just started a business meeting."

"With whom?" Daryl asked.

She tossed him a half-smile. "Sorry, didn't catch the vamp's name; it was a bit hard to pay attention to anything coming out of his mouth as he was too damn hot. I mean, really, that kind of deliciousness is distracting and should be illegal."

A man approached the waitress. "No time for chatting, Emily. Back to work," he barked at her, and his eyes moved to me. "You, the new human, take off your jacket and come with me. Asgard wants to see you."

"Good, let's go," Tess said, taking the jacket from me.

"Alone," he told her. "You know his rules: no more than ten people in his room. He hates it when it's too crowded. Besides, Bill wants to see you and Daryl upstairs in his office."

The blood drained from her face as she took out her cell. "Yeah, right, no problem. I'll call and tell him we're on our way up." To me, she said, "We'll see you later. Good luck."

The man gestured for me to come with him, and my fear increased, beating against my nerves.

To follow him alone was the last thing I wanted to do; nonetheless, I did just that. I maneuvered my way through the crowd until we reached a wooden door at the far end of the cave. He knocked, waited two seconds, opened it, and ordered me inside. He stayed outside, closing the door behind me. The music died at once.

I was in a big room with a high ceiling. A dude in a brown button-up shirt and black pants with flawless, milky-white skin sat on a button-tufted couch placed against the rocky wall. The man's blond hair was pulled back in a ponytail at his nape. His blue eyes moved to me. Power radiated from him like heat from a fire, flushing my skin. Expressionless men with black suits stood on either side of his couch, three on his right, three on his left.

In front of the blond vampire, Asgard I assumed, there was a low glass table with an open case, and across from that there was a man clad all in black: black shirt, long black leather coat, black pants, black boots. From his profile, I could see that his skin, the color of porcelain, was unblemished too—a vampire. About three inches over six feet, he was standing even though a chair was next to him.

At Asgard's stare, I mumbled, "I'm, uh, Sydney. I, um... want to work as a Donor."

His eyes went to the vampire across from him, as if I hadn't spoken. "I'm at a loss here," he said to him with a faint trace of a foreign accent. "I was under the impression you intended to buy The Dark Night. We've agreed you'll pay half the money now and the rest next month, but the case is empty. Why?"

Rather than answering, the vampire dressed all in black asked, "Does the human really need to be in here?" He sounded displeased.

"You can speak in front of her. She's insignificant, just a mortal. Why is the case empty?"

Insignificant? I can hear you, asshole.

My eyes moved to the other vampire. It seemed like Asgard's reply didn't satisfy him. He didn't voice his discontent, though. Instead, he answered the question. "Because I didn't bring the money with me. I know the club is in a financial crisis—"

A flicker of surprise passed across Asgard's face before his expression was back to serious. "Who has fed you those lies? Didn't you see the queue outside my club? I assure you, the financial records of The Dark Night will prove that your source is unreliable, Mr. ...?" Asgard frowned as if trying to recall his last name.

"You mean the falsified financial records and the fake line outside the club that you staged to impress me?" the vampire said. "Seeing as I was the one who spent significant time and effort over the past few months ensuring The Dark Night would lose money, I think I can say I'm a reliable source. My apologies for the trouble I've caused you, but it was necessary."

What the hell is he talking about? I wondered.

Asgard's irises grew bright gold. "To hell with you. You never wished to buy my club, did you?"

The other vampire let out a soft chuckle. "Of course not. The Dark Night is a terrible investment. But driving your club to the brink of bankruptcy was a good cover story to get you in a room like this. Where there are no cameras and everyone knows you won't allow more than ten people in your office at once. That makes what, six bodyguards?" The vampire drew a dagger from inside his coat.

I gasped, shocked by the unexpected turn of events.

"It was a good thing I made sure only I can buy The Dark Night," he continued, playing with the weapon in his hands. "You were so desperate to sell that you let me in without having your security team search me. You'd have done anything to make me feel welcome. Oh, and call me by my first name, Gideon. No need for formality. After all, I'm going to be the last person you see before you die."

Asgard's bodyguards were already moving in, but their boss raised his hand to signal them to stay put, his eyes blue once again. "How old are you, vampire?" Asgard sniffed the air and answered his own question. "One hundred and sixty-five years old. A baby. And you think you have the physical power to eliminate me? An Ancient? A Ruler?" His tone was scornful and patronizing.

"Actually, I do. Maximus and Ferdinand would have attested to that if my dagger hadn't turned them into a pile of ashes."

Asgard shot up on his feet. His eyes turned back to gold, spitting fire. "You! You are the traitor who killed Maximus and Ferdinand? It is impossible; you're a mere baby!"

"Technically an Adult," Gideon said. "I'd love to continue our lovely chat, but the clock's ticking, my lord." He gave him a mocking bow. "And it's time to end your existence."

Fangs thicker, sharper, and longer than Daryl's tore from Asgard's gums. "I will cut your hea—"

"Nobody's killing anybody. Not tonight anyway." A familiar voice stopped him. It took me a few seconds to realize it was mine. What the hell was I doing? I shifted my weight nervously when Asgard's gold eyes jerked in my direction, his expression furious. He fired a how-dare-a-human-interrupt-my-threats look at me. I swallowed hard.

I had to defuse the situation. I needed Asgard alive. He was my permanent cure for my cancer. "Everybody just calm down," I said, but of course everybody didn't just calm down. Gideon, who evidently was the Rulers' killer Tess had referred to, seemed unhappy—to say the least—that I had drawn attention to myself, and Asgard looked even more pissed.

"Drain the mortal dry for not knowing her place, then burn her body," the Ruler ordered.

"But, my lord, we're in charge of your protection. We mu—" one of the bodyguards started to argue.

"He's an *infant*," Asgard barked. "Don't insult me. I can end him myself. You kill the mortal."

Gideon muttered a curse and turned to move in my direction, as if to help me, but he was stopped.

In a blur of motion, Asgard was near him, kicking his stomach hard and sending his body sailing across the floor away from me. His bodyguards closed in. Terror sliced through my body as they circled me. Oh God, I was going to die. One of them grabbed my arm and yanked me to him, lips curling into a vicious smile.

He reveled in my fear—which transformed it into anger. "Let me go." I scratched his face with my free hand. He snarled and punched me in the chest, knocking me to the floor. I gasped for air.

Hissing, I scrambled to my feet and moved to the door. It was locked, so I pounded on the wood. "Tess, Daryl, help!"

"Save your energy," one of them said behind me. I turned around. The vampires stood in a semi-circle around me. "Your thief friends are dead, and the room is soundproofed."

"Dead?" My voice was almost a whisper.

"Yes," the bloodsucker replied. "We caught them on camera stealing blood bags. Tess thought if she told Bill they brought you as a gift to Asgard and not to work as a Donor, it'd soften our Ruler. He ordered their deaths anyway before you came into the room. Too bad for you, Asgard doesn't like it when his sex slaves don't keep their mouths shut. He hates to be interrupted."

A sex slave? I was aghast. Tess and Daryl had betrayed me to save their own skins. Which meant I was completely on my own. In an underground cave teeming with vampires. The irony that I'd been safer held by a psycho in a prison cell did not escape me.

The vampire in the middle neared me. My back pressed against the door. I had nowhere to go, and he clearly enjoyed my helplessness. They all did. His fangs jutted out as he wrenched me to him. His head dipped to my neck. Sweat gathered on my brow. Each beat of my heart sent adrenaline pumping through my veins.

I expected to meet my death. Except I didn't. What happened next shocked me. On reflex, I moved back, squatted, spun, and with a low, spinning sweep kick—which I performed flawlessly—I knocked him off his feet. Before he had a chance to get back on his feet, I took off my left shoe, quickly straddled him, and plunged the heel into his chest. Blood poured from the wound and he screamed with anger, but he didn't die. If anything, I'd just managed to piss him off. As his eyes narrowed in rage, changing color, something slid across the floor toward me. It stopped near my bent knee.

"Silver through the heart will do the job," Gideon's voice said. As I grabbed the stake on the ground, I caught a glimpse of Asgard wrapping one arm around Gideon's neck while he tried to stab a dagger through his chest with the other.

The vampire underneath me pulled out my heel while telling me all the nice things he'd do to me, like ripping my head off, tearing me limb from limb, and gouging out my eyeballs. Not giving him enough time to make good on his word, I swiftly drove the silver stake through his heart.

I leaped back to my feet with the weapon and stared at the dead body, stunned. The vampire on the floor hadn't exploded into ashes, but he was dead. I'd definitely killed him. How the hell had I done that? I'd never taken any self-defense classes. He was twice my size, yet I'd managed to overpower him—in a minidress and heels, no less.

I snapped out of my shock when one of the leeches swung a fist toward my face. With reflexes I never knew existed, I dodged it and stabbed him in the heart while two other bloodsuckers charged at me. I took off my right heel to fight barefoot, turning to them. They stopped to glance at Tess's sister's dress, which was covered with their friend's blood. Their eyes changed to bright silver.

"Yeah, I know, I don't think a stain remover will fix it, either," I said and jerked to the side, avoiding another blow. I kicked out a leg and hit the vamp on my right in his stomach, sending him staggering back. The one on my left, I punched in the throat, grabbed him by the shoulder, and kneed him in the side of his rib cage. Then their friends joined the fight.

I expertly moved right, left, down, up as I blocked, dodged, and deflected blows from every direction, then punched, kicked, smacked, and struck back. I neutralized two leeches by breaking their necks with a swift pull of the jaw and then killed them with the stake. I did the same to the next two bloodsuckers who met my fist. I blew a wisp of hair off my face as I looked down at the floor. All of Asgard's bodyguards were dead. I snorted in disbelief. How? How was it possible? How had I kicked their asses in a matter of a few minutes?

The tattoo on my palm started to glow white, in and out, drawing my attention from the endless questions swirling in my head. I ran a finger along the ink. Was it responsible for my new martial arts skills?

A loud thud broke me out of my musing, reminding me I was not alone. I snapped my head up. Asgard and Gideon were still fighting, but the latter's focus was on my left hand. Looking surprised and distracted by my glowing tattoo, he got a punch in the face. The number ceased to glow. Gideon spat blood and went back to concentrating on Asgard. He dodged Asgard's next blow and struck him with a flying sidekick. When he recovered from the hit and charged at him, the sound of a phone ringing filled the space. Gideon whipped out his cell from the pocket of his pants, glanced at the caller ID, and pressed the device to his ear.

"A little busy here, Kate," he answered as he kicked Asgard in the stomach and knee. Then he picked up the dagger lying on the floor. "No, don't open the cave yet. Keep stalling," he responded to whatever Kate had said. Wincing in pain, Asgard growled when his opponent's blade sliced deep into his thigh. He collapsed to the ground. "I'll be there in five minutes," Gideon added. Asgard got up in spite of the severe injury in his leg, which caused Gideon to roll his eyes. "Make it six."

He hung up, slipped his phone back into his pocket, and fought Asgard for a few more moments before he thrust his weapon into his chest. I watched Asgard's body explode into ashes—along with the cure for my cancer. Gideon knelt beside Asgard's remains and slid his hand into his coat pocket, pulling out a vial as the door behind me opened. Music flooded the room. My gaze turned to the guy standing in the doorway. He was a vampire, no doubt.

"You gotta get out of here," he urged Gideon. "Bill's just killed a vampire and his girlfriend, a Donor, and now he's waiting to hear from Asgard. He's starting to get suspicious. Kate can't stall anymore." He glanced over at me. "Who's this?"

Gideon, who was now on his feet and no longer holding a vial, ignored the question. "Change of plan. Tell Kate to compel the blue-haired waitress and bartenders so that they'll forget I was ever here. Also, I want Mike and Bill dead and this room cleaned."

"Consider it done," the guy said. The door closed, and he was gone, the music too.

"This place will be crawling with vampire cops soon," he told me. "If you stay here with blood all over your dress, they'll assume you helped kill their Ruler. You'll think that too since your memory of me will be erased. You won't leave here alive. But your second option is to come with me, and I'll get you out of here—alive."

I considered my situation. Vampires shared a common desire: human blood. My blood. So, no, I did not trust him, not by a long shot. My initial impulse was to refuse, but he had a point. At the moment, he was my best option.

"Okay, I'm coming with you," I said. "Get me out of here."

"Wise choice." He opened the door. "Don't move. I'll be right back." He was out of the room before I could utter a word and returned a few seconds later, a pack of wet wipes in his hand. "Clean the blood off your face and neck. Hurry up."

After I did as he'd instructed, he took off his coat, revealing a tight black shirt, broad shoulders, and a narrow waist.

"Put it on over your dress."

I enveloped myself in his coat, a blended scent of leather and musk emanating from the collar. I looked down at my feet. "Wait, my heels."

He glanced over at them, his face twisting at the sight of the ugly neon-green shoes. "Leave them."

"Leave them?" I would be barefoot.

"Yes. Trust me, you should be thanking me for this. Now, stay close to me." He took my hand and drew me to him. "Act as my Donor."

Right. Like I knew what Donors were supposed to act like. His other hand landed on the door handle when I stopped him. "Doesn't Asgard have security cameras outside his room?"

"No. Down here, there is only one camera, a hidden camera, and it's in the room where the blood bags are stored. Upstairs, though, there are cameras, so keep your head down when we reach there," he replied, and we were out of the room. Passing through vampires and Donors, we walked to the other side of the cave where the entrance was. A woman with a blonde wavy bob haircut waited for him.

"Kate." He nodded at her. She touched the wall, and a portion of the rock disappeared, creating a gap leading to the narrow tunnel with scented candles. Gideon, Kate, and I stepped through, and the cave closed behind us.

"My men took care of the security team upstairs. The humans will be compelled; none of them will remember you." She glanced at me. Curiosity flicked across her face, but she didn't ask questions. "Rick is cleaning the room as we speak. The compulsion and getting rid of the evidence wasn't part of our original deal. As you know, my men and I are not cheap, so I'm afraid it's gonna cost you ext—"

"Just send the bill when you're done here," he said.

The corners of her lips turned up in a smile. "Pleasure doing business with you, handsome. As always." She winked at him, and we continued down the tunnel without her, then climbed upstairs. There, we waded through the crowd, and when we were outside the club, he swept me up in his arms.

"Hey! What are you doing? Put me down!" I demanded, which he ignored.

In a blink—literally—he'd crossed two blocks, and in the next blink, I was straddling a black motorcycle.

"What the hell?" I raised my voice, feeling the cold air on my legs and feet.

"What was that? Thank you for being a gentleman and not making me walk barefoot on a dirty street? You're welcome," he said with a sarcastic smile, then hopped on and sat in front of me. "Hold tight," he ordered.

"I'm not holding tight to anything because I am not going anywhere with you."

I was about to get off his bike when he revved the engine and drove off. The wind bit deep into my flesh, threatening to freeze me to death as he sped off like a maniac. Muttering about his bad driving skills, I held on to his midsection as his body quaked with laughter. At an alarming speed, his bike weaved back and forth, threading between the moving cars. A police siren began screaming after us, but his motorcycle picked up even more speed, and we whooshed down the road as he maneuvered the bike with ease. After blowing through a few red lights, we exited the urban area and lost the police car.

There was a short moment of silence before I heard him say, "Hold on tighter!" and then he tipped the bike to its side. My bare leg almost grazed the asphalt as we made our way around a sharp curve. I held on for dear life. Forget creepy prison cells and fatal diseases and vampire clubs. *This* was going to kill me. Then we were flying down a long road lined with green trees. Although he still drove like a lunatic, the rest of the ride was less frightening. When we turned down a street in what looked like a low-income neighborhood, he slowed and pulled into the driveway of a two-story house, then killed the engine. The next thing I knew, he was standing and swinging me up over one shoulder.

Alarm flared inside me. I pummeled his back with my fists, wriggling my hips down along his chest. Apparently all the freaky martial arts skills in the world did no good when you're flung over a muscular shoulder like a sack of flour. "What do you think you're doing? Put me down! Now!"

Paying no attention to my shouting as he absorbed my blows like I hadn't even hit him, he moved to the front door of that house, unlocked it, stepped inside, and flipped the light on. Hung upside-down along his back, I saw a foyer containing a set of stairs that led to a second floor. The entryway was simple and empty with no rug, table, or any other accessories. Passing the stairs, he opened a set of battered and warped French doors, stepping inside a large living room with white paint peeling from the walls. Like the foyer, it had limited furniture and decor: a black couch against a wall, a glass coffee table, and three white chairs. No TV, pictures, or flowers filled the room.

He strode to the couch and the second he put me down, I sucker punched him in his face, kicked his side, flipped around, and scuttled toward the French doors. I was halfway to them when he caught me on the back of my shin, just above the ankle. I lost my balance and toppled over onto the hardwood floor, hitting it hard face-first. *Son of a bitch! That hurt!*

Suddenly, on top of me from behind, he pinned me down, saying calmly, "Settle down. I mean you no harm. Your name is Sydney, right?"

I nodded.

"Okay, Sydney, I just want to talk to you."

"And I'm supposed to believe that because...? You brought me here against my will, and I happen"—I tried to draw in air, his body crushing me—"to be, you know, your food source."

His weight lifted off my chest, and he let me turn over. I faced him, breathing easier. Still on top of me, he propped himself up on his elbows. I exploited our new position and kneed him in the groin. His eyes squeezed shut as he moaned loudly and rolled to his back. I lurched to my feet and ran for the French doors for the second time. A string of curses directed to someone named Amelia flew out of his mouth. Amelia? Who was Amelia?

When I started to open the door, a blade whizzed past my ear—so near I felt the wind—and the tip of the knife thumped into the wood of the door, closing it shut with a bang, glass panels shuddering. I slapped a flat palm on the door and yanked the knife out with my other hand, then turned around. One second he was lying on the floor where I'd left him, the next, he was in front of me. *Damn him and his preternatural speed!*

I held up the knife. "Don't come any closer, or I swear to God, I'll kill you."

"I know you believe you can do that. You're good. The way you handled Asgard's guards, who were highly trained Adult fighters, was impressive. And surprising. Your fighting skills are excellent, no argument about that, but Sydney"—a small cocky smile bowed his lips—"I am not Asgard's guards. You'll be needing much more than a knife to take me out."

"We'll see about that." I peeled off his coat and dropped it to the floor, then swung at him. Or tried.

Every smack, every punch, every kick I delivered hit the air. The real damage I managed to do was to his pants. He glanced down, his fingers examining the cut in the fabric, and then his gaze returned to me. The mocking look on his face said, "That's the best you can do?"

Frustrated, I leaped at him. The knife in my hand poised to slash him, my fist ready to fire into him, but yet again, at the last moment he shifted his balance, and I wound up assaulting the air. I flipped over and tried to stab him once more. He caught the hand that held the knife, twisted my wrist, and forced me to let go. The weapon fell to the ground. He stepped on it and sent the knife skidding across the room, out of reach. Not giving up, I continued to fight him, using my new knowledge of martial arts. He wasn't hitting me back, though.

After a few minutes, it was clear he was waiting for me to become exhausted and admit defeat. I didn't. So he finally went from avoiding my blows to actually fighting back. And when that happened, I realized he hadn't been kidding earlier: he was not one of Asgard's bodyguards. It'd been less challenging to kick six big vampires' asses at the same time than the one before me. Gideon's strength was immense. At some point, his powerful kick tossed me across the room, smashing my body against a wall. Doubled over, I coughed. Everything hurt.

"Are you ready to talk now?" he asked, already in front of me.

As an answer, I gathered the little strength left in me and whipped my leg out, but he swiftly reared back and grabbed my ankle. Holding it, he pulled me forward, and I fell on my ass, shrieking. I got back on my feet, but before I could do anything, his hand shot out to my neck, cupping it and slamming my back against the wall. The force of the impact pressed all the air from my lungs. I saw stars.

His hand pinned my neck to the wall. "Have you had enough?" he snapped. I felt the restraint in his body; he was being careful with me. If he wanted, he could snap my neck like a twig. Yet I wasn't scared for my life anymore. He'd had many opportunities to kill me, including now; however, he hadn't. Then again, I'd thought the same thing about Daryl and Tess, and it turned out they were just using me. Still, a layer of tension peeled away from me. He wasn't going to kill me right now, at least. I let myself look up at him for a moment, or two.

The blue-haired waitress had been right. He really was gorgeous.

His face was chiseled with high, sharp cheekbones, a firm jaw, a strong brow, and milky-white skin, smooth and perfect. His straight ear-length hair was thick and pitch black, setting off two ice-blue eyes framed with black lashes.

"Good," he said, taking my silence as an affirmative answer and releasing me.

"I haven't had blood over the last twenty-four hours, and the smell of the bleeding cut from your leg doesn't particularly help."

"If I'm not your dinner, why did you bring me to your house?"

"Two years I've been waiting for you, so you can be damn sure I wasn't gonna leave The Dark Night without you," he answered and started toward the kitchen set on the left side of the living room, leaving me gaping after him in shock.

Chapter 5

Barefoot, dirty, and in a bloodied dress, I sat on Gideon's couch. Across from me, Gideon sank into a chair, holding a glass full of blood. He'd set a glass of water on the coffee table for me. I eyed it suspiciously. I was thirsty, sure, but after everything that had happened to me over the past three weeks, like hell was I drinking anything a total stranger set in front of me.

"Waiting for me for two years? What did you mean by that?" I asked.

"Two years ago, Amelia contacted me, offering a solution to a problem she knew I had. Sh—"

"Amelia?" I remembered the name. He'd cursed her when I ran toward the French doors. He sipped from his glass. "A powerful witch, well known in our world. She shared a vision with me. In it, she saw that in an unknown future, I'd come across a girl with a number, dark magic, on her left palm. Though she couldn't tell me when or where the encounter would take place."

"Did she mention that the tattoo would glow?"

"She said nothing about glowing dark magic. She did, however, emphasize the importance of taking you with me."

I was even more puzzled than I'd been at the beginning of this conversation. "Why?"

"Because you're the solution. Your blood has powerful dark magic in it, and I'll need to drink it in the future."

My hand shot to my neck, and I shrank back. "Hell no!"

He brought the glass to his mouth, finished his drink in one gulp, and set it down on the coffee table. He leaned back in his chair while linking his hands together across his stomach, extending his long legs and crossing them at the ankles. "Let's talk business, shall we? You have no money or a place to go to, according to Amelia, and now"—he smelled the air—"I also know you are gravely ill. Cancer. The smell is not strong, but it will be. It must be more than fifteen hours since you last took BFB. Soon the Ancient's blood won't be able to mask the rotten smell of cancer at all. I bet you don't have more pills on you, or an Ancient vamp willing to contribute his blood for you.

"To me, Sydney, it seems your days on earth are pretty... well, numbered. But they don't have to be. You don't have to die. Here's what I'm offering: in about two weeks, maybe three, I'll cure you—permanently. Until you're healed, you can live here and have anything you need: BFB pills, human food, clothes, money for personal spending, et cetera. In exchange, after I kill Djar, a US Ruler, all you gotta do is give me a half-pint of your blood. Nothing more. Just that. If you think about it, this deal is actually more of a favor for you I'm doing here."

My eyebrows lifted higher. "Wait a second. Cure me for good? How? I've been told only Ancient vampire blood can heal permanently, given the human drinks from his or her vein."

"Which is correct."

"I don't understand. Asgard said you were one hundred and sixty-five years old. Was he wrong? Are you an Ancient? How old are you, really? When did your Change occur?"

"When I was twenty-five, and in vampire years, I'm one hundred and sixty-five years old," he replied. "Asgard wasn't wrong; I'm an Adult vampire. However, I have different abilities from them—better abilities—like permanently healing humans from terminal diseases and severe injuries."

Yeah, right. How convenient. It sounded like some grade-A bullshit. "And what will assure me that you're not bullshitting me right now, that you're really not the same as other Adult vamps?"

His icy-blue eyes penetrated mine, his voice taking on a husky undertone. "Strip off your clothes, straddle my lap, and kiss me, then look at my eyes. This, I believe, will provide you with sufficient proof that I'm not lying to you."

His stunning features morphed into a smirk and, for a moment, I forgot the person sitting in front of me was not human.

Ignoring the heat spreading over my cheeks, I asked, "And how will that prove you're not lying?"

His head tilted to the side, as if he'd just realized something. "You don't have much knowledge about my kind, do you?"

"How would I? I didn't know about the existence of the supernatural world until last night."

"I see," he said and explained, "Vampires' eyes are affected by strong emotions, like arousal. An Adult's eyes will turn silver, whereas Ancients' will turn gold. Mine become gold as well."

My gaze dropped to his lips. "Why not show me your fangs for proof? I suppose they're in the same size range as Ancient vampires' teeth too, right?"

He rested an elbow on the chair's arm. "Wrong. They're like the Adults' fangs."

The room grew silent. He was waiting. Would I take him up on his suggestion and check whether the bright blue turns to gold when aroused? Of course I wouldn't.

There was another way for me to tell if he was lying. It wasn't perfect, but it was better than nothing.

"Okay. I believe you. I don't need to check your eyes."

I inspected his reaction. Slight disappointment—not relief—appeared on his face, which meant that he might be telling the truth. Though, I was still skeptical.

"Why do you need to drink blood that contains dark magic? And why are you killing the Rulers?" I asked, curious.

"I have my reasons," he said in a clipped tone, ignoring my first question.

"How come you're not like the other Adult vamps? What kind of vampire are you?"

"The kind who needs sleep when the sun is up, which will happen soon, so let's return to the deal. Do we have one?" The tone of his voice made it clear that he wouldn't elaborate about himself more than he already had. Fine. Whatever his story was, it didn't matter. To have a supply of BFB and a place to stay for a while, on the other hand, did.

If I accepted his deal, it'd solve half my problem. And there was the possibility he was not lying about his blood.

"Yes, we have a deal," I agreed, then said, "But why do we have to wait two weeks before you heal me?"

He nodded to my tattoo. "It's pure dark magic. Very strong. And rare. Therefore, destroying your cancer will entail strengthening my healing ability. For that, I'll have to go on a detox diet for two weeks, maybe three.

I'll be drinking blood bags of healthy humans with no high cholesterol and triglycerides. In other words, dull blood without flavor."

Right, Daryl had said something about that. "Is it safe for vampires, for you, to drink from a human who has BFB in his or her system, like my blood?"

Humor danced in his eyes. "Why? Considering offering yourself as my Donor? If so, don't worry; drinking a vampire's or Daywalker's blood doesn't affect other vampires in any way. Though it doesn't nourish our body."

I shot him an annoyed look. "Be your Donor? You wish. I'd let fangs pierce my throat only if I absolutely have to."

He shrugged. "Pity. Humans find it rather pleasurable."

"I guarantee you, I won't be one of them. In fact, after I give you my blood, I think I'll start eating tons of raw garlic every day." My social life would go extinct, but hey, at least the garlic would ward off vampires.

A soft laugh broke free from his chest before he said, "We have no aversion to crosses, holy water, or garlic, and they're not lethal to us. Same for wooden stakes, electrocution, poisons of any kind, drugs, and regular bullets. We are pretty hard to kill. Unless you stab, stake, or shoot us through the heart with silver, or decapitate us, we won't die. Our eyes, though, are very susceptible to pain. If you stab a vampire there, it won't kill him, but it'll hurt long after it's healed and regenerated."

"What about the sun?"

"We won't burst into flame, but we'll contract the UV virus, and it'll end our existence painfully."

"The UV virus?"

"All vampires are born with a virus in a dormant state. Once the Change happens, it becomes active after exposure to sunlight for more than an hour, give or take. This is why direct rays from the sun cause excruciating pain to vampires. Like a reflex, it intends to protect our body, to force us away from sunlight.

"The UV virus is the only disease vampires can be infected with, and it has a few stages. First, you feel weakness, then you experience more severe symptoms such as aggression and extreme bleeding from the nose and mouth. The final stage is when your internal organs melt as you beg for death to come."

"God, it sounds awful," I said as I scratched my left palm.

"Indeed, it's a nasty disease." His eyes slipped down to the tattoo. "Does it hurt?"

"No. It sometimes itches, though."

"I'm astonished you survived the spell. Most humans wouldn't have."

"Yeah, but now I have cancer, courtesy of the dark magic on my hand. Does the witch, Amelia, happen to know how to take it off?"

He put his elbows on his knees, clasping his hands together. "It cannot be removed. It's a potent spell that even Amelia wouldn't be able to undo. What I don't understand is how you ended up with it in the first place."

"Someone kidnapped me," I told him, "and I woke up alone in a small room with a number tattoo going down by one every twenty-four hours. Now that I've escaped, my family is my kidnapper's leverage. If I try to contact them or the police, he'll hurt them. Did Amelia say why I was kidnapped or why the tattoo is counting down?"

He shook his head. "The vision was limited. Her Voice didn't reveal much." At my confused frown, he said, "Every witch has an inner voice. It whispers whenever it senses things, especially during a vision. In your case, Amelia's Voice whispered that you'd have no money, that you'd have nowhere to go, and that I'd need your blood."

"And my consent to take it," I added. Why else would he strike a deal with me when he could just draw my blood without asking? He was way stronger than I was, and I doubted vampires had moral rectitude.

"That too," he reluctantly conceded. Yeah, we needed each other *equally*.

"So I guess our deal is not a favor you're doing for me," I pointed out.

"I guess it's not," he agreed with a tiny smile, then changed the subject. "Did you know your abductor?"

"I didn't," I answered. "And I have no idea why he chose me. I mean, before all this crazy shit, I was a normal sophomore in college, living a boring life, nothing out of the ordinary, really."

"Not that I'm hinting you don't have a... lovely personality," a corner of his lips quirked up a little, "but perhaps you managed to piss off someone who later orchestrated your abduction."

Um, maybe he was on to something. Why hadn't I thought of that during my time in captivity? Probably because my mind had been honed in on other things, like why the number on my hand was changing every twenty-four hours.

I chewed on my bottom lip. Who could I have angered so badly that he or she would do this to me? A name popped into my head: Jared, my jerk ex-boyfriend from high school.

It'd been an ugly breakup. We'd been together for two years. I believed he loved me. I loved him. Loved everything about him: his smile, his look, his patience.

He never pressured me into having sex. As a matter of fact, kissing was all we ever did.

When I was ready to have sex for the first time on the night of our senior prom, he insisted we keep waiting. Since he wasn't a virgin, I'd thought it was weird, but I said nothing until last year when things exploded between us. His parents were out of town, and I went over to his empty house with a box of condoms in my purse. After we went up to his room, I initiated the first contact, as I always had, kissing him, taking off my shirt. He pushed me away from him. I was humiliated. Did my touch repulse him?

"Are you even attracted to me?" I'd asked him, hurt.

His answer had shattered my heart into tiny fragments. "Sorry, Syd, it's not you I want; it's Zoey. She's the reason I started dating you. I'm in love with her, I always have been, but she turned me down. I had to make her fall in love with me. Being with you meant being close to her, but now you had to ruin everything. Zoey would never have me if I slept with her sister."

Anger flooded me. "Your chances with her dropped to zero the minute you started dating me, you moron. Zoey would never go out with her sister's ex-boyfriends, especially the jerk ones."

I stomped out of his house and ran to mine, tears exploding in a hot rush. All night I'd cried as Zoey comforted me. It really threw her for a loop to hear what Jared did, and the next day she'd screamed at him, saying she wouldn't date him even if he were the last guy on earth.

I imagined he was mad at me, but enough to have me kidnapped and poisoned with powerful dark magic? No, he wasn't *that* crazy. Or sophisticated. So if not him, then who? I hadn't gone out with anyone else since Jared, my first and only boyfriend, and there was no bad blood with any of my friends, no—

"Must be a long list," Gideon's teasing voice said, earning him a roll of my eyes.

"I don't think it's someone from my past, and I doubt anyone in my social circle developed a sudden desire to infect me with dark magic that on the one hand weakens my immune system but on the other, turns me into a kick-ass fighter."

His brows drew together. "Hold on. You have never learned any martial arts before?"

"No, never. Why?"

"Remarkable," he muttered, his gaze on the tattoo. "Dark magic sometimes enhances physical strength, so that the host will protect it, but rarely does it affect the brain by sending it knowledge of fighting movements. Whoever cast the spell must be very powerful, even more so than Amelia. How did you escape him?"

"There was someone there. I think his name was Oberon. He freed me."

"Oberon? The king of the fae?" He leaned back, his head cocking to the side, no doubt wondering if he'd heard me correctly.

"Yes. Him. The king of the fae."

"Impossible. Mortals will die from fear if they look at a royal fae, not to mention that royal fae rarely bother themselves to cross over to our world."

"Cross over? Where do fae live?"

"The realm of faerie is in another dimension," he answered.

The image of the girl with golden tears appeared in my mind. She'd called my rescuer Oberon, the king of the fae. Had she been wrong?

"I'm not sure if it was actually him who freed me, but whoever he was, he spoke in my head and got me out. A girl—do you have ice cream in your freezer?"

What? Why had I just asked him that?

A dark brow arched at me. "Ice cream? Now?"

I shook my head and opened my mouth to try again. The words that should have—but didn't—come out of my mouth were: I'm sorry, I meant to say that a girl with golden tears referred to him as Oberon, the king of the fae. However, what Gideon heard was, "Yes, I really, really, really want ice cream." *What gives?* He looked at me. Blinked. *I know what you're thinking, and you're right. I just lost it.*

"Okay," he said slowly. "When I buy the BFB, I'll also pick up some—"

I made another attempt. A failed attempt. "No, you don't understand. I want ice cream like now. I crave it!" I gasped at my unintentional outburst, then heaved a big breath and tried once more. But four times, it was ice cream, ice cream, ice cream, ice cream. Son of a bitch! I couldn't even ask why it was impossible for me to mention that girl. Damn it! She'd done something to me, maybe cast a spell or whatever, but why?

Gideon's cell rang, cutting me off. He answered it, still eyeing me warily, and a few seconds later, asked the person on the other end, "When and where?" He received a response and before hanging up, said, "Okay, I'll be there."

He stood up, his attention on me. "Unfortunately your craving for ice cream will have to wait. That was Philippe, a vampire who sometimes sells me useful information. He wants to meet up, and you're coming along." He nodded to my left hand. "He may know something about the tattoo."

"Go with you now?" My gaze dropped to the bloodied dress and my bare feet.

"We'll leave after you've showered and changed clothes."

"What clothes? I don't have any."

"Follow me."

As we moved to the second floor, he explained that after Amelia had estimated my size, from her vision, he'd purchased clothes and shoes for me in advance. I murmured a thank you as we reached the top of the stairs. He pointed out a bathroom, his bedroom, and the room I'd be sleeping in for the next two weeks or so.

He opened its door for me, not coming inside with me. "I'm heading out to buy a few things. I'll be back before you finish getting ready. Philippe is having a party now, so put on something sexy. Wear one of the black dresses and the black heels." It sounded more like an order than a suggestion.

"I think I'll..." My voice faded away as I turned and faced an empty doorway. "Jerk," I said under my breath and studied my temporary bedroom.

It had a twin-sized bed, a walnut nightstand next to it, a built-in closet, a mirror dresser, and a window with a view of the street. I stepped to it and stared up at the bright moon and stars, then at the neighborhood. I was far away from my home. A twinge of sadness crept into my heart. I wished I had a way to reach out to my family without risking their lives. On second thought, maybe not being able to go back home was for the best.

After all, what would I say? "Hey, Mom, hey, Dad, I have cancer, final stage, caused by dark magic. Yup, magic is real. Vampires, fae, and witches exist too." I envisioned their reactions: my mom crying, my dad freaking out, Zoey hugging me. *What a mess.* No, they couldn't know about my cancer and the supernatural world. Ignorance is sometimes bliss. Until I was cured for good, until I was sure they were safe from that man, I wouldn't try finding a way to contact them. A gentle wind brushed my face, and I closed the window, heading outside the room with a clean towel.

In the bathroom, under the hot spray of water, I felt the tightly knotted muscles give way to relaxation, arching my neck and soaping my hair and body. After I finished, I returned to the bedroom.

In the first drawer of the dresser, I found bras and underwear, along with some cash. I pulled them on and went to open the closet door. I scanned the high-end clothes: several pairs of jeans, T-shirts, sweaters, blouses, pants, jackets, coats, and three black dresses. On the floor, sneakers, heels, and boots were lined up against the wall of the closet. I looked at the heels. There were six pairs in two different colors: silver and black. Which color of shoes had he ordered me to wear? Oh, right, black. I picked up a pair of silver heels and dragged out a classic black dress.

I slipped them on and examined myself in the mirror, wondering how he could afford to buy designer clothes and shoes. And BFB pills, which were pricey as well. Nothing in his house, much less the neighborhood, indicated that someone wealthy lived here. I made a mental note to ask him about it later, pulled a gray jacket from the closet, and headed back to the living room.

"Gideon? Are you here?" I whirled around when I felt him behind me.

His eyes raked over me, face, dress, legs—a long pause at the silver heels. My lips curved into a satisfied smile. So did his. Wait. What?

"Excellent. Perfect color combination," he said. Pleased. He was pleased. My eyes narrowed, then widened. He'd tricked me. The silver Jimmy Choo heels had been precisely what he'd wanted me to wear all along.

"Why the reverse psychology?" I asked angrily.

"I had a feeling you wouldn't like being told what to wear. Apparently, I was right."

I threw him a dirty look. "Oh, go to hell."

"Perhaps another time when we're not in a hurry." He chuckled softly, and I struggled not to strangle him, even though it wouldn't kill him, before we took off.

Chapter 6

Gideon parked his bike at a street corner, and we walked a few blocks, passing two homeless men, a few hookers, some sketchy-looking people, and liquor bottles and beer cans scattered along the sidewalk. We turned down a dark moonlit alley, and a chill skittered up my spine. The smell of piss and garbage surrounded us as we moved down the alleyway. He halted in front of a metal gate flanked by two large Dumpsters and opened it. We went down a few steps leading to a door. Gideon turned to a corner-mounted security camera and extended his fangs. Five seconds passed, and a male vampire opened the door, music blaring out. He sized me up.

"She's with me," Gideon told him.

The vampire bobbed his head once. "Come on in." He moved aside, and we stepped into a large, loft-style basement with exposed ductwork and brickwork, concrete floors, and brick columns. In the living room, people were dancing, some socializing, others relaxing in a love seat and chairs while drinking from glasses with red liquid. Two girls in bikinis carrying usherette trays filled with red Popsicles stood near a small bar tucked away in a corner.

"Ew, is that frozen blood those girls are offering?" I asked Gideon over the music, following him across the room. He nodded as we turned down a short hallway and stopped in front of a vampire with a sleeve tattoo going up his neckline.

The vampire jerked his head at the door behind him. "Can't enter. Philippe's busy."

"Not anymore," Gideon said in a curt tone as he moved around the vampire to get to the door. When a hand landed on his chest to stop him, Gideon grabbed it and twisted, almost breaking the vampire's wrist.

"Ahhhhgh!" The tattooed bloodsucker jerked his hand back. "Fuck this, I'm out of here," he grumbled and moved out of our way.

Gideon flung the door open, barging in. I walked inside after him and gasped at the sight across from me. A large, muscled man stood behind a smaller guy bent over a desk, both of their pants shoved down to their knees. As the big one pumped into his partner at a steady rhythm, they moaned with pleasure until they noticed us. I pivoted around to step out of the office, wanting to give them privacy. Unlike me, though, Gideon didn't seem uncomfortable with the situation at all.

Eyes on the couple, he caught my arm and pulled me back to his side. "No need to leave. We're not interrupting. They were just finishing up. Isn't that right, Philippe?" Impatience colored Gideon's voice, yet his lips curved into a smile.

Chestnut hair falling past his collar, his skin white as snow, the smaller vampire said, "Gideon, you've arrived, and as always have a knack for ruining a good time. Henry, please, leave us." I detected a slight French accent in his voice.

The vampire behind him pulled his pants up, stare trained on Gideon, clearly assessing whether he was a threat to his partner. "You sure you want me to go?"

Philippe worked his pants back up too and ran his fingers through his hair. "Yes, *mon cher*, it's okay. He's a friend."

"I'm a lot of things, Philippe, but your friend is not one of them." Gideon moved his gaze to Henry. "But he's not my enemy either, so you'll get him back in one piece when we're done here."

Henry passed by us and closed the door behind him.

As if noticing my presence for the first time, Philippe surveyed me. "So young." His focus shifted to Gideon. "You finally decided to adopt a pet?"

A pet? *A pet?* I was about to give him a piece of my mind when Gideon spoke. "Careful there. I wouldn't underestimate her. She only looks harmless."

A condescending grin spread across Philippe's chiseled face. "Warning me? Your pet is a mere breather."

He suddenly stood a few inches away from me. Startled, I backed off, but he gripped my arm tightly, pulling me close to him. He sniffed my hair.

"Mmmm, heaven," he whispered. His fangs slid free, telling me he wasn't an Ancient. "And you're not his. I don't smell his mark in your blood, only a faint smell of illness, which means I can have a taste of you, *ma belle*." He brushed my hair to the side, lowering his head to my neck.

I quickly maneuvered out of his hold, elbowed his face, and flipped him to the ground, his mouth landing on the dusty rug. "Taste that, asshole."

He was back on his feet in a blink, but not to hit me. He stood still with a disbelieving expression on his face. "She's strong, much more than a human, yet she is one." He looked at Gideon. "My God, you were right."

"I get that a lot," Gideon told him.

Philippe regarded me as if I was an alien with four heads. "But... how... how is it possible?"

"You see," Gideon started, "when someone is brilliant, like me for instance, he tends to be right most of the time. Believe it or not, it's actually exhausting to always be—"

I rolled my eyes and showed Philippe my left palm. "This is why I'm strong."

After the stunt he'd just pulled, I wasn't inclined to explain anything about myself to this asshole. But Gideon had said he might be able to help, and really, what did I have to lose?

His eyes grew larger.

He drew closer and took my hand, then trailed his fingers over the ink, fascinated. "*Incroyable,*" he muttered in French and in English said, "Dark magic. The rarest, the most powerful, I've ever seen."

"Do you have any idea who could be responsible for it?" Gideon's tone was serious again.

Silence fell in the room as Philippe examined the tattoo, muffled music in the background.

"Less drooling, more sharing your thoughts, Philippe. *Tonight,*" Gideon said after a while.

Philippe let go of my hand and turned to look at Gideon. "No. I have no idea who may be behind it, but whoever cast the spell is either not afraid to be caught by the Watchers or knows how to cover their tracks very well."

"The Watchers? Who are they?" I said.

"They're the law enforcement officers of the entire Hidden World, which is how we refer to the supernatural world. Practicing dark magic is illegal," Gideon explained, and then addressed Philippe. "Okay, let's move on to the reason I'm here. Where is it?"

"Djar's hideout?" Philippe asked.

Gideon lost his patience. "No, the tooth fairy's. What do you think? Of course Djar's hideout. You called, claiming you know where he is. Ring a bell?"

Philippe seemed insulted by his response. "Could you be any ruder?"

"You'd be surprised. Now, talk," Gideon replied.

"First, let me start by saying how hard it was to obtain the intel."

"I'll double the pay. Where. Is. Djar?" Gideon demanded.

"It's not money I seek." When Gideon's eyebrow cocked in surprise, he elaborated. "My lover, a female human, has disappeared."

"A human?" Gideon interrupted, his tone suggesting it wasn't like Philippe to have a human girlfriend.

"She is. I know. It baffles me as well. How an inferior creature like her caught my heart is beyond me. But she did. The last time I heard from her was a week ago when she called to end our relationship, not sounding like her usual self. She said she was starting a new life away from everyone and asked me not to look for her.

"I wanted to make sure she was all right, so I called her the following night, but she wasn't taking my calls. Now her mobile phone is out of service, and all her social media accounts have been deleted too. She just disappeared off the face of the earth. I need to be reassured that nothing bad has happened to her. I've been searching for her everywhere, used every connection I have, even sent a human to her house to check if her parents know anything about her whereabouts. They don't.

"I questioned her friends, too, especially the Newborn vampire, Kelly, who swore to me she didn't hurt her and that her blood craving was under control. I don't know if I believe her. It's hard to trust baby vampires around humans. Newborns are unstable. I fear for my lover's safety. I will give you Djar's whereabouts if you give me hers."

"What makes you think I can find her if you couldn't?" Gideon asked.

"I've been told I'm too emotionally involved. It affects the way I work, and useful information eludes me. I can't see things clearly. I am positive you'll have more productive results than I had," Philippe answered.

"All right, I'll do it, but you goddamn better have Djar's location. Your human, how close was she to you? Have you shared a blood connection with her?"

My eyes furrowed in confusion. "Blood connection? What's that?"

"In our fangs," Philippe explained, "all vampires have two types of substances that can be injected into humans, or witches. The first type is called Erasure. Adults and Newborns use it whenever they feed on humans who have no knowledge of our existence. It stays in our victims' system for thirty minutes and obliterates the memory of us drinking from them.

"The second type is unique to each vampire, like fingerprints, and is called Bounding. It's a precious gift we can choose to give to our mortal. Once it's out of the fangs, our body won't generate new Bounding liquid until our human dies. Three things happen to the mortal when this substance enters him or her: one, the body stops aging but is still vulnerable to injuries and diseases and remains fragile.

"Two, the blood turns poisonous to other vampires. And three, it also becomes the sole source of food for the vampire who gave him or her the Bounding liquid. No other blood will nourish that vampire as long as the human lives. The two are bound together. We refer to it as having a blood connection." Philippe's eyebrows clenched together as he observed me for a moment, then turned his head to Gideon. "She's rather ignorant of the way our world works. Odd considering she's with *you*. If not a pet or a Donor, what is the human to you? Who is she?"

Gideon's forehead wrinkled in question. "Didn't I introduce her when we came in?"

"I'm afraid you failed to do that," Philippe answered.

"Oh, then it must be none of your goddamn business," Gideon said and switched the subject back to his missing girlfriend. "The girl, do you have a blood connection with her?"

He mumbled something about Gideon being ill-mannered, which was accompanied by a few French words sounding like curses, before answering. "No. She was my Donor, and I love her deeply."

"Yeah, so much so you needed Henry to calm your sorrow," I commented in contempt.

"He was just an enjoyable fuck. Nothing more," he said calmly, then asked Gideon, "Why is my lover's status relevant?"

"If you're not bound to her, it's unlikely someone took your Donor to starve you," Gideon answered. "To trace her, I need at least the basics: physical description, home address, age."

Philippe walked behind the desk and opened a drawer, picking up a cell phone. "She used to aim it at us at various angles and take pictures. She referred to it as..." His face contracted with thought.

"A selfie," I offered.

"Yes, a selfie," he said and padded to Gideon to hand him the cell phone. "There are plenty of photos of her on it."

I neared Gideon to take a look at Philippe's Donor, and my stomach dropped to my toes. With long, wavy chocolate-brown hair and blue eyes, the girl who was making funny faces at the camera was my sister.

Chapter 7

I couldn't believe it. I rubbed my eyes and looked at the screen again, but it was still Zoey on it.

"What's her name?" Gideon asked.

"Zoey," I said, my voice suddenly hoarse. "Her name is Zoey." My gaze moved up to Philippe. "How the hell did my sister get involved with you?"

"Your sister?" both Gideon and Philippe said simultaneously, and I wasn't sure which one sounded more surprised.

I snatched the phone from Gideon's hand and scrolled down. One by one, I went over the pictures. Zoey smiling at the camera, Zoey laughing, Zoey hugging Philippe, Zoey kissing Philippe. Kissing! I shook my head. No, this was not happening. She looked happy. She looked in love. With him, a moron, a jerk, a cheater—a leech! What had she been thinking? It didn't make sense. All her life guys had been throwing themselves at her feet, so why had she settled for an idiot vampire who didn't really seem to care for her?

"Aren't you supposed to be missing?" Philippe's voice interrupted my thoughts. "She was searching for you. We had many fights over it, actually. I did not want her to continue her search; I was afraid for her safety. It is a job for the human police, not for a human without the skills to defend herself."

My eyebrows clenched together, and my lips pursed in anger. "Where did you meet my sister?"

"At a nightclub called The Dark Night," he began. "One night, I spotted a human, magnificent, so beautiful, from across the cave. She was with Kelly, the Newborn I mentioned, and another human, a female, less pretty. Her name was Izzy. I approached and introduced myself. After that night, we spent quite some time together. She became dear to my heart, and I offered to allow her to be my Donor and my lover. My offer filled her with joy and excitement. After a while, she confessed her love to me."

I tossed him an appalled look. "Confessed her love to you? Did she know about your enjoyable fucks? About Henry?"

"Of course she did. Unfortunately, Zoey wished to have me all to herself and was upset when I didn't give her exclusivity." He stopped and wrinkled his nose, as if the smell of my cancer got worse. "However," he continued, "not wanting to lose our beautiful relationship, she finally accepted that my body could never be chained to one person."

His words repulsed me. Zoey loved him and wanted monogamy. Rather than setting her free, he kept her in a toxic relationship where she was miserable. Now, Zoey was probably in her dorm room—no, wait. She wasn't. She'd left for an unknown place! But why? It was uncharacteristic of her to act like that. Fear crept into my heart. Had my abductor done something to her because I'd escaped?

My gaze jerked to the douche leech. "When did you last hear from Zoey?"

"A week ago," he replied.

I felt a slight relief. A week ago, I had still been locked up. Besides, my kidnapper wouldn't hurt my family now that I was free; they were his only insurance I wouldn't go to the cops. He'd said so himself when he threatened me.

"The human you sent to my house. Did he talk to my parents?" I asked him.

"He did. Zoey called them too, also about a week ago, saying she'd decided to leave school because she met new friends and wished to go live with them. She asked to be left alone."

Clearly, she had gone through something, and her jerk of a boyfriend hadn't been there for her. I stepped up to him and slapped the phone to his chest, not gently. "You disgust me. I'll make sure my sister will never take you back." I turned to Gideon. "Are we done here?"

"We are," Gideon said, then looked at Philippe. "I'll be in touch."

"Bear in mind that in the next few weeks, I'll be away for business and can only be reached via my electronic mail," Philippe told him.

Gideon nodded, and we walked out of the room. As we moved through a sea of people, too distracted by thoughts of Zoey, I bumped into someone. A girl, I thought. Mumbling an apology, I continued walking toward the front door.

When we reached the alley, Gideon stopped me. "His Donor is your sister, and understandably, you'll want to help find her. But we are doing it my way." His tone left no room for argument, but I wasn't going to, anyway. Whatever the reason behind Zoey's weird behavior was, it might be connected to the supernatural world. Gideon was part of it, knew its rules, knew how it worked, knew its creatures. I didn't.

"Okay, your way, so long as it brings us to her. I just have one request. The man who kidnapped me may still be watching her every move. When we find her, before approaching, we have to double-check whether she's being watched or not. If she is, we need to be careful. I don't want to risk my parents' lives, or hers."

"Okay," he said, and we headed to his bike.

During the ride back to his house, I brooded over my parents. Their only two children were in trouble. One daughter had gone missing; the other suddenly decided to drop out of college, cut off all ties with the people in her life, and then disappeared. They must be going out of their minds with worry.

The cold wind stopped whipping through my hair, and I noticed Gideon had parked his bike in his driveway. After we got inside, he gestured to the kitchen.

"In the refrigerator, you'll find two bottles of BFB."

"Two? Not that it's any of my business, but how can you afford those pricey pills? And the designer clothes while living here?" I asked.

"You think I purchased a house in this neighborhood because of money issues?"

"Why else then? I doubt having drug dealers around the corner, gangs, and graffiti everywhere would appeal to anyone," I said.

"No, it wouldn't, but for some people, less noisy or concerned neighbors would. Let's put it this way: screams coming out of someone's house around here probably won't lead to human cops knocking on your door."

"You've tortured people in this house?"

One dark eyebrow arched, saying, "Duh." Then he stepped to the coffee table and picked up something.

"I surmise you don't have a phone on you," he said and handed me a brand new cell. "I programmed its number and mine in. Also, there is a tube of sunscreen and sunglasses for you on the kitchen counter."

"Sunscreen and sunglasses? Why?"

"Since a small quantity of vampire blood is running through your veins, you'll be sensitive to sunlight."

I became alarmed. "Wait, will exposure to the sun's ultraviolet rays infect me with the UV virus?"

"No, only vampires can contract it. You're still human, but because of the Ancient's blood, you'll experience some pain in the sun."

He slid his coat sleeve up to his wrist and checked his Rolex, then headed toward the French doors. "I have to go out to buy healthy blood bags before sunrise. You go to bed, get some rest. Tomorrow night is going to be busy." His hand was on the door handle when he turned to me. "Almost forgot, I packed the freezer with chocolate ice cream. Hope you like the flavor." A smile tugged at the corner of his mouth, and he left.

Great. Tempting, empty calories stuffed in the freezer. *Thank you, girl with the golden tears, whoever you are. Couldn't you have come up with a healthier choice of food for the spell? Broccoli, for instance?* Sighing, I trudged upstairs. After I brushed my teeth and changed into comfortable pants and a shirt, I crawled into bed. I set the alarm for seven a.m. to take the BFB and then let sleep take over.

A vivid dream pulled me back into the all-white hallway. Standing in front of that girl's room, I had blue pants and a black T-shirt on me again. However, she was shirtless and in a sheer white dress, her long hair concealing her breasts.

"Don't look at Oberon," she whispered to me, tears of gold trailing down her cheeks. Gossamer wings spread from her back.

"Are you fae?" I asked her. Light snow started to fall from the white ceiling, the temperature dropping. I shivered. "What's your name? Who are you? What are you?"

She opened her mouth and beeps poured out of it. They grew louder and louder until the sound jerked me out of the dream.

I sat up and reached over, tapping the "Off" button on the alarm and hauling myself out of bed. I made a quick trip down to the kitchen, swallowed a BFB pill, and returned to the bedroom, filled with curiosity. The spell didn't prevent my brain from thinking or dreaming about the girl with the golden tears. Would it allow me to search her on Google?

I took the cell phone from the nightstand and unlocked its screen, praying for an internet connection. I brought up a browser, content when my prayers were answered, then cursed when my fingers typed in "I want ice cream" rather than "a girl crying golden tears."

I pinched my nose and closed my eyes. *Think. How can I rephrase it in a way that won't trigger the spell?* A few seconds later, I typed in, "Do fae cry golden tears?" Damn it! The words "ice cream" appeared once more. *Okay, if not her, then Oberon.* I set up a new search: the king of the fae. Obviously, I didn't expect to get reliable information, but it was worth a try. A string of hits popped up on the screen.

I slowly scrolled down the first page. Result number one, not relevant, number two, the same, number three, nope, number four... um, sounded promising. Its name was The Mysterious World of the Fae. I tapped on the link. An image showing beams of moonlight shining down through a dark wood filled the home page. The site's sidebar menu presented the following: About Me, Oberon, Royal Fae, Common Fae, Humans and Fae, How to Protect Yourself from Fae, My Blog, Contact Me.

The About Me page revealed that the owner of the site was a twenty-four-year-old guy with a buzz cut and brown eyes. Although all the creatures in the supernatural world fascinated him, he was most obsessed with the fae. "Yes, folks, they have wings, and they exist," he assured his readers and added, "Fae are beautiful creatures, and they possess the powers of magic, like witches."

On the Humans and Fae page, he explained the danger of humans looking at a royal fae. "They're creatures of incredible power, so much so that one glance at them and fear will overwhelm your body. You'll die from a heart attack." A fae commoner, however, was safe to glance at, at least according to him.

I moved on to other pages, exploring. The data on the site matched what I already knew about the supernatural world. The more I read, the more I was convinced that the information was reliable. And there was a lot of it.

The guy even provided details about the fae's appearance. Curious, he'd asked his friend, a vampire, about it and learned that fae were humanoids with pointed ears and wings. Their skin was flawless, their hair thick and shiny. The fae's social class could be recognized by their wings: the commoners' were gossamer, while royals' were angelic.

"Um, interesting," I commented to myself, then searched for anything mentioning golden tears. There was nothing about it, so I went to Oberon's page.

Just one short paragraph appeared on the screen. Oberon: the king of the fae, a powerful, ruthless being with white-feathered wings. Only once in a blue moon does he visit our dimension, which was why few supernatural creatures had ever seen him. The paragraph ended with the owner of the site hoping his readers would never encounter the king of the fae. *Yeah, too late for this reader, pal.*

Why on earth would a mighty being such as Oberon trouble himself to break free a mere human? Was it because of the rare dark magic on my hand? That train of thought jolted to a halt when I spotted a folded piece of paper lying on the floor near the dresser. I rose from the bed and went to pick it up. Someone had written me a note.

I heard your conversation with Philippe about Zoey at his party. We need to talk. It's important. Meet me tomorrow at Pardee Seawall Park, 4:00 p.m. Take a seat on a bench and wait for me.

That was it? No name? No physical description of him or her? No explanation as to why he or she wanted to meet with me? I turned over the piece of paper. Nothing. I looked at the jacket draped over the back of the chair near the dresser. The paper must have fallen out of a pocket. Someone had slipped the note inside while I was at Philippe's party. But when? Even as the question arose in my head, I remembered the girl I'd bumped into at the party. It must have been her who had slipped the note—no doubt. Whoever she was, she might shed light on Zoey's whereabouts. I had to go see her.

At four p.m. Gideon would be sleeping, being a vampire and all, so I'd have to go alone. *I'll bring him up to speed with the latest developments when I return.*

I unlocked the cell phone to look up Pardee Seawall Park. *Okay, not too far from here.* And it was public, somewhat safer when meeting a stranger. I stepped back to the bed, got in, and set the alarm for three p.m.

Chapter 8

The cab driver pulled up at Pardee Seawall Park, and I paid him with the money Gideon had left me in the dresser drawer. Then, I hiked to a walkway with a wrought-iron fence lining it. A long row of benches and brass streetlamps along the coastline faced the ocean water, overlooking the harbor. I sat down on one of the benches, a cold breeze brushing my face.

As I waited for the girl, I glanced up at the sun. The side effect of BFB was a bitch. I could still feel the burning sensation that had gnawed at my eyes and skin when I stepped out of the house earlier. I'd rushed back inside—as far away as possible from sunlight—and applied sunscreen. I had to wait until the pain let up before I could put sunglasses on. Only then had it been tolerable for me to walk out into the sun again and get here.

Fifteen minutes of watching people stroll along the fence passed without her showing up. I became restless. Where was she? As I glanced at my watch for the millionth time, someone sat next to me.

"Are you really Zoey's sister, the one who went missing?" the stranger asked.

I looked up and recognized the girl I'd bumped into at Philippe's party, remembering that dark brown hair tipped with bright pink highlights.

"She has only one sibling, and it's me, yes. Who are you?" I demanded.

"I'm Izzy, and I know your sister. We had a few classes together and used to hang out sometimes."

My eyes went wide. Philippe had mentioned her name. "Do you know why Zoey suddenly decided to leave everything and disappear?"

She shook her head, her brown eyes apologetic. "No, I don't," she answered, and disappointment swept over me. "Zoey was fine," she continued. "Everything was cool until one day I found her in her dorm room, crying. She explained that she was worried 'cause her sister, you, didn't come back home from a trip with some friends. So what's the deal? Why didn't you return home?"

"It's complicated. Do you know where she may be now?"

"No clue."

I sighed. Then why did she drag me here?

"I'm worried about her," she said. "After that day in her dorm room, we didn't talk much since she was busy looking for you. The last time we spoke was when she called me. It was a week ago. All of a sudden, she dropped out of school, went AWOL on social media, and demanded that I wouldn't contact her again. I was sure she was joking around, so three days later, I stopped by her dorm. Her roommate said that Zoey had left and taken all her stuff with her. I called her. When she didn't pick up for two days, I stopped by Philippe's basement loft. He claimed he didn't know where she was either and that he was concerned about her. Yet he was in a mood to plan a party. He even invited me."

"Why did you slip the note into my jacket? Why not just talk to me at the party?" I asked.

"Too many eyes, too many ears. I don't trust Philippe and his friends."

"You think he had a hand in Zoey's decision to leave?"

"I'm not sure," she said. "He might have. I eavesdropped outside his office door when you were there. He sounded devastated, asking your vampire friend to find her, but it could have been just an act. He's hiding something. I've never liked him. She cried a lot over that shithead but wouldn't dump his sorry ass. She was so in love with him. To be honest, I feel guilty. She met him because of me. I introduced her to the vampire world and brought her to The Dark Night, a vamp club."

A couple holding hands walked by as a gust of wind blew Izzy's hair across her face. She brushed it out of her eyes.

"How'd you get involved in that world? Are you a Donor?" I asked.

She shook her head. "Before Zoey and I became friends, I used to go out a lot to The Dark Night, where humans hung out. There I met this girl, Kelly. We hit it off immediately. At first, I didn't know about her, but she later confessed to being a Newborn vampire. Her Change happened last year, in the middle of her midterms. She's still adapting to the transition but swore she wouldn't hurt me and that her bloodlust was under control. Funny, but I was more fascinated than afraid. She'll be nineteen forever. How awesome is that?

"Anyhow, when Zoey started to hang out with us, Kelly thought it'd be cool if I brought her to The Dark Night. Strangely, your sister didn't freak out, like I did, when she discovered that vampires were real. She was pretty casual about the whole thing and wanted to explore the cave. Kelly managed to get us downstairs. We had good times. That is until Zoey met Philippe."

Two children playing with each other came close to our bench, and Izzy paused. A woman near the fence called out to them, and they ran back to her.

"As always," she went on, "every other guy hit on her. Zoey turned them all down, but not Philippe. She was totally into him, charmed by his accent, by his looks." She rolled her eyes. "God knows why. He's a world-class jerk. They started dating. She fell head over heels for him, but once the honeymoon period was over, troubles came. She found out he had a number of fuck buddies, and it broke her heart. He told her he doesn't believe in monogamy. She was devastated but didn't dump him."

I huffed out a sigh. "Ugh, that asshole. After I find Zoey, I'll put some sense into her. What happened after the night you went to Philippe to ask about her?"

Her stare drifted to the ocean before it returned to mine. "I left his house and called Kelly, thinking maybe she had talked to Zoey and knew what was going on with her, but it kept going straight to her voicemail. The following day, I waited till night and drove over to her apartment. The door was busted in, and the inside was trashed like someone had been looking for something. When I stepped into her bedroom, I heard a man in the bathroom. I quickly hid under her bed, and a man's boots came into view. He moved to Kelly's dresser and ripped open the drawers. Then he made a short phone call."

"Did you see what he looked like?" I asked.

Her head bobbed up and down once. "I got a peek at him. He was tall, about forty years old, brown hair, definitely a vampire. He held something in his hand, but from under the bed, I couldn't tell what it was."

I zipped my jacket shut as the wind picked up. "What did he say on the phone?"

"Something about finding *it*. Have no clue what *it* meant. Before he ended the call, he mentioned a date and time of a meeting and confirmed that he'd be there. After he took off, I followed him," she answered.

"Any idea who he may be?"

"No. That's why I was at the party yesterday, to ask Philippe if he knew anyone who matched that vampire's description, but he didn't even listen to me, telling me to leave him alone," she answered.

"You said you went after the vampire intruder. Where did he go?"

She pointed at the hundreds of houses sitting near the waterline a few miles away from us. "Over there. His home is at the end of the walkway. That's why I'm here. That meeting he mentioned? It's today at seven. Look, I don't believe in coincidence. Both Zoey and Kelly suddenly went MIA. It must be connected, so I stalked him for the last couple of days. As soon as he leaves the house for the meeting, I'll trail him. My car's parked nearby. You want to come with?"

My recent experiences with strangers weren't the best, but with my new martial arts skills, I felt more confident, so I nodded.

Thirty minutes later, we were in her Jeep, following a black BMW to an industrial district, the sunset coloring the sky in soft orange and purple. By the time he pulled up outside an abandoned building with broken windows and graffiti painted on the brick walls, the moon and stars were out in a cloudless sky. I took off the sunglasses while Izzy parked the car at a safe distance from the BMW. The area was empty of people.

Out of the car, we crept through dead grass, ducking as low as possible, passing several streetlamps casting a soft light. We hid behind the corner of a small decaying building next to the deserted one the vampire was standing in front of, like he was waiting for someone.

"Izzy? What are you doing here?" a low voice said behind us. We both jumped and snapped our heads back.

Izzy gasped. "Kelly?" she whispered sharply. "What are *you* doing here? Where have you been? Why haven't you picked up any of my calls?"

"My cell broke when Philippe beat the shit out of me while grilling me. I bought a new one and changed my number because of him. Sorry I didn't have time to talk to you. Gosh, you were right about him; he's a total ass."

Kelly's hazel eyes were weary, her skin white, her dark brown hair wrapped in a messy bun. Jeans and a shirt with long sleeves encased her slender body, a pearl necklace around her neck.

"He hit you? Why?" Izzy's voice rose above a whisper.

She shushed her and answered, "Three nights ago, as I was walking to my cousin's house, Philippe jumped me. He dragged me over to a dark corner. He's balls-out crazy. Did you know Zoey dumped him over the phone? Turns out he has no idea where she is now and is convinced I had something to do with her disappearance. He thinks she's scared of me 'cause I hurt her. I swore to him that I didn't, that I controlled my bloodlust around humans even though I'm Newborn, but he kept hitting me, demanding I reveal the truth. I was lucky my cousin saw us. Shelley's got a few hundred years on Philippe, so he let me go and took off.

"I was afraid of him and stayed at my cousin's house for a while. When I returned to my apartment, I found out that someone had broken into it. They trashed everything and took all my jewelry. Shelley hired Ian. He's the best PI there is, a bit expensive but worth every penny she paid him. After six hours, I got all the information I needed. It was Philippe who sent a man to break into my home. Maybe he thought Zoey was there, I don't know. The greedy fucker who tore my apartment apart wasn't just looking for Zoey. He also stole my stuff to sell it. Ian told me that the vamp thief found a buyer and that they were meeting here tonight."

"I came over and saw the mess in your apartment," Izzy said. "I was under your bed when he stole your stuff and I overheard him set up this meeting. He also said he found *it*. What is *it*?"

Kelly's mouth opened in shock. "You were in my apartment? Thank gosh he didn't see you. 'It' probably refers to my grandma's necklace. It's worth a fortune. I was an idiot not to lock it away in the safe. I saw how Philippe's men had their eyes on that necklace the night I wore it at that party Zoey invited us to."

"Yeah, I remember. The diamonds on it were gorgeous," Izzy said.

"Did Zoey call you too? Before she disappeared?" I asked Kelly.

She rolled her eyes at me. "Like I already told Philippe, I don't know where she is. Who are you anyway?"

"Sydney, Zoey's sister," I replied.

Her brow shot up. "Sydney? Didn't you go, like, missing?"

"It's a long story," I said.

Izzy glanced at Kelly. "So, wait, you're here to get your jewelry back?"

"Yes. Before I spotted you, I was about to threaten him into returning my stuff." Kelly's trembling hand drew out a small handgun from her purse. "With this. My cousin would kill me if she—"

"Someone's arrived," I cut in as a car pulled up near the vampire. A man got out.

"Kelly, listen to me," Izzy said. "Don't do anything stupid. If the buyer's an Ancient, we'll end up dead."

"She's right," I agreed. "The jewelry isn't worth your life. Our lives." Kelly watched the men as the buyer opened a suitcase full of what seemed like money. A moment passed before she put the gun back into her bag.

"All right, all right. Let's get out of here." She gritted her teeth, and then her cell phone rang in her purse. Her hand shot into the bag, but it was too late. The vampires' heads whipped our way.

"Hurry to my car," Izzy urged and we sprinted toward her Jeep. The two vampires were dangerously close when we jumped inside the car. The engine roared to life, and Izzy slammed on the gas, speeding off. As we moved farther away from them, I felt relief. But also disappointment. The vampire in Kelly's apartment wasn't connected to my sister's disappearance. Zoey's whereabouts remained unknown. At least Izzy had discovered that her other friend, Kelly, was fine.

"Phew, that was a close call," Kelly said.

"Sorry I dragged you into all this. I thought Kelly had been taken by that vampire and that it might be related to Zoey," Izzy apologized, still driving fast.

"He didn't kidnap me, but I was tortured by that monster, Philippe," Kelly added with a shiver. "I'm staying at my cousin's house until he gets off my back."

"Probably for the best. Let him cool down," Izzy said and then asked me, "Where do you need me to drop you off?" I gave her Gideon's address, and then my phone number when we reached his house, in case they heard from Zoey.

After that, I waved goodbye and stepped inside the house. The light in the living room was on. I walked through the French doors. Gideon was sitting on the couch, a glass of blood in his hand.

"Oh, look at that. You're alive." He looked calm. His tone, however, was anything but.

Apparently, he'd called me ten times when he realized I wasn't in the house. My phone being on silent, I hadn't heard it. I apologized and recounted everything that had happened with Izzy and Kelly.

"You escaped two vampires, one of whom might have been an Ancient?" he repeated, his voice somehow even angrier. "Goddamn it, Sydney, you should've woken me up, or waited until the sun set, so I could come with you. Do you have any idea how extremely vulnerable you are near Ancient vampires?"

Why was he so agitated? "Which part of succeeding in escaping them did you fail to understand?"

He stood up, setting his glass on the coffee table with a thud that rang with irritation, then stepped to me. "Which part of being extremely vulnerable near Ancient vampires did *you* fail to understand? Sydney, an Ancient can control the human mind easily, make you spill all your secrets, or worse—kill yourself just for the fun of it. Ancient vampires can *own* you. Your body and your mind." This shut me up. The thought terrified me. He dragged a hand down his face and sighed. "If you insist on following up on new leads without me," he continued, "you will learn how to block compulsion. It'll take some time to teach you, but it just became our top priority."

Surprise filled my voice. "It's possible for humans to learn how to block it?"

"With hard work, you might be able to. It's not a guarantee, though."

I was easy prey for Ancients. Before I could go on with my search for Zoey, I had to fix that. ASAP. "When do we start?"

"The first step is knowing how to reach a state of heightened awareness. Have you ever meditated?"

"Meditated? No," I answered, and my first lesson started.

Chapter 9

Breathe in, breathe out, I instructed myself, sitting on the floor of the living room in a lotus position, my eyes closed. For the first time, my mind was empty of thoughts for a whole hour. It'd been three days since my training started, during which I'd done meditation and mindfulness exercises from sunset to sunrise while Gideon guided me. Unfortunately, I'd been failing, not able to wipe my mind clear of thoughts for more than a few moments. However, today, waking up two hours earlier than usual, before the sun was down, I'd been determined to make it. And I did. My mind had been silent for over two hours.

Super excited, I hurried upstairs to Gideon's bedroom door. Without knocking—or thinking—I flung it open. Two steps in, I froze. There, in the middle of the king-sized bed, Gideon lay motionless on his back and on top of the covers. Also, he was naked. Very naked. My mouth went dry as my stare drifted down his hairless chest, then to the trail of hair from his navel to his groin. I explored his stomach, flat and lean, his perfect six-pack, the trim muscles of his torso, the V of his hips, and the seriously impressive, erected pe—

"You're welcome to do more than just stand over there and ogle." Eyes closed, he suddenly spoke, startling me.

He was awake? Crap. "I am not ogling." How on earth did he know I was ogling? *Never mind, change the subject and focus on his face.* "Uh, sorry I didn't knock"—*his face, Sydney, his face*—"but I wanted to update you. I did it! I can have no thoughts in my head." *And no shame in you. Look up. Have you forgotten where his face is?* "I'm ready."

When he opened his eyes, mine jerked up to his. Finally.

"It's good progress, but you're not ready yet." His words squashed my excitement. With a smooth movement, he got out of bed. His nakedness didn't seem to disturb him as he stood in front of me. Too close. I backed up a little, swallowing. Had the temperature in the room risen?

Resisting the need to fan myself, I said, "But I've done every mental exercise you gave me, and I managed to have zero thoughts in my head for more than two hours, so yeah, I—will you please put some clothes on? It's... it's inappropriate."

An eyebrow lifted. "Like entering someone's bedroom without knocking?"

"I already said I was sorry," I told him.

He turned around and headed to his closet, pulling out a white towel and wrapping it around his waist.

"Thank you," I said. "Anyway, if you ask me, I'm ready. I feel it. I know I'll be able to protect my mind in the future, especially after all that training. I'll just empty my head and push Ancients' compulsion out."

He glided back to where I was and, on its own accord, my gaze dropped to his bare chest and lingered for way too long before returning to his face. I wet my lips.

His blue eyes burned into mine while a tiny smile played on his lips. "You like what you see?"

Ugh! What an arrogant jerk. I opened my mouth to tell him he wasn't nearly as hot as he clearly thought he was. "Yes, you have a gorgeous face and a body to die for." My eyes widened as the filter between my head and mouth ceased to work, and words started to spill out. "Your body is a masterpiece, and your face... You look like a fallen angel. I want to touch, lick, and explore every inch of—" Horrified, I slapped my hand over my mouth to shut the hell up.

"Still convinced you can block the compulsion?" he asked, amusement lacing his voice. That he could do compulsion didn't surprise me. It did, however, piss me off to no end.

"How dare you get into my head and put those... those words into my mouth."

"Those words are all *yours*, not mine. I simply prevented you from lying. I said the compulsion in my head, so you didn't hear it." He passed by me and stopped at the doorway. "You have a lot of work ahead of you, but you're ready for the next step. I'm going to take a shower. Go get dressed. We're leaving in an hour to visit a friend of mine. Unless," humor sparkled in his eyes, "you prefer to join me and do some... exploring."

I scoffed. "When hell freezes over."

He laughed and walked into the bathroom—alone.

Soon after, in jeans and a sweater, I came downstairs. His hair damp, Gideon was already there, a black leather jacket over a black shirt and dark jeans, leather boots on his feet.

"Time to go," he said, and we headed out to see his friend.

The ride was short and before long, he parked in front of a bookstore. A woman met us at the door. She was stunning, dressed in a gray pencil skirt with a white silk button-down shirt tucked in at the waist, and black heels. We stepped inside the store, and a bell chimed. She flipped the sign on the door to "Closed."

Wooden floorboards creaked beneath our feet as we followed her, passing pine bookshelves with old books that filled the room with a musty smell. She unlocked the door behind the vintage shop counter and flicked the light on.

We entered an office, and she moved to a desk in the corner, placing her keys on it, near a computer, then turned to face us. Her lilac hair was long and wavy, gathered at the nape, her eyes bright green, her mouth a cupid's bow. Her fair skin was smooth and perfect, though not vampiric perfect. Looking at Gideon, she grinned, and the vibe I got was that they were more than just friends.

"You forgot to mention she's human," she said. Her gaze flicked to the tattoo on my hand. "And infected with dark magic."

Gideon stepped closer to her, an apologetic expression on his face. "I know, much more difficult. But I'll be in your debt."

The two dimples decorating her cheeks deepened. "Yes, you will be." She neared him and stretched her body up to reach his face. Her plump lips touched his mouth for a brief kiss, and then she regarded him with narrowed eyes, as if he wasn't reacting to her affection as usual. Her eyes moved to me and back to him. "Oh... I see," she said and backed away from him, her mouth crooking up in a little smile.

See? See what? Did she think something was going on between Gideon and me?

Instead of correcting her very wrong assumption, he said, "Audrey, it'll mean a lot to me if you do this."

She waved a hand in the air. "Don't be silly, G. Of course I'll do it. Leave her here"—she pointed a manicured finger at him—"but don't expect miracles."

"I knew I could count on you." He leaned down to kiss her gently on the forehead and then handed me a BFB pill. "Don't forget to take it at seven a.m. I'll come back tomorrow night to check in on you."

"Tomorrow night? But..." My voice fizzled out when a whoosh of air brushed my face and he vanished from the room. I sighed and turned to her. "Um, just so you know, my relationship with Gideon is strictly professional."

She chortled as if I'd said something funny. "The spike of jealousy in your eyes after I kissed him says otherwise."

"Jealous? No, I was not."

"It's okay, I don't mind. There wasn't anything serious between us, just casual sex." She leaned her backside against the desk, crossed her ankles, and clapped her hands. "All right, let's begin with an introduction. I'm Audrey, an illusionist, and you are Sydney, right?"

"Right. Uh, clueless human over here." I motioned at myself. "What's an illusionist? Like a magician?"

"Close, but no," she answered, and suddenly, green grass replaced the floor. Birds emerged out of thin air, flying around in the room, which was morphing gradually into an exotic forest. My mouth opened, and I gasped when a ray of sun touched my face. The sound of a waterfall filled the space, and colored butterflies moved between tall trees. Speechless, I spun in place, inhaling the scent of damp earth mixed with pine resins and wild jasmine.

"An illusionist is a witch who masters the art of creating magical illusions," she explained. "We're experts at mind reading, as well."

I stilled, and my eyes went to hers. "You can read my mind?"

"If I wish to, yes," she said, and at once the forest disappeared, bringing back the office. Right then, the door behind me flew open. Gideon? I gulped air. He was naked!

"W-what's going on? Why aren't you dressed?" I asked, my eyes going large. He glided toward me, and his hand caressed my jawline. My skin tingled beneath his touch. Then, he started to fade away like smoke evaporating into the air.

"And your deepest desires too." Audrey's voice was playful.

My cheeks burned. "Get out of my head!"

"Technically, I'm inside your soul, not your head."

Confusion wrinkled my brow. "What?"

"It's not like compulsion. To manipulate or read someone's mind, an illusionist witch uses the human's soul. An Ancient, on the other hand, gets straight into the human's mind," she said and went to sit behind the desk. "The soul and the mind are connected, so if you want to learn how to resist compulsion, you must first know how to protect your soul from intruders like illusionist witches. That's what Gideon's asked me to teach you."

I raised a hand. "Let me get this straight. Anyone who can protect their soul can resist compulsion?"

"No," she answered. "Resisting compulsion requires full control over your mind *and* soul. The human mind is a powerful tool, not like that of supernatural beings, but powerful nonetheless. Your mind has the ability to create a strong force around itself and the soul. Gideon's taught you concentration through deep meditation. It's the first step before learning how to reach and feel your soul in order to protect it. This is where I come in. After you've learned that, Gideon will continue his training. But I gotta warn you. As a human, you'll have your work cut out for you, and it's not a sure thing that in the end, you'll know how to shield your soul."

"It's okay; Gideon already told me that I may fail despite the hard work," I said, and then wondered, "Are vampires naturally immune to illusionists?"

She shook her head. "Those who are immune, mainly Ancients, have gone through hard training. It's a skill: either you have it, or you don't."

Gideon was a powerful Adult, and her magic was probably useless against him, but maybe he'd shared some personal details about himself, like what kind of vampire he was.

I sat in the chair across from hers. "What's the story with Gideon?"

She reached around for her handbag hanging on the chair's back and pulled out her cell phone. "Gideon? Oh, he's an enigma. Wish I knew. He's not much of a talker, tends to keep to himself. Plus, he's immune to my powers, so I can't get into his soul."

Gideon had used compulsion on me. It was an indication he was not like other Adult vampires, but I wanted to be sure, so I asked, "Is he really different from other Adult vampires?"

"Yes, he is. Don't know why, though." She tapped the screen of her cell then put it to her ear, looking at me. "I'm starving, and it's gonna be a long night. I'm ordering a pizza. You okay with pepperoni?"

I nodded and waited until she finished the order, then asked, "How'd you meet him?"

She put down her phone and settled back in her chair. "Every witch at fifteen must go through a test that assesses his or her personal attributes. If the witch has a tendency for illusion powers, they can apply for the prestigious Magic Academy. I got in, and six years later, on the night of my graduation, I went out to a bar with my girlfriends to celebrate. After a few beers, I spotted a dark-haired hottie sitting alone in a booth across the room. He was too gorgeous to ignore, so I walked over to talk to him. Halfway to his booth, I realized he was a vampire. My mother always warned me to be careful around them. They're dangerous creatures, but I was curious, especially about Euphoric Bites."

"Euphoric Bites?"

A look of surprise covered her face. "He never gave you a Euphoric Bite?"

"Hell no. Why would I let a vampire bite me?"

"'Cause when they draw blood from you, it's..." Her voice died away as she searched for the right word to describe the feeling. "Intimate. A sensual, erotic experience. And a Euphoric Bite is..." she sighed dreamily, "wow. Orgasmic. Ecstatic. It's in their fangs. They all have two kinds of substances. The vampire can use the first, called Erasure, in two ways: as a roofie, making you forget he or she has ever bitten you. Or as sexual pleasure—provided the vamp knows how to cancel the roofie effect and turn his liquid into an orgasm inducer while it's in the mortal's bloodstream.

"It's a damn shame most of them don't know how to do it. The process takes a lot of energy and concentration from of the vampire and requires special skills that, as I said before, you either got it or you don't." A lopsided smile tilted up a corner of her mouth. "If Gideon offers you a Euphoric Bite, don't think twice—say yes."

Her cell rang, and she picked it up. It was the pizza delivery guy. He was outside, so she went out to him. After a few minutes, she came back with a pizza box. The smell of cheese filled the room and made my mouth water. She returned to her seat.

When we started eating, I asked, "What happened next with Gideon at the bar?"

She chewed and answered, "I reached his booth and took a seat across from him, but before I could uttered a single word, he blew me off, saying, 'I'm waiting for someone. Perhaps another time.' I stood up, and as I stepped away, I saw a woman walk up to his booth. She was a demon."

My eyebrows shot up. "A demon? As in, evil spirits possessing humans?"

"Demons are an ancient race, not spirits," she explained.

Another species? Great. As if vampires, fae, and witches were not enough.

"What do they look like?"

She wiped her mouth with a napkin. "They're a humanoid species."

"Are they dangerous?"

She nodded fast. "Very. Particularly when they need to feed. They eat the souls of humans and witches. If they're not under a time crunch, they prefer to suck it over the course of a week or more. The unfortunate victim dies slowly and painfully. It's an excruciating way to go."

A chill slithered up my spine. "Why, aren't they a ray of sunshine?" I let sarcasm roll out of my mouth and finished my slice then grabbed another one. "Why was Gideon meeting a demon?"

"Demons and vampires don't exactly get along, to put it mildly," she told me. "So I wondered the same thing. I went back to my girlfriends, but I watched Gideon and the demon, and eventually I formed a theory. Demon blood is addictive to vampires, just like heroin is to humans, so I thought maybe the demon lady was selling him her blood.

"I was fascinated, so when they stood up and moved together toward the exit, I followed them outside and into the alley. I hid behind a Dumpster, and then suddenly someone caught me by my throat and pulled me out. My mother always warned me that vampires were super fast, but damn, I wasn't prepared for Gideon's speed. I tried to use my powers against him but it was futile. He didn't have a wall surrounding his soul; he had a fucking impenetrable fortress. I've never seen anything quite like it. As I clawed at his hand around my neck, he kept asking me who I was working for: Heather, Damon, or both. And why an illusionist was working for demons."

"Who are Heather and Damon? How could Gideon tell you're an illusionist?"

"Supernatural beings can sense one another. Damon is the demon king. A seriously powerful demon. Unadulterated evil, cruel, and sadistic. The gorgeous princess Heather is his daughter. Her nickname? The bitch from hell. Some say she's worse than her father and even more powerful. She's ruthless. The stories I've heard about her..." She shuddered. "You really don't want to get on her bad side.

"Anyway, Gideon assumed I was working for them, and he was ready to kill me. I was so scared." There was a glimmer of fear in her eyes as if she was reliving the moment. "Come to think of it, you don't want to get on Gideon's bad side either. I don't know how, but somehow as he tightened his grip on my neck, I managed to explain that I was not a spy. I told him that I was just a twenty-one-year-old illusionist witch celebrating her graduation. A mortal. I asked him to confirm my story with my classmates at the bar. Thank God he believed me, or else I wouldn't be alive."

"But why would he assume you were working for the demon king and his daughter?" I asked.

"The demon in the alley was Heather's minion. She was there with Gideon to provide him with valuable information about her masters, Heather and Damon. Since I suspiciously had followed them, Gideon was afraid they were on to her and that they'd sent me to spy on the demon," she answered.

"Why did the demon betray them?" Weren't vampires supposed to be her enemy or something?

"Because she loathed Heather even more than she hated vampires. The demon king, by the way, badly wants Gideon dead, but I've no idea why. Gideon never talks about his past or himself. Anyway, after that night, we actually became friends. He even taught me how to tail someone properly." She chuckled, a warm expression spreading across her beautiful features.

"You care about him," I said.

"I do care about him, a lot, but not romantically. I've known him for four years now, and we both preferred to keep it casual between us. He had his own reasons, and I had mine. I like my men less complicated, and Gideon is... well, a complicated, Outsider vampire with too many secrets."

"Outsider?" I repeated.

"Oh, I forgot you're a newbie to the Hidden World. In vampire society, ten days after the Change, Newborns are given two choices: be part of them or be an Outsider. If you choose the first option, you have obligations like paying taxes, following the vampires' laws, et cetera, but in return, you get the protection of your Ruler and the vampire police. If you pick the second option, you're on your own. It's the Wild West out there for you. All crimes committed against an Outsider are unpunishable, at least by the Ruler. The culprit won't be brought in front of a Ruler to be judged. He or she won't be killed, forced to compensate the victim, or thrown into prison," she replied.

"And Gideon *chose* to be an Outsider." Why?

"He did, but I wouldn't lose any sleep over him; he can take care of himself. Believe me," she said as she leaned forward to close the empty pizza box on the desk. A necklace with a carved dragon pendant swung forward.

I nodded at it. "It's beautiful."

She touched the pendant. "What, this?"

"Yeah, I like it."

"Thanks. My aunt gave it to me for my sixth birthday. She's so superstitious. I assume you've never heard about the seven dragons, right?" I shook my head, and she went on, "Dragons are magnificent beasts. Unfortunately, there's not a lot we know about them. One of the few things we do know is that they maintain an unchangeable ratio between good and evil on Earth. They make sure our planet will never be populated with only bad people or good people. There's a certain balance the dragons keep."

My mouth drifted open, and my face slackened in shock. "Whoa, hold on a sec. Dragons? You mean the giant, fire-breathing kind?"

"Yes. According to the textbooks I read at school, there are seven of them in different colors: red, blue, gray, gold, purple, black, and white. Whoever tells you they have seen a dragon, they're probably lying to your face. Dragons can take a human male appearance, and they will never be in their true forms near us."

"How do they keep the balance between good and evil?" I asked, still stunned.

"Whenever it's disturbed by having more people do good deeds than bad or vice versa, a dragon will receive a magical list. It contains random names of good and bad people, including supernatural beings. Then the dragon shifts into a human form to reap their souls. That's why the seven dragons are called the Soul Reapers." She fingered her pendant. "It is said that if you wear a necklace with a carved dragon, your name will never be on their list, but it's just a superstition. There is only one thing that can keep you off their death list: consuming five drops of the red dragon's blood."

"Okay, wow. I... I... wow. Dragons are real, and they're the Grim Reaper," I mumbled.

"Yes," she said, then stood and put her hands to her hips. "Right then. Ready to learn how to protect your soul?"

For the next week, I stayed at her small apartment across from her bookstore. My meditation skills had been improving, which helped with the other tasks I was given. Gideon came over almost every night, checking my progress. He also brought me clean clothes, more BFB pills, and anything else I needed or asked for. Since my eyes were sensitive to sunlight, my sleep pattern changed. At night, I spent hours practicing Audrey's exercises, and during the daytime, I slept. It became my new routine.

Until one evening Audrey announced to Gideon that her part was done and I was ready for his next training.

Bewildered, I asked, "What? That's it? How can you tell I'm ready?"

Gideon said, "Sydney, what do you see around you?"

My brow furrowed in puzzlement, but I looked around the living room. "A couch, a coffee table, four walls, nothing out of the ordinary."

"And that is how she can tell you are ready," he told me.

"I had a feeling you'd pass this test. And I was right." Audrey sounded content.

I turned to look at her. "Whoa, your eyes. They're white."

"It's my magic," she explained. "I'm using it right now. Your mind learned how to resist it by blocking your soul, so what you see is the magic itself and not the illusion I'm creating at the moment, which is a tree standing in the middle of the living room.

"But you're not immune to compulsion. Gideon still has to teach you how to build a wall around your mind." Her expression grew serious when her gaze dropped to the number 744 on my palm. "Three nights ago, I accidentally touched the tattoo, and my Voice whispered something. I debated whether or not to bring it up, then opted to wait until we were done here, so you wouldn't be distracted."

"What did it say?" I asked her.

"Eternal gods."

"Eternal gods?" I echoed. "What does it mean?"

She shrugged. "No idea."

Before Gideon and I left Audrey's apartment, I thanked her for everything and hugged her goodbye. She wished me luck with the rest of my training. And boy, did I need it.

Chapter 10

I'd forgotten Gideon was an exacting teacher, way more than Audrey, demanding excellence and hard work. Complaining about lack of sleep or breaks was pointless; everything went his way anyway. Two weeks of tackling challenging mental exercises had passed, and I was exhausted.

Mentally preparing myself for another night of Gideon torturing me, I fumbled for the alarm button when it went off at six p.m. and dragged myself out of bed.

So what is waiting for me tonight? I wondered. Probably more of him saying, "Pay attention to your breathing, Sydney. Sit straighter, Sydney. Stop chewing on your bottom lip, Sydney," I imitated Gideon's voice while trundling toward the bathroom. After I brushed my teeth, showered, and wrapped a small towel around my body, I stepped out of the bathroom. Then I closed the door and turned around to cross the hallway, almost knocking into Gideon.

I sucked in air, my hand flying to my chest. "Sweet Baby Jesus. You scared the crap out of me! What the hell are you doing outside the bathroom?" And so close to me. I swallowed. In dark jeans, a taut T-shirt, and black leather boots, he was gorgeous.

He stared down at me. The color of his irises flared an unnatural bright green. Antifreeze green. Confused, I stared up at them, then cried out as something pressed inside my mind. Feeling like my head was about to explode, I clenched my eyes shut.

"What are you doing to me? Stop. It hurts!" I shouted.

"You saw it, the compulsion in my eyes, didn't you?"

"Yes. Now, please stop!" I growled with pain.

"Open your eyes. Look up at me."

I did as he'd asked. Beads of sweat gathered on my forehead as I tried to push him out of my mind. It was agonizing. "You're hurting me!" I yelled. Tears spilled from my eyes.

"Repel the compulsion. Build a wall. Do it," he ordered.

I averted my gaze from his. "I c-can't. Too much pain. Why does the compulsion suddenly hurt so much?"

He tucked a finger under my chin, gently lifting it and turning my face toward his. Eyes bright green, he said, "Because it's the first time you're resisting it. You're trying to push me out without realizing it, but you need to fight harder; build a strong wall to throw me out of your head. Disregard the pain and clear your mind. Concentrate." He withdrew his hand from under my chin.

I breathed in and out slowly. *Ignore the pain. Ignore the pain. Ignore the pain.*

"Good. Keep going," he encouraged. His compulsion thrust against my mind harder. I squealed with agony. *Ignore the pain. Ignore the pain. Ignore the pain. Focus.* I inhaled a deep breath and channeled all my concentration into the breathing. As I imagined a brick wall forming around my mind, I searched for my soul's energy as Audrey had taught me.

Her words floated into my head. *It's harder for Ancients to get into your mind when your soul is protected.* It took me a while, but I found its energy, and I surrounded it with a wall too. The pressure inside my head started to ebb away. I thickened the bricks, my concentration absolute. A few seconds later, the pressure ended altogether.

The edge of his lips curved up, his eyes icy blue again. "*Now* you're immune to compulsion and illusion."

I jumped with excitement, then stopped cold as I remembered what I was wearing: a tiny towel that barely covered my assets. While I adjusted the fabric, a thought occurred to me. He had lots of superhuman abilities. Could he...? No, there was no way.

But just to make sure, I asked, "You can't see through clothes, can you?"

Amusement brightened his features. "I'm a vampire, not Superman." His gaze skittered down my almost naked body, then back to my face. "Though with this towel on you, I don't really need x-ray vision to enjoy the view."

Heat hit my cheeks. "Hey, don't loo—"

He cupped his hand around my nape, drawing me against him and lowering his head. His mouth slanted over mine. I knew I should push him away and tell him off. I did neither. Instead, I parted my lips, inviting him in. His tongue darted inside. My stomach fluttered. One hand swept down the line of my back while the other tangled in my hair, and he stroked my tongue with his, sucking gently. I moaned, wanting more. A steady throb was building between my legs. His touch was cold; my insides, though, were burning. I didn't want the kiss to end. Disappointment surged inside me when he broke it. He looked down at me. His eyes flickered gold before he released me.

"You don't need to take BFB anymore. In a few minutes, you'll be healed for good," he said.

My eyebrows flew upward. "What? How?"

"My saliva."

"Your saliva?"

"It's been three and a half weeks. My blood is clean now, and my saliva is able to destroy your cancerous cells."

"So that's why you kissed me? Because it was the only way to pass it into my body?" I asked.

"Actually, I could think of another way, a little more fun if you ask me." His eyes went down and paused between my legs, then traveled back up to my face. "But I surmised that you wouldn't approve."

"Your assumption was correct," I said quickly. Too quickly.

He laughed softly. "And to your other question, yes, it was why I kissed you."

I hated that this bothered me. I gave myself a mental shake. *What is wrong with you? For God's sake, he's a vampire. A predator. A killer.*

To my horror, his eagle eyes caught my reaction to his last words, and he said, "However, I can kiss you again, and this time it'd be for an entirely different reason." He reached out, caressing my cheek. "Anything to wipe the disappointment from your lovely face." His tone was teasing.

My lips pursed as I swatted his hand away. "I am not disappointed." *Liar.* "I'm just confused. I thought the process of healing would involve your blood, not your saliva."

"I'm not an Ancient. My blood can't heal, but my saliva has the same healing abilities as their blood. And like them, it too needs a cleansed body to enhance those abilities."

"I'm really cured for good?" I wanted to be sure.

"Yes, for good. A small amount of my saliva will stay in your body as long as you have the tattoo."

Happiness mixed with relief washed over me like a tidal wave. I wouldn't die of cancer! And no more BFB, which was what had prevented me from feeling fully human. Now it was like I had regained my humanity back.

Itchiness in my hand punctuated my thoughts. I gazed down at my left palm. "Wow, the number went up to 744," I said.

"Your body has been cured, and it seems to affect the dark magic." He took my hand and examined the ink. "Eternal gods," he whispered like he was trying to figure out what it meant for the millionth time. Then he said, "I didn't get answers. No one I've asked had any idea as to what "eternal gods" might refer to, or what might occur when the dark magic countdown is over."

"Yeah, I didn't have any luck either scouring the internet for 'eternal gods' and 'dark magic,'" I told him.

"I'll keep looking into it." He let go of my hand. "For now, get dressed. We're going to Philippe's. He returned from his business trip and called. He has something to show us regarding your sister."

I nodded and hurried to my bedroom to slide into a pair of blue jeans and a cashmere sweater.

Thirty minutes later, we parked on Philippe's street. After passing two homeless men and a blonde hooker, we reached Philippe's front door. It was ajar. Gideon pulled out a silver stake from his inner jacket pocket, moving me behind him while cautiously stepping inside. The lights were on, and an eerie silence filled the living room. I noticed a trail of blood leading to the hallway. Alarmed, I padded to Gideon's side and gazed at his profile. He spotted the blood too.

"Stay here." His voice was low. He moved toward the hallway. I went after him, and he came to a halt, turning to me with a look that said, "Didn't I just tell you to remain in the living room?"

"You actually thought I'd stay put and do nothing? That's cute," I whispered sarcastically.

"Fair enough," he said, and we followed the blood trail together. The drops took us to Philippe's office. The door was open. Gideon stepped inside, scanning the room for threats. When I got inside too, he placed his weapon back in his jacket. Then, I gasped. Near the desk, Philippe's dead body lay on his back in a pool of his own blood, a silver dagger deep in his chest.

"Oh my God, he's dead. Like, really dead. Who would murder him?" I said.

"Well, he wasn't exactly short on enemies." A thump followed Gideon's words, and then a clatter of heels echoed in the basement loft. The sound came from the living room and got closer and closer. Gideon's body tensed up, his hand whipping inside his jacket.

"Philippe? You here?" a scared, feminine voice asked. "Philippe, I'm glad you found my new number and called me. I swear to God I didn't do anything to Zoey." In skinny jeans, red heels, and a brown jacket zipped up to her neck, Kelly appeared in the doorway.

Surprise colored her features. "Sydney? What are you doing here?" She stepped into the room and screamed. "Oh God, oh God, oh God, h-he, he's... dead... like dead dead."

"Who's this?" Gideon asked me, his head inclined to Kelly.

"She's Zoey's friend, the Newborn Philippe suspected had harmed her," I answered him.

Kelly rushed to a corner, bent over, and vomited red liquid. When finished, she straightened, her lips crimson. She wiped her mouth with her jacket, then held her stomach as her eyes moved back to Philippe's body. "Jesus, look at all that blood, so much blood. It makes me sick."

Gideon's gaze moved to me. "She is aware of the fact she's a vampire, right?"

At his mocking expression, her mouth tightened with irritation. "Yeah, I know I'm a vampire. But what can I do? Dead bodies still make me sick."

He ignored her and stepped closer to Philippe's body.

"What is it?" I asked, stepping even with him.

He picked up a cell phone, and with a sweep of his thumb across the screen, he woke it. Not locked, the screen displayed an email:

Hi Philippe, it's Skye, Zoey's roommate. You wanted me to contact you if I remembered anything else. So, yeah, I forgot to mention that a while back, a man with a long scar on his face and pale skin, really pale, asked questions about a missing freshman girl who lived in my dorm. He talked to Zoey. She told him her sister was missing too, and they exchanged numbers. I know she hid all of this from you. When I asked her about it, she explained you wouldn't approve of her searching for her sister. I'm so with you on that, by the way. It's a job for the cops, not for civilians like us. I hope the new information helps.

FYI, I'm free this Saturday. Maybe you'd like to grab a drink?

Unbelievable. Did she seriously have the nerve to ask him out while he was looking for his missing girlfriend?

Standing next to me, eyes on the email, Kelly seemed puzzled. "A man with a scarred face? She never brought up anything about a man with a scar on his face."

"So he's in town and didn't drop by to say hello," Gideon murmured, looking annoyed and worried.

"You know him?" My voice rose in surprise, but I was ignored.

"Why did Philippe call you?" he asked Kelly.

"Somehow he got my new number, and about an hour ago, I received a call from him. He told me he believed that I didn't hurt Zoey and asked me to come over 'cause he had some questions for me. Of course, at first, I thought no way in hell was I coming to his place, but then I remembered it was Philippe; I couldn't hide from him. He would eventually find me if I said no. He's good at this stuff. To not make him angry, I agreed to come by. I guess he wanted to ask me about the scarred dude."

"Gideon, who is he?" I repeated my question, my tone demanding.

"Later," he said. I opened my mouth to argue, but he told me, "Philippe dialed our police before he was murdered. Vampire cops will be here any minute. We gotta go."

We hurried outside and as we turned the corner at the end of the alley, five vampires in long black coats and black pants marched into it. Looking over at us suspiciously, the tallest one stopped.

Gideon turned his back to him and mouthed to us, "Play along." Then a flirtatious smile spread across his face as his stare slid to the blonde prostitute in a short fake-fur jacket, a tight miniskirt, and a low-cut top. She stood near the wall, at the corner of the alley.

He approached her. "Hello, there. My ladies and I are looking for some fun tonight. How much will it cost?" His voice was loud enough for the vampire cop to hear him.

She checked him out, then me and Kelly. She removed the cigarette from her mouth, flicking it to the dirty concrete and squashing the butt with her heel. A grin curled her lips as she named her price.

With two fingers, he beckoned us to come. "Ladies, we've got ourselves a new friend and her name is..."

"Call me Lust." She threw him a seductive smile.

"Lust," he rolled the name around on his tongue. "One of the seven deadly sins. I love it. Shall we go? Our car is just a block away."

Gideon's plan was working. The vampire cop who had stopped walked on, disappearing into the alley as we strode away.

At his parked bike, Lust's brow pinched together. "Where's your car? And I ain't getting in without seeing the dough first."

Gideon pulled out his wallet and gave her a wad of cash.

She counted it, and her eyes popped wide open. "It's five times more than what I asked." As if she realized something, her excitement dissolved. "Oh, fuck no. Y'all look nice and all, but I ain't doing no shady stuff. Uh uh, no strangulation and things like that."

Gideon's irises turned bright green as he looked down at her. "Chloe, how old are you?"

"Twenty-one." Under compulsion, she answered him without hesitation.

"Why are you here, selling your body?" he asked.

"I need the money, and my boyfriend said it'd pay the rent." A tear escaped her eye. She wiped it, and I noticed a beaded name bracelet around her wrist. Chloe.

"Leave your boyfriend. Pack your things, use this money to get a new apartment, then find another job, a job that doesn't require people touching your body sexually and making you feel bad," he instructed, eyes still glowing green. "Understood?" Her head bobbed up and down once. "Good. Now go." She put the money in her purse and spun around, walking away.

"Did you just compel her?" Kelly asked Gideon.

"His eyes turned green, so yeah," I said.

Kelly seemed surprised. "You an Ancient?" she asked, then swung her stare to me. "And you saw the green in his eyes? You immune to compulsion?"

"You bet I am. I busted my ass off to be able to resist it."

"The cops will be out of Philippe's home soon. It's best we aren't here when that happens," Gideon told us.

Kelly nodded. "You're right. I'm gonna go. You should, too. Sydney, if I hear anything from Zoey, I'll call you right away."

I thanked her, and after she took off, my attention went to Gideon. "Before we leave, I need to know; the man with the scarred face, who is he? Is he dangerous?"

He handed me a helmet and threw his leg over his bike. "He is, but I don't believe he'd hurt your sister. Hop on. I know where he may be."

Gideon drove us to a middle-class neighborhood and parked across from a two-story Victorian-style house. I was expecting a scary scarred dude, so I was surprised when a woman opened the door. A human, she looked to be in her late forties, black circles under her eyes. Aside from a few wrinkles, her dark brown skin was smooth. She donned blue pants and a finely knitted white cardigan, her brown, curly hair reaching her shoulders. The dude's wife, maybe?

A warm smile broke across her lips. "Oh, my dear lord. Gideon, is that really you? Come over here." She rose to her toes to hug him.

"Olivia, good to see you, too." He leaned down to return the hug. She motioned for us to come in and led us to the living room.

A large couch sat against the wall to our right. A flat-screen TV was opposite it. In front of us, there was a fireplace with a framed wedding photo on the mantel. The groom was tall with short, natural blond hair, blue eyes, and no scar on his face. He was behind the bride—Olivia—arms wrapped around her in a loving embrace. His wife was Olivia, and she was not a vampire. Who was she?

Gideon sat on the couch. I joined him. A picture of a girl about my age rested on the coffee table before us. Shiny curly hair hung down to her shoulders, and a wide, white grin plastered her face.

"B negative? Or do you prefer O positive like Thomas?" Olivia asked Gideon.

"I've already fed. I'm good."

She looked at me. "And you, dear?"

"A glass of water, please. Thank you."

When she stepped out of the living room, I whispered, "Who is she? Why are we here?"

He opened his mouth, then seemed to register the picture on the coffee table. Focus switching to it, he stayed quiet.

"Gideon?" I prompted.

Olivia returned with a tray holding a bottle of water and a glass.

"Where's Kyla? Why is her picture here and not in her bedroom?" Worry laced his tone.

Looking confused, she put down the tray on the coffee table and sat in the love seat in front of us. "I thought you came by because Thomas spoke with you."

"He didn't. I heard he was in town, so I assumed he was here. What's going on, Olivia? Where's Kyla?"

So the man with the scarred face has a name: Thomas.

Olivia rubbed her eyes tiredly. "A few months ago, I got a call from her. It was Nathan's one-year death anniversary. Can you believe it's been a year since he died in that car crash?" She paused. Sorrow filled her eyes as she turned to look at the wedding photo on the mantel. Turning her gaze back to Gideon, she continued. "Kyla sounded different. At first, I thought it was because she missed her father, but she didn't mention him at all.

"She told me it'd be our last conversation because she'd met new friends and was going to start a new life with them far away from here." Olivia took a deep breath, as if it'd give her some inner strength, then went on, "She was seeing a boy behind my back. I can't fathom why she'd hide him from me. On the phone, I asked her if he had anything to do with her abrupt decision. She wouldn't answer, only demanded I didn't contact her ever again. I did, though. Her cell phone is disconnected, and none of her friends know where she is."

What Kyla said to her mother sounded similar to what Zoey told Philippe and my parents.

"Why was I kept in the dark?" Anger raised Gideon's voice an octave.

She sighed. "You had your hands full with other matters. I didn't want to burden you with this."

"For God's sake, Olivia. You and Kyla are more important. If I had known, I would've left everything to help."

"There was no need; Thomas flew in to help. It was enough."

"My sister suddenly decided to leave and cut all contact with her friends and family," I piped up. "Thomas was in touch with her before it happened. Has he mentioned a girl named Zoey?"

"I'm sorry to hear that, dear, but no, he hasn't. I'll pray for her as well."

"Where is he now?" Gideon asked her.

"Back in New York City. Yesterday someone messaged him, saying they had information that might help find Kyla. Thomas set up a meeting with him tonight at a place called Wo Hop. It's in—"

"Brooklyn." I finished her sentence, my voice trembling a bit. It was my mother's favorite Chinese restaurant. When Zoey and I had been younger, we used to dine there a lot with my mom and dad. Memories flooded my mind, making me sad. I missed my parents.

I felt Gideon's stare on me when she said, "Yes, in Brooklyn. Are you from New York City?"

"I am," I answered, hoping I didn't sound depressed.

"Olivia, I apologize," Gideon said, "but we must go now. I need to talk to Thomas to see who he's meeting with." He stood up.

She followed suit, tears rolling down her cheeks. "Please find my baby. I can't lose her too."

He put a comforting hand on her shoulder. "I guarantee you I will do anything I can to find Kyla."

Outside her house, Gideon exchanged texts with someone as we moved toward his bike.

When he stuffed his cell phone back into his jacket, I faced him. "There are lots of similarities between Zoey and Kyla's disappearance. It could be a coincidence, but I don't believe that. Who's Kyla? You and her mother seem pretty close. Who is she to you?"

I saw the reservation on his face and expected him to refuse to answer, yet he did. "Olivia was married to Nathan, and Nathan's fifth great grandmother,

Clara, saved my life once. I'll be forever grateful to her and always protect her descendants." He fished out his motor key from his jacket pocket.

I caught his arm before he mounted his bike. Hoping he'd open up to me, I pushed. "What's the whole story?"

He grew silent. I retrieved my hand, staying in my place. Silence.

"The demon king, Damon, and I were never on the best terms," he finally said. "Damon constantly tries to kill me, and I kinda wish he'd stop because quite frankly, it's getting tiring." He leaned against his bike, his expression turning dark. "One of those attempts happened in 1858. I was tricked into drinking demon blood, which is highly addictive to my kind. One pint of it is enough to weaken any vampire, making us incapable of thinking clearly or fighting.

"Too weak to resist, I was captured by Damon. He threw me into a cage, and I was deprived of blood. After a week and a half of starvation, he released me in a densely populated rural area. Any starved vampire—Ancient, Adult, or Newborn—is like a wild animal, controlled by basic instincts and not reason. In that state, I was dangerous, loosed in a village full of sleeping people, frantically searching for blood, for killing. Then Damon showed up with a child who appeared to be about five years old, fragile, and innocent. Damon pushed him toward me and left."

I was horrified. "Why not just kill you and be done with it?"

"He wanted me to suffer. Murdering an innocent child would've tormented me for eternity."

"Whoa, he really hates your guts. Why?"

"We have a complicated history." Clearly not going to expand on this, he continued with the story. "When my eyes fell on the child's pounding artery, my senses went crazy. I leaped on him, drinking like a savage while he screamed and cried. I couldn't control myself. His heartbeat slowed, and he was close to death. A young woman emerged from the darkness. Her name was Clara, and she knew what I was. 'Drink from my vein. Take me instead,' she shouted, slitting her wrist.

"Her frightened voice helped me regain control, enough to detach myself from the boy's neck. Resisting the smell of her blood, I screamed at her to take the boy and run away from me. She picked him up in her arms and disappeared back into the darkness. Before I murdered everyone in that village, I pulled out my silver dagger Damon let me keep in the cage. I was ready to die when the young woman returned without the child. She hit me over the back of my head and knocked me unconscious, so I wouldn't kill her.

"When I woke up, I was restrained to a bed. She nursed me back to sanity, giving me her blood every day until I had full control over myself again. That night Clara saved the boy, my existence, and my soul."

What Clara had done was noble. She hadn't had to come back for Gideon, a stranger and a crazed vampire. I looked at Olivia's house. The lights were out, however, I doubted she was getting some shut-eye. How could she? Her husband died last year, and now her daughter had left. I understood why Gideon felt obligated to help, but what about Thomas's reasons?

"What's Thomas's connection to Olivia?"

"A few years after Clara saved me, she got married and had a daughter, Josephine. When Josephine was ten, she wandered off while playing with her friends. Being in the wrong place at the wrong time, she witnessed a human named Arthur Price, a corrupt local politician, committing a murder. Josephine screamed, revealing herself, and he chased after her. After she escaped him, he hired a contract killer to do his dirty work for him. Josephine told her mother about the murder. Afraid Arthur would harm her daughter, Clara reached out to me. I took her family into my house where they'd be safe and then went to Arthur's mansion to kill him.

When I sneaked into his house, I heard him talking to an assassin vampire with a scar on his face."

"Thomas is one of you? How come he doesn't have perfect skin?" I stopped him.

"Yes, he's a vampire. For an unknown reason, the Change didn't erase his scars as it should have."

"Is he really a hit man?"

"One of the deadliest. He was a member of an elite organization of vampire assassins." How could Thomas agree to murder Josephine? She'd been just a kid. It disgusted me.

"What happened next? Please don't tell me he offed that little girl," I said.

"I was about to dagger the vampire and slit the human's throat when the latter collapsed to the ground. Thomas had drained him of blood and life."

"He killed the dirty politician? Why?" I asked.

"Thomas has a code—no children. When Arthur contacted him about Josephine, Thomas didn't turn down the job since he figured if he did, Arthur would hire someone else. Intending to kill him to protect the child, Thomas demanded a meeting in person under the pretense of wanting half of his payment in advance."

"And then Josephine was saved?"

"No, she wasn't out of the woods yet. Before Arthur died, he divulged that he'd hired a second vampire assassin for the job because he sensed the reluctance in Thomas's voice on the phone. As Thomas and I searched for the other assassin, Elijah, to kill him, the demon king's spies were snooping around, asking questions about who I was guarding. To protect Josephine and keep her away from the demons, Thomas offered to take her and her family to his house in London while I dealt with the demons and Elijah. It was a good plan. However, after I killed the assassin and Damon's spies, I found out that Clara and her husband didn't survive the journey to London. They died from consumption." There was sadness in his voice.

I shook my head. "Poor Josephine. Not only was she ripped from her home, but she also became an orphan."

"Thomas raised her as his own since I couldn't. If Damon knew she was important to me, he would have used her as leverage against me." He pulled out the helmet from his bike's side, then handed it to me.

I took the helmet but didn't put it on yet. "So that's Thomas's connection to Olivia? He's her husband's great-great-great-great-great-grandfather?"

"Yes."

My mouth opened to ask more questions about his past, but he swung his leg over his bike, ready to leave. He wasn't in a sharing mood anymore.

"Gideon, it's important I speak with Thomas about Zoey," I said instead.

"And you will. I already texted him."

I sighed and put on the helmet, then hopped on behind him, and we drove off. I thought we were heading home, so I was confused when we parked outside Audrey's apartment building.

"Why are we here?" I asked, pulling off the helmet.

He slid off the bike. "We're flying out to New York City to meet Thomas at Wo Hop, which is where he's arranged a meeting with the human who has information about Kyla. Before we do that, though, we'll make a quick stop at your parents' house." He started walking toward Audrey's building and added, "Audrey will cast a spell to change your appearance, so you can talk to them."

I caught up with him. "You mean I'm gonna see my parents when we're in Brooklyn?" My voice boomed with excitement.

"You miss them, don't you?" he said as we were buzzed inside Audrey's building.

I nodded, smiling at him, and we got into the elevator. Opening the door to her apartment, Audrey regarded us with confusion. Gideon apologized for coming unannounced and explained why we had dropped by. Without hesitation, she agreed to help.

"What do you want to look like?" she asked me.

"A girl my age, the rest I don't care."

"No problem, but unlike a regular illusion, this will take some time. It's a hard spell, which by the way works only on mortals." Her eyes turned white as she mumbled something that sounded like Latin. After a short while, she said, "It's done."

I looked down at my hands and body. The tattoo was still there, and my body hadn't changed. I stepped to the mirror in the entryway. My features looked the same.

"You won't see the new face," Gideon said.

"Because you're immune to illusion magic, my spell can't get to your soul to fool your brain," Audrey elaborated.

I turned to Gideon. "Do you see my new appearance?"

"Yes, I see it, and you could too if you switch off the protection you've built around your soul."

"How?"

"You break your wall the same way you built it," Audrey answered.

"Break my wall? It was hard as hell to build it, so I think I'll pass," I told her.

"It won't be difficult like the first time you did it," Audrey said. "You have already learned how to put a wall around your soul. This time, it'll be different."

I hesitated, but after a moment, I closed my eyes, breathing slowly, concentrating. I imagined my protection around my soul breaking down.

Brick after brick fell, and when I opened my eyes, they widened. A girl with curly red hair, green eyes, and freckles stared back at me in the mirror. I reached up and touched my new face, examining it.

"Wow, it's amazing," I murmured.

Audrey grinned. "I'm glad you like it."

"Yeah, I don't look like me. It's so weird," I said, then gasped. "Wait. My abductor. He probably has a wall around his soul as well. He'll see my real appearance."

"Only if he stands close to you. This spell is very strong and can fool anyone—and I mean anyone—who is looking at you from afar, or on a TV screen," Audrey said.

"You sure?" I asked.

"Yes, don't worry," she replied, and I calmed down.

"Okay, now, bring back the wall," Gideon told me.

I concentrated again, and the protection around my soul was back a few seconds later.

I smiled at Audrey. "You were right. It was easy." Then I asked, "How long does the spell last?"

"Two days, give or take. It depends on many factors, like stress, illness, or lack of sleep. All of these will weaken the power of the spell and shorten its effect," she warned.

"Okay, duly noted," I said, and Gideon moved to the front door.

After we thanked her and left the apartment, he told me, "Thomas's private jet is waiting for us at the airport."

My jaw dropped. "We're flying to New York on a private jet?"

He checked his watch. "In an hour."

I whistled softly. "Impressive. Apparently being a hit man pays off."

He twisted his lips into a lopsided grin. "Considering a career change?"

"If it means I'll own a freakin' private jet, hell yeah," I said as we reached his bike.

He laughed. But before he climbed onto the motorcycle, his expression became serious. "Sydney, remember: when we get to your parents' house, don't say anything that would raise suspicions. They cannot know it's you."

"I know." I nodded, and sadness suddenly clouded my joy.

I wished I had more than just a short moment with my parents. I wanted this nightmare to be over. I wanted to find Zoey and get my life back. Despite the sudden gloominess, I chose to keep the smile on my face. Seeing my parents, even for a short time, was better than nothing.

Chapter 11

We didn't use the main airport terminal. Instead, we headed for the FBO. According to Gideon, it stood for a fixed-base operator. Which meant we skipped the security lines and walked right onto the plane. Flying on a private jet was freaking awesome. We weren't packed in like sardines. I had plenty of legroom, and no one was snoring in the seat next to me. *Thank you, Thomas!*

Fifteen minutes after landing, we were in a cab on our way to my home, thoughts racing through my head. Would I be able to fool my parents into thinking I was somebody else? Would I control my emotions near them?

"You remember our cover story, right?" Gideon's voice jerked me out of my reflections as we arrived.

"Yes, I'll introduce myself as Zoey's classmate, and you as my friend," I said as the cab driver pulled up two houses down from mine. Gideon instructed him to keep the meter running. I climbed out of the car, glanced around, and heaved a big breath. I grew up in this neighborhood. *Here my dad taught me how to ride a bicycle, my mom taught me how to drive, Zoey and I played with our friends in the backyard, and Jared broke my heart.* Memories, so many of them, surfaced.

"Sydney? You with me?" Gideon asked.

"Yeah, sorry." I shook my head to clear it as Gideon and I walked toward my house, scanning the area. Was my abductor watching it? I wondered when a woman passed by us, hugging a stack of flyers close to her chest. I caught a glimpse of her profile, and my heart skipped a beat.

"Mom?" My voice was a whisper, yet somehow she heard it.

With her back to us, she froze, then turned to face me. I almost didn't recognize her. The sweater and pants on her slim body were rumpled. She looked at me through a tangled mass of matted blonde hair, her eyes puffy and red-rimmed. Lines of worry and fatigue adorned her face.

Gideon nudged me gently, and with haste, I corrected myself. "Mrs. Newbern?"

She stared at me for a moment before her lips formed a strained smile. "Yes, how can I help you?"

"I, uh, I... I'm Zoey's friend, Britt. I have—had, uh, a few classes with her." I stopped, struggling to contain the storm of emotions stirring inside me.

"Are you all right?" Concern filled her voice.

No, I'm not. It's me, Mom. Sydney. I'm alive, and I've missed you and Dad. I want to—

Gideon came to my rescue. "Mrs. Newbern, we hope we're not interrupting, but Britt's just worried about Zoey. She left without a word."

"My husband and I are worried as well. It's unlike her to shut everyone out and disappear. We think her recent behavior is related to what happened to her sister, Sydney. She went missing. Never came back from a trip with her friends."

"I'm sorry to hear that. If there's anything we can help with, Mrs. Newbern, we'll be happy to," Gideon told her.

"Thank you. I appreciate it," my mother said. She was about to hand us some flyers when my dad stepped out of my house.

In faded jeans and a jacket, he approached us. "Honey, is everything okay?" Lines of weariness etched his face too. They both needed a good night's sleep.

"This is Britt, Zoey's friend," my mother introduced me.

His stare swung to Gideon, inspecting him, and then returned to me. "Has my daughter spoken to you? Do you know where she is?" He sounded desperate for some good news.

I felt bad I didn't have any to give him. "No. I'm sorry. One day she stopped coming to classes and answering her phone." At that, my father sighed with disappointment.

"When was the last time you talked with Zoey?" Gideon asked them.

"About a month ago. She called us and..." My mother's voice cracked, eyes glossing over.

My father continued for her. "She said she was leaving for another country and never coming back home. She demanded that we don't look for her."

"First Sydney and now Zoey. Oh, Robert, we've lost our daughters. Zoey's gone, and Sydney must be scared, all alone out there." She burst into tears.

My father drew her close to him and stroked her hair, comforting her. "We can't lose hope, hon. We raised two strong girls. They're survivors and resourceful. They'll be fine, and we'll find them."

They were a wreck. I burned to reveal my true identity to ease their pain, but I couldn't risk it. Not when *he* might be watching. Seeing my parents falling apart was too much for me, so after my mother stopped crying, I apologized and told them we had to go.

Back in the cab, Gideon gave the driver the address of Wo Hop, and we drove off. I looked outside the window, silent. A swirling vortex of emotions reeled through me. Gideon, sitting next to me, stayed quiet too, letting me have some time to myself. When we reached the city, the cab driver pulled over on a side street. Gideon paid him as I got out, noticing we were two blocks away from Wo Hop. It was nine p.m., and the street here was mostly empty of people.

"Is Thomas expecting us inside the restaurant?" I was still in emotional turmoil, and it showed in my voice.

"He is, but we don't have to go over there right now. If you need more time or anything else, just say so."

"No, I'm fine. Really," I lied. "I don't need anything." I turned around to start walking, but before I took a step forward, he grabbed my hand and flipped me around to face him again.

"I think you do." In one motion, he pulled me into his arms for a deep hug. His musky, woodsy smell engulfed me at once. I inhaled it deep into my lungs, closing my eyes and burying my face in his rock-hard chest. He was cold; his touch, however, spread heat throughout my body. For the first time since my ordeal had begun, I felt safe. Protected. He was right; I needed this. His embrace. Arms wrapped around him, I stared up into his eyes. So blue. So bright. So beautiful. Silence fell over us until a pedestrian walked past us, breaking the spell between us.

He released me, and a cold breeze blew a strand of hair across my face. He reached out and tucked it behind my ear. Then he pulled a small dagger from a sheath in his jacket pocket and handed it to me.

"It's important you keep it on you the whole time we're in Wo Hop."

Confusion crinkled my brow. "Why? Does Thomas pose a threat?"

"Not Thomas. At night, Wo Hop turns into a vampire brothel. Some vamps may be aggressive toward a female human."

A brothel? I'd eaten with my family in a freaking vamp brothel? I ignored the nausea rolling through my stomach and tucked the dagger under my waistband. We then moved along a row of stores until we reached the restaurant. I peered through the glass doors. The place was closed, the lights out. Gideon knocked twice.

A few seconds later, the door opened. We stepped inside and the door swept closed behind us. Light from the streetlamps streamed through the glass, and from what I could make out, Wo Hop looked the same as I remembered it: a large elegant room with Chinese decorations.

Out of nowhere, a big vampire suddenly appeared in front of us. He glanced down at our hands and said in a placid tone, "No invitation, no coming in. Leave."

"Well, this is awkward," Gideon started. "We came all this way. So what should we do?" He crossed his arms over his chest and tapped his pursed lips thoughtfully, then said, "I know!" He held up his index finger. "Here's a solution: you are going to let us in anyway."

"Leave," the man repeated with a blank expression.

"It's a bit problematic since we really need to get in."

The big vampire bared his teeth in a snarl.

"Oh, please," Gideon responded with a roll of his eyes. "Put away those baby fangs before you hurt yourself."

Heels clacking across the tiled floor filled the room. An attractive tall woman in a black, latex miniskirt and a halter top emerged from the back of the room, which was completely dark.

"What's the problem here, Igor?" she asked, stepping closer to the vampire in front of us, her mouth stained with blood. She licked her lips and dragged the tip of her tongue across the ends of her upper teeth as she sized Gideon up with thoroughness, obviously liking the sight.

"They don't have invitations," Igor answered. The sound of two raps on the door behind us tore her attention from Gideon.

She peered over her shoulder. "Slave, go get the door." A shirtless guy appeared out of the blackness in the back of the room. He was human, in his early twenties, wearing jeans and sneakers. He shuffled toward the front door, and when he passed by me, I registered the two bite marks on his neck. He opened the doors, revealing three men in the doorway.

The one on the right had dark glasses on his face. He held a long white cane out in front of him and swept it back and forth as he walked inside the room. Unlike the other two guys, he wasn't holding a card.

When they entered the restaurant too, a vampire came out of a room at our left, green leather pants and a tank shirt molding to his built body. His shoulder-length brown hair was tied in a low ponytail.

He pointed at the newcomers who held cards. "You two, you may proceed to the hallway in the back."

Without saying a word, they moved to the back of the room and disappeared into the blackness.

His attention switched to me. "As for you, breather. I assume you're here for a Euphoric Bite. I have five vampires who are skilled in Euphoric Bites, but alas, they're all fully booked for the next three months. You should've made an appointment and come with an invitation. However, since you're already here, beautiful..." Stepping closer, his mouth widened in a carnal smile. Long, wide fangs protruded past his lips, and I sucked in a breath. He was an Ancient. "I'll make an exception and offer myself for the service, but I'm not cheap. It'll cost you seven hundred dollars for the pleasure."

His fingers trailed down my jawline, and then over the vein in my neck. Just when they were about to reach the swell of my breast, Gideon's hand whipped out, grabbed his wrist, twisted his arm behind his back, and threw him across the room with a brutal kick to the back. The sound of shattering glass exploded in the room as the Ancient smashed into a table, sending silverware and broken plates scattering across the floor. My stare moved to Gideon, but he was no longer near me.

Standing over the Ancient, he said, "Sorry, Alexander, but she already has someone who can give her a Euphoric Bite. And it's free of charge."

Alexander leaped to his feet and swung at him. Gideon caught his fist and squeezed until the sound of breaking bones echoed through the room. The Ancient vamp's face twisted with pain. "That's for putting your dirty paws on her." Gideon's voice was gruff with irritation.

Alexander slipped from his hold and shouted, "Gideon, you're dead. You're not getting out of here with your head intact!" Bright gold colored his irises.

"Watch out," the blind guy warned as he pushed me to the side, taking a blow meant for me from the very pissed-off female vampire. She growled and leapt at him, and her big friend, Igor, joined her.

Two vampires against a blind man. *Yeah, leeches, real classy.*

I pulled out the dagger under my waistband, but to my amazement, there was nothing for me to do. Like a ninja, he kicked their asses. Then, with a silver stake he whipped out from the inside pocket of his suit jacket, he killed both of them in a matter of seconds. There was no freaking way that dude was blind.

His head turned toward the sound of a fight coming from the back of the room.

"Need a hand, mate?" he asked in an English accent.

In response, Alexander was hurled out of the darkness. His body hit the floor. Gideon blurred as he moved from the blackness and stabbed Alexander through the heart with a silver dagger. The Ancient vampire burst into ashes.

"Guess not," the ninja guy murmured, and the shirtless human, who had huddled in a corner, hurried to the front door and left the restaurant. Gideon approached me. Many deep cuts covered his face, but they were already mending.

His eyes were on the ninja dude. "Next time, you think you can arrange a meeting at a nicer place, like somewhere that is not a brothel owned by an Ancient I'm not really fond of?"

Whoa, the blind guy was Thomas? My head snapped to him, and I looked him over. He wore an expensive Italian suit, a black tie, and a white shirt stained with drops of the dead vampire's blood. His features were strong. Fiercely masculine, he wasn't handsome in the usual way. His medium-length brown hair was slicked back, and his white skin was not flawless. He was tall, about six foot five, and it looked like the Change had happened in his early thirties. When he turned to pick up his cane lying on the floor, I got a peek at his deep scar. It ran across his left cheek and ended at his chin.

"Oh, flap off," he said to Gideon, cane back in his hand. "It was the only location where the bloke was willing to meet with me."

"The bloke?" I repeated, putting the dagger back under my waistband.

"The boy with the information about Kyla," Gideon said.

"Who's the human?" Thomas asked as he headed to the back of the room, then added with annoyance, "We don't have time to bloody babysit."

"She can hold her own," Gideon said as he went after Thomas, who had disappeared into the darkness. Not all of us have vampire-level night vision, so I took out my phone and illuminated the way with it, to a door at the end of the room.

"The human is Zoey's sister," I said. "Do you know where she is?"

Thomas paused with his hand on the doorknob. "Zoey's sister? You're Sydney?" There was a note of surprise in his voice.

"That would be me. Do you know where she is?" *Please say yes, please say yes, please say yes.*

"No," he replied. "Her phone has been disconnected for over a month, and all of her belongings are gone from her dorm room."

"It sounds like you two spent a lot of time together. What kind of relationship did you have?" I asked point-blank.

"I assure you, Miss Newbern, it was solely platonic. The first time I met her, she brought up her concern about you and wished to get my help as her impotent boyfriend refused to assist. But here you are, all safe and sound." His tone was accusing, hinting that I'd gone away for a vacation while my family was worried sick about me.

I opened my mouth to explain that I'd been kidnapped when Gideon said, "Not now. I'll fill him in later." He opened the door, and we followed him through a dimly lit passage.

I put my phone away and after a minute or two, we reached another door. It opened, and soft electronic music poured out, along with a scantily clad woman. Gideon held the door as she passed through.

Her eyes fell on Thomas. "A blind vamp? That's a first." She touched his shoulder. "I'm Sharon, and I can make you scream with pleasure for ninety bucks." Her fingers trailed the fine fabric of his suit.

He shrugged her hand off him. "Sorry, luv, I'm not in the habit of paying for shagging. Here for business only."

Pouting, she continued on her way, and we entered into a space that looked like the reception area. It was dimly lit by glass-beaded lamps and surprisingly, saturated with the scent of flowers, not blood. The place was filled with a subtle, erotic atmosphere, and the air felt warm and cozy. Two girls, one blonde, the other brunette, sat behind a desk ten feet ahead of us. Both of them wore a black, long-sleeved blouse.

Thomas folded his cane as we walked to the desk. "We're here for Lucas Smith," he told the receptionists.

"The human bartender?" the brunette said.

"Yes, him. Where is he?" There was a tinge of impatience in Gideon's voice.

Their gazes moved to me, and suspicion crossed their faces. The blonde's focus returned to Thomas. "May I see your cards, please?"

When he told her we didn't have invitations, she looked at her coworker. "Page Alexander."

"Don't bother; he's dead," Gideon said. Then, suddenly, screams erupted from a hallway to the left of the reception desk. Vampires, some naked, others partially clothed, stampeded out of it, running from... something. Thomas, Gideon, and I rushed in the opposite direction. We weaved our way down the hallway, which was lined with rooms on either side, trying to spot the source of their fear. When we found it, Gideon moved in front of me protectively. Someone was throwing things out of the last room: clothes, handcuffs, shoes, even a nightstand. Thomas and Gideon slipped inside the room, and I stopped at the doorway, careful not to get hit by anything.

A woman in black leather leggings, strappy heels, and a red top held a guy by his shirt collar as four men trashed the room. "Where'd you hide it, you filthy lowborn?" she demanded from her victim. His face was in bad condition, eyes swollen shut, mouth all busted up, cheekbones bruised.

"Please, I swear to God, I don't have it." His voice was choked with pain.

Noticing our presence, they all glanced over at us. One pair of green eyes grabbed my attention, and from that moment on, nothing else mattered. Everything else became a blur. Except for him, the owner of those green eyes, the color of life.

"Look at me, just me." He spoke in my head.

"Yes, only you. Only you," I whispered. I would obey his every command, wish, and desire. Without him, I'd cease to exist—I'd die. "No! No! No!" I screamed when someone plucked me by the waist, pulling me away from my lifeline. I clawed at the arm circling my midriff. Fear, anger, panic—all burst inside me like an erupting volcano. I was flipped around to face the doorway. The green eyes were gone, and pain ripped through me. I cried and thrashed. Whoever held me tightened his grip. I was rocked from side to side, up and down, as my captor kicked and punched obscure figures coming at us.

"Bloody demons. How bad is she?" I heard a distant voice ask.

"Pretty bad," my captor answered. "I gotta get her out of here, or she won't make it."

"Go. You know who to call. I'll deal with these cockroaches," the man fighting alongside the one who held me said.

The noises in the room became weaker, as if I was sealed inside a bubble, the pain almost too much to bear. Where were those green eyes? Those eyes would eliminate all my agony. I *needed* them! I kicked and screamed, but it was useless. My abductor wouldn't let me go. My heavy eyelids fluttered closed. It was cold, and I shivered in his hold. The pain lessened as I drifted in and out of consciousness, and at some point, objects around me stopped moving.

"Lay her down on the bed. I'll start the IV," I heard someone say.

"Be careful when inserting it; she's weak," the man who had me in his arms ordered.

"I'm a nurse; it's not my first rodeo. Dr. Harrelson has worked with your friend many times before. He'll take good care of her," the nurse promised him.

I was gently deposited on a bed, and I opened my eyes. Familiar blue eyes looked down at me, filled with worry. My lips parted to speak. Nothing came out. My whole body hurt.

"Don't try to talk," the man with the blue eyes said, and blackness engulfed me.

Chapter 12

When I woke up this time, it was not to vomit or squeak in pain. The weakness in my body had ebbed away, as had the soreness. I inhaled the clean scent of fabric softener. Surrounded by softness, lying under a thick comforter, I rubbed my eyes.

"How are you feeling?" someone asked.

I sprang up in bed and glanced around the dark room. One moment it was only me in bed, the next, a male's body was sitting beside me.

"It's just me, Gideon."

At his voice, flashes of memory flooded my mind: him feeding me, him bathing me, him changing my clothes. I pushed the embarrassment aside. *You were sick, and he took care of you. Nothing sexual about it.*

I touched the unfamiliar bed. "Where am I?"

"In Thomas's guest room. Let me turn on the light." A moment later, the modern ceiling lamp above the bed turned on, although Gideon didn't seem to have moved an inch. God, I could never get used to his inhuman speed.

"What happened to me?" I asked, trying to make sense of the hazy, incoherent memories.

"Do you remember being at Wo Hop?"

I nodded. "Chinese restaurant by day, vampire brothel by night. We were there to speak with a guy who claimed to have information about Zoey. But before we found him, there was a commotion. And a room, and a woman in red." Or was it green? I frowned as my memories after that jumbled together in a haze of green. What had happened?

Gideon's voice was contemptuous as he said, "She was a demon. A royal, actually. Her minions were with her, and they attacked us. The one with the green eyes reached your soul and sucked half of it before I could stop him." Anger tightened his features.

"Jesus! That thing ate half of my soul?" A cold shiver ran up my back. "I don't get it; I built a wall around my soul. How did the green-eyed demon get past my protection?"

"He didn't attempt to obtain control over your soul. He sucked out its energy. The wall doesn't protect you against that."

"So what can?" There was fear in my voice.

"Having BFB in your system. Ancient vampire blood makes the human soul inedible to them."

"I see. And what kills them?" *Knowledge is power, my father always used to say to Zoey and me.*

Gideon replied, "They're immortal and as strong as vampires, but a bullet—any bullet—to the heart, and they're dead. They have another major weakness: once they start feeding on a soul, they must finish it up. If for some reason the victim dies or escapes before the demon finishes eating his or her soul, that demon will die."

I smiled with satisfaction. "Good. Then the bastard who attacked me is dead. But how did I survive with only half a soul?"

"Most humans would have been left with permanent brain damage after such a demon attack, but the doctor who treated you is one of the best. He's human but has extensive experience in healing supernatural beings and humans who've been attacked by them." He paused, then added, "Demons are forbidden to set foot on vampire territories and vice versa. If I had known there was a chance demons would be there, I wouldn't have let you come near the brothel without taking BFB first."

"God, what an odious species." An image of scared vampires running away from the demons surfaced in my mind. "Even your kind were scared of them…"

"She was royal," he said. "Those demons are really powerful, and most of the vampires in that hallway were Newborns. They were also surprised to see them in our territories. Even though we're not at war, they're still our enemy."

I scooted back and leaned against the headboard. "So I guess that by being there, the royal chick and her minions risked starting a war with your kind. But over what? Why were they at Wo Hop?"

"The human who contacted Thomas had something in his possession she wanted," he told me. "We don't know what it is, or why a royal demon would seek it. She escaped before Thomas could touch her. The rest are dead, including the human. She sliced his throat open before running off."

"What did the guy tell Thomas when he contacted him?"

"That he knew he was looking for Kyla and that he had something to show him. He didn't specify what it was. Before he died, he gurgled some words to Thomas. They didn't make sense. It was about visiting the mysterious world of the fae. Thomas has been searching for more leads in the past week."

"Whoa. A week? I was out for a whole week?"

"Up until two nights ago, you had an IV attached to your arm, and the doctor thought you were gonna suffer permanent neurological damage. After he increased the dosage of the medicine he'd concocted for you, your body started to recover, and he said the worst was behind you. You'll be fine, but you need to rest."

"Couldn't your saliva heal me, like with the cancer?"

"No, it was your soul that was gravely sick, not your body. Though the doctor did give you BFB a few hours ago to help your heart get stronger."

He reached out and took my left hand to glance at the tattoo. I noticed his skin seemed whiter than usual. He felt colder to the touch too. *Odd. Is he ill? No, he can't be.* Aside from the UV virus, vampires were resistant to diseases.

My thoughts came to a stop as I looked at the ink on my hand. I inhaled sharply. The number on my palm was 650. It had dropped to 650!

At my look, he said, "You were sick, and your body was weak. Now you're better, so let's hope the sharp decrease stops."

"God, yes." I sighed, and with my head down, I scrubbed a hand over my face, tired of everything.

When I looked up, the fancy bedroom I'd been in for the past week caught my attention. All the furniture was gray, including the platform bed I'd slept on. A chaise lounge with two toss pillows sat in a corner near a large window covered with a gray blind. The closet was opposite the bed, and on the left, there was a door, which I assumed led to an en-suite bathroom. Beside the bed, I saw a high-back bedroom chair. Gideon had probably sat there while I slept.

"Thank you for taking care of me this week," I said and then looked over at the covered window. "Are we still in New York?"

"Yes, in Thomas's penthouse."

Remembering the way he'd fought, I asked, "Is he really blind, or was it all an act?"

"Not an act. Illness took his eyesight when he was five. He's completely blind. He doesn't need the cane, though. He uses it sometimes to appear harmless."

I crossed my legs under the covers. "But he fought like a ninja, and how can he be a hit man? He's blind."

"His other senses were amplified because of his blindness. After the Change, they became even more acute. In a way, he sees better than those who have their eyesight."

"How old is he? Did he grow up in London?" I was curious.

"He's two hundred years old. When he lost his eyesight, his aristocratic parents, powerful vampires, disowned him. They didn't wish to raise a blind child and were ashamed of his disability. Not patient enough to wait until the Change would fix his eyes, they threw him out of their house when he was five. Forced to live in the slums of London, he fended for himself, learning how to fight and survive on the harsh streets by relying on his other senses."

"Gee, parents of the year." I was appalled. How could they abandon their own child? I felt sorry for Thomas. He grew up with no love, no family, all alone in the world. "Are there other blind vampires besides him?"

"As far as I know, no. His case is rare. The Change should've fixed his eyes. It's a mystery that he has tried to solve."

The door to the room opened, and a woman in a maid uniform entered. She set a tray with a soup bowl down on the nightstand.

She smiled politely at Gideon. "As you've requested. Warm soup for her." Steam rose in a fragrant cloud as she took off the lid. "I'm very pleased you're awake, miss," she said to me.

Gideon thanked her. When she stepped out of the room, he took the tray and handed it over to me. "Eat. You need your strength."

The smell of onion, carrot, and celery wafted to my nose. My stomach rumbled. I dipped my spoon into the bowl and gulped the soup down as he went to sit in the chair near the bed.

"Where's Thomas now?" I asked.

"In Boston, chasing a new lead. He found out that in the past thirty years, there have been many reports of missing human girls in a few towns in Boston. They were all between the ages of eighteen and twenty at the time of their disappearances. The human police didn't take their cases seriously because, like Kyla and your sister, the girls called their parents and asked them not to look for them. Then they cut all contact with the people in their lives. Thomas's theory is that Kyla, your sister, and all the other girls were forced to call their parents. He also thinks that their cases may be connected to your abduction."

I scooped up a spoonful of soup. Could it be? *No, wait, if it was, wouldn't I be forced to call my parents too?* "I don't think it's related to my abduction," I said. "In their cases, there was a clear pattern. Unlike them, I didn't call my parents and ask to be left alone." I sipped at the soup. "I don't know. It sounds to me like they were brainwashed into submission by a charismatic leader and joined some old, secret cult. The whole thing may not even have anything to do with the supernatural world."

"It's a possibility, but don't forget the demons are now part of the equation," he reminded me.

The image of that demon torturing the poor guy popped into my head. "Did Thomas ask the guy whose throat was slit how he was involved in all this?"

He nodded. "Last year, his sister abruptly decided to cut ties with everyone the same way Kyla and your sister did, and his search for her led him to Thomas."

A thought occurred to me. "Could the royal demon be behind Philippe's murder?"

"It's one thing to enter our territory; it's another to murder a vampire who is not an Outsider. I doubt a royal demon would do that. Damon doesn't need a war with vampires right now."

I sighed. "Zoey, Kyla, and the other girls are out there somewhere. If they joined a cult tied somehow to demons, we gotta get them out of there." I leaned over to put the tray on the nightstand.

"We will," he said, getting to his feet. The ceiling light flooded over him. His skin was paler and thinner, almost transparent. I hadn't imagined it before.

"Are you feeling okay?" I asked.

"I'm fine. There are clean clothes for you in the closet in case you wish to take a shower, but then get some rest. Your body is still recovering. I have my phone if you need anything," he said and headed for the door.

"Are you leaving?" I grimaced at the disappointment in my voice.

He stilled, then turned to look at me, a question in his eyes.

"Uh, I-I mean I don't mind you leaving, but, um... where are you off to?" I hoped my tone conveyed indifference this time.

"To a vampire bar offering Donors."

"Doesn't Thomas keep blood in his fridge, like you do?"

"He does, but I finished the last bottle three nights ago."

And you haven't fed since then?"

He shook his head.

It explained his sick appearance. A spike of worry and alarm passed through me. "Why didn't you buy more blood?"

"You were unwell and barely conscious. Leaving you was not an option. And it's been only three nights. I may be a bit weak, but I'm in full control of myself. I'm nowhere near starvation. I wouldn't have put you in danger," he told me.

"I know that. My point was that I don't think it's healthy for your body."

"Don't worry about me. I'm all right. I'll be back in a few hours to check in on you," he said and then he left.

Would he be drinking from a female Donor? Would his lips touch more than just her neck? I threw back the covers and swung my legs over the bed. The floor felt cold to my bare feet as I rushed after him in sweatpants and a T-shirt.

I caught up to him in the hall. "Wait." Standing in front of him, I blurted the first thing that was on my mind. "Has a Donor ever offered to pay you to give 'em, um, a Euphoric Bite?"

The smug smile spreading across his face made me want to smack myself for the stupid question.

"Yes," he replied.

"And?" *Did he agree to do it? Who was she? Or maybe it was a he?* I felt like I was going to explode with curiosity. Judging by his satisfied expression, this was exactly what he'd aimed to achieve with the lack of details. *Damn him.* "Oh, never mind. Don't answer, I don't care," I said but three seconds later changed my mind. "You know what? No, I do care 'cause I just don't get what the fuss is all about. Why would a bite cost freakin' seven hundred bucks?"

His fangs slid down as he bared his teeth. "Want me to show you why it costs seven hundred dollars?" His tone was husky.

I opened and closed my mouth several times then mumbled, "Y-you're weak from not feeding... a-and I'm... I..."

"Your blood will restore my energy while I give you a Euphoric Bite, and my saliva, which will pass into your body while I drink from you, will speed your healing processes."

My eyes dropped to his fangs. I stared at their razor-sharp edges long enough that I heard the ticking of the wall clock. I opened my mouth to tell him no, but gasped instead when he moved, suddenly a few inches away from me. One hand at the back of my head, the other on my waist, he bent his head, and his fangs hovered over my neck, his breath touching my skin. Goosebumps raced down my body. His fingers knotted in my hair and tilted my head to the side, exposing the jugular vein. My heart raced as he slowly dragged his fangs along my neck, and then his mouth found my earlobe, his lips caressing it. My breathing quickened.

"All you have to do is tell me yes, and I'll show you." His voice was a low rasp in my ear. Mine, on the other hand, was nowhere to be found. Questions swamped my mind. Would it hurt? Would it be addictive? Would things between us change?

A quiet moment passed, and he released me. His fangs retracted as he stroked my cheek with his knuckles. "Whenever you're ready, just say the word." And with that, he turned and left. This time, I let him go.

I inhaled and exhaled several times to regain my senses, then trailed my fingers where his fangs had touched. *No, don't think about Euphoric Bites. Don't think about his mouth, his lips, his fangs. Just don't think about him.* But I did—oh, I did—and it took several long moments before other things finally occupied my mind. One of them was the guy who had been killed by the royal demon.

What had he whispered before he died? Fae exist? No. Fae are mysterious? No. Come on, what was it? Fae something... fae... mysterious... the mysterious world of the fae! Yes, it was the mysterious world of the fae. It sounded familiar. Why? I massaged my temples with my fingers, and the answer came to me. It was the name of that website I'd visited.

I searched for my cell phone. Finding it in the first drawer of the nightstand, I unlocked the device and went through the internet history, then pulled up that site. I navigated to the About Me page. Even though I hadn't gotten a good look at the guy the demon had killed, I still recognized him in the picture displayed on the phone. His name was Lucas Smith. Why had he wanted Thomas to go to his website? I tapped on the Contact Me page, which provided a cell phone number and an email address.

"If you witness a supernatural event, contact me," it read at the top of the page. Lucas was dead, but I dialed the number anyway.

Four rings in and a hesitant female voice picked up. "Yes?"

"Oh, uh, hi." I was surprised someone answered me. "Um, who am I speaking with?"

"You're the one who called me, lady. Who the hell are you?"

Whoa, what was up with the hostility? I checked the time. Six p.m. It certainly was a decent hour to call someone.

"My name is Sydney. I got your number from The Mysterious World of the Fae. It was on the Contact Me page. You know, as in you are *welcome* to call me." I was being rude, but hey, so was she. A long silence followed. Was she still on the line? "Hello?"

A heavy sigh. "Sorry, can't help you. Don't call this number again."

"Wait! Don't hang up. Please. I'm looking for Lucas."

A lengthy pause, then she broke the silence with, "He's dead." Her voice quaked, and I heard a sniff. "A word of advice? Stay the fuck away from all the supernatural shit. It's not a game. This crap is real."

"No—it's not a game. I'm so sorry for your loss. I was there when Lucas died, and I wish I could've saved him," I told her.

"Oh my God," she whispered. "It's you, isn't it? The red-headed chick, but your appearance changed when that demon stared at you. You transformed into a different person. What are you?"

My jaw dropped in disbelief. She'd been there, witnessing everything? "I'm human. What you saw is magic, but not mine. A witch cast a spell on me because I needed to look different. What were you doing in Wo Hop?"

"I was..." She faltered.

"You were..." I prompted.

"I don't know if I can trust you," she said at last. "You claim you got Lucas's number from his site, but did you really? He warned me to be careful. Those demons scared me shitless, and they could be after me."

"He was right to warn you, but I'm not working for her, nor any other demon. They tried to kill me too. One of them sucked my soul. You witnessed it yourself, didn't you?" I reminded her.

"Yeah, it was weird the way he stared at you, and that vampire fought them while holding you in one arm. He was with another undead."

"Yes, Thomas," I told her. "We were all there to meet with Lucas. Listen, I know you're terrified. I wanna help you, but you're gonna have to trust me and give me your address, so I can come over. We should talk in person."

For the next few seconds, all I heard was her breathing. *Please, please, please, don't hang up.* She might know what Lucas had been about to show Thomas, and maybe more.

"Okay," she finally said. I looked upward and mouthed, "Thank you."

She gave me Lucas's address, where she was staying at the moment, and her name, which was Natalie. Then she told me she was heading to the bus station in forty minutes whether or not I made it.

I swiftly went to the closet and changed into the clothes I had on me the day the demon attacked me. The money I'd kept in the pocket of my jeans was still there. I shoved Gideon's dagger under my waistband and picked up the cell phone from the bed. I was about to tap on Gideon's name when my finger paused over the screen. If I talked to him, he'd probably order me to stay in bed and then tell me that he would go to Natalie while I rested. I didn't have time to argue with him, so I closed the cell phone, put it in my pocket, and strode out of the room.

I went down the sweeping stairs leading to an enormous living room with floor-to-ceiling windows showing panoramic views of Manhattan and beyond. Thomas must have sunscreen roller blinds on the windows or UV protection because in the daytime, this penthouse, which was at least nine thousand square feet, would be flooded with sunlight.

At the bottom of the stairs, I smelled faint lemon oil in the air. Everything was squeaky clean. I glanced up at the barrel-vaulted ceiling and then at the opulent furniture, the spotless fireplace, and the fine artwork on the walls. I was impressed. From London slums to this wealth? *Good for you, Thomas*, I thought as I darted toward the private elevator.

Outside the high-rise building, I hurried to the subway and hopped on a train. When I arrived at Lucas's building, an old lady was walking out. I held the door for her and stepped inside. The elevator was out of order, so I trudged up to the fifth floor, where I walked down a musty hallway with dull overhead lighting. Passing by doors, I heard a loud TV, a man yelling at his wife, and a baby's cries. I stopped at Lucas's apartment and knocked on the door.

"It's open!" Natalie's voice called out, and I let myself in. A frightened girl stood in a small living room. She was about my height and age, with honey-blonde hair in a bun, bronze skin, and mascara smudged under red, puffy eyes.

With a shaking hand, she was pointing a handgun at me. Oh, great. Just my luck.

Chapter 13

I raised my hands up. "Whoa, put it down. It's me, Sydney. We talked on the phone earlier, remember?"

"I don't know what to believe anymore. You might be a demon. Close the door." I did as she asked and stepped into the living room.

"Natalie, I am not a demon. I'm a human like you. Here, touch my skin." Whether demons had different skin texture, I had no idea, but it was a good excuse to get closer to her to disarm her.

"T-t-that's close enough. Don't take another step, or I'll shoot," she threatened and drew back, almost stumbling on something.

I exploited the split second of distraction and grabbed the barrel, redirecting it away from me. Out of the line of fire, I twisted the gun toward her, and with my other hand, I chopped into her wrist and disarmed her. Natalie looked at her handgun, which was now in my hand. She cowered backward.

"Calm down. I'm not here to hurt you," I told her. "I'm human. I swear. I just wanna talk. That's it."

When she seemed to relax, I stepped to the stained beige couch. Perching on it, I scanned the room. Over a cheap rug, there was a coffee table with three empty beers on it. An old TV was in front of the couch. To my right, there was a small kitchen containing a dining table and a fridge.

To gain her trust, I laid the gun on the coffee table. "Let's start from the beginning. What were you doing in that brothel with Lucas? Was he your boyfriend?"

Still standing near the wall, she shook her head. "We were close friends. Lucas has... had," she cleared her throat, "an obsession with the supernatural, fae in particular. About a month ago, this damn obsession got him in trouble with some demons, and they were after him. He wouldn't say why. James, who was his roommate, wanted to help him out, so he confessed to him that he was a real vampire, or a day walker, or something like that. I don't remember the exact term. Anyway, he told Lucas he worked at a vampire whorehouse.

"James was the one who fixed him up with a job as a bartender over there, saying it'd keep him safe because Wo Hop was their territory. No demons are allowed in. That's why in the last couple of weeks, Lucas had spent most of his time there. He really thought he'd be safe at Wo Hop." She stepped to the coffee table, picked up a bottle, then cussed when she discovered it was empty.

She went to the kitchen and opened the fridge. "Wanna a beer?"

"Thanks, but I'm good."

She returned, gulping from a fresh can of cold beer. Wiping her lips with her sleeve, she sat next to me on the couch and said, "A few hours before Lucas was murdered, he called me, hysterical. He found out the demon bitch had killed James because he refused to give away his hiding place. He sounded so scared, begging me to come over to the brothel.

"When I arrived there, I saw him at the bar, working. I walked up to him, and he took me to his friend's room for privacy. He said he was meeting with a vampire and planned to leave for Texas after that. He asked if I could lend him some money. Before I could answer, the door flew open. It was his friend. All worked up, he warned him that there were demons at the restaurant entrance. To get in, they offered their dick of a boss a large amount of money in a case."

"Was the boss's name Alexander?"

"Uh, I'm not sure. Maybe. I remember he had a ponytail and wore green leather pants that night."

Definitely Alexander. "Go on."

"Lucas was shocked that his boss had accepted the demons' money. He quickly hid me in the closet. There wasn't enough room for him in there, so he closed the closet door and..." Tears streamed down her cheeks. She sniffed. "Through a small crack, I saw everything. That bitch beat the shit out of him as the other demons tore the room apart, looking for something. Christ, I almost shit my pants. I was so fucking scared. There were so many screams outside the room. Then, the three of you came in. Your friends fought them while you were in that vampire's arms... and your face... it changed, and your boyfriend, or whatever, left with you, and that demon bitch killed Lucas." She choked on her tears.

"I'm sorry you had to go through that." I felt for her. Watching your close friend die couldn't be easy.

She knuckled away her tears and stood. "Look, I really need to get the hell out of here, but before I go, there's something I think you should have." She disappeared into the room near the kitchen.

When she came back, she said, "Before Lucas shoved me into the closet, he handed me his phone and a flash drive. I have no idea what's on it since he didn't have time to explain everything, but I know he planned to show it to your vampire friends.

"After he was killed, I ran to his apartment. Not the smartest decision, I know, but I couldn't return home and face Lucas's mother. I just couldn't. So, I stayed here for the past week, trying to figure out how to explain his death to his family. Today I finally came up with something and was ready to get on a bus back home, but you called." She drew a deep breath. "Anyway, here, it's yours." The second she handed me the thumb drive, the front door flew open with a bang.

Two men appeared in the doorway. Demons? I wasn't worried about my soul being eaten again as I had BFB in my system, but it didn't mean I wasn't alert or that Natalie's soul was safe. I quickly put the thumb drive in the back pocket of my jeans.

The big man on the left stepped closer to us. "Where is she? Where's my daughter?"

My eyebrows drew together. "Who?"

"That will be all," his friend, a lanky guy with black sunglasses told him, then glanced at the name tag on the dude's uniform. "Liam, I don't need your muscle anymore. You may return to your boring life as a store manager."

"But my daughter's cries came from here. They took her," Liam insisted and, as if hearing his phone ringing, he pulled it out of his pants pocket and looked at the screen. "Lisa? Lisa, you okay?" he answered, paused for a few seconds, then said, "Home? With Aunt Ruth?" He sounded relieved. "Okay, good, good. Stay there. I'll see you when I come back home from work." He hung up.

"See? She's fine," the skinny man said. "Go back to work now."

Liam's gaze went to me as though I'd spoken to him. "You sure? Okay, thank you for not calling the cops on me. Sorry about the door." He turned and left the apartment.

"What's wrong with him?" Natalie asked.

The man pulled his sunglasses up to the top of his head. His eyes went from white to brown. Of course, an illusionist witch. "It's so much easier to have someone else break down doors. It hurts my shoulder, you know."

He crossed the room and stuck out his hand to me, his palm up. "The flash drive in your back pocket, please."

I played innocent. "What flash drive? What are you talking about?"

He expelled an impatient breath. "I know you have it. I saw you with it when I barged in."

"Who the hell are you? Why would a witch be after it?"

"For the dough, darlin'. The name is Ian Robinson. I'm a private investigator," he said.

"Were you hired by a royal demon?" I asked.

"As a matter of fact, I was. Three nights ago." He stretched his hand out to me once more. "The flash drive, if you please."

I reached back into my jeans pocket, but instead of giving him what he wanted, I pulled out my empty hand and flipped him the bird. "*This* is the only thing you're gonna get, so you better leave."

His lips tightened with anger, and his eyes turned white. A slight pressure pushed against my body.

"Hasn't anyone told you it's rude to enter someone's soul uninvited?" I said as I easily blocked his attempt to reach my soul.

His eyes slit while his head cocked to one side, as if trying to figure out how I was immune to his magic. "It can't be... You're human."

"So I've been told—a lot," I grumbled.

His gaze snapped to Natalie.

She started to scream. "Oh my God, cockroaches! Get 'em off of me! Get 'em off of me! They're crawling under my shirt! They're all over me!" She flailed around the apartment. I hurried after her as she frantically slapped her arms and legs to get the imaginary insects off her, starting to undress.

"Natalie, look at me. They're not real! Don't hurt yourself." From firsthand experience, I knew how real illusion magic felt.

"Oh, God! They're creeping under my skin!" She scratched her arms until they bled.

"Stop it! Stop the illusion, or I swear to God I'll kill you," I warned the witch.

"The spell won't die with me, darlin'. Hand me the flash drive, and I'll free her. Do it now before she does more damage to herself," he said.

Natalie squealed in pain. Shirtless now, she cried as her bloodied nails dug deeper into her arm.

I cringed. "Okay, okay, I'll give it to you. Just stop the illusion." I drew out the thumb drive. "Here, take it." I hurled it through the broken front door. I wanted to kick his ass but was afraid he'd cast another spell on Natalie, so I rushed to the kitchen instead.

I rummaged through drawers and cabinets for a clean hand towel but found something better: a basic first-aid kit. When I came back to the living room, the illusionist and the thumb drive were gone. Like he'd promised, he'd undone the spell.

Natalie was sitting on the couch, seemingly out of it, her expression blank. Her bra, belly, and pants were smeared with blood. I went to sit next to her while she mumbled incoherently. I opened the first-aid kit and pulled out gauze pads, a strip of tape, a small pair of scissors, and a bottle of hydrogen peroxide.

"This is going to sting a bit," I said before I cleaned the wounds on her forearm. She hissed as I took care of her injuries. Then I returned to the kitchen for a glass of water.

She drank it, snapping out of her shock and standing up. "I can't be here anymore. I need to get away, take a bus back home."

I got to my feet too. "Yeah, you do that. And stay away from the supernatural world. Live a normal life."

"Oh, I'm done with all this stuff, for good," she said.

After she put her sweater back on, said goodbye, and took off, I cursed the illusionist out loud for stealing the thumb drive. I searched Lucas and James's bedrooms, then the living room, hoping to find a copy or anything related to the disappearance of Lucas's sister. There was nothing, though, not even a laptop.

Exasperated, I was about to take off when a woman stepped through the broken front door. My gaze swept over her clothes, a slim-fit, black leather vest, leather shoulder armor, and tight black pants. The look was completed with lace-up black knee-high boots. She had a fit body, her hair pulled up in a high ponytail. She was a vampire, no doubt, but something about her was off. Her skin was pale gray, her eyes bloodshot, her nose bleeding.

"Who are you? What are you doing in this apartment?" she asked, glancing at the mess in the living room. Her eyes narrowed at me. Not giving me time to respond, she launched herself at me with visceral fury, then kicked me. I flew across the room and slammed up against a wall. I coughed, and my head spun. I scrambled to get up but failed. My bones hurt. Everywhere. Gideon had been right; I hadn't fully recovered from the demon attack.

The vampire was near me in an instant. Before I could utter a single word, she seized me by my shirt and lifted me off the floor, thrusting my body up against the wall. She flipped me over and pressed my head to it while twisting my arm behind my back.

"What'd you do to him?" she demanded.

I groaned in pain. "Who ar—" A cough. "Who are yo—" Another cough. My chest hurt like hell, and it was hard to breathe. She caught my hair and pulled my head back with a snap. I cried out.

I guessed she assumed that inflicting pain would encourage me to be more talkative. She was partly correct; the pain did spur me into action. But I was tired of being attacked by vampires and demons and witches, and I was in no mood to talk. Pissed off, I gathered all my strength and delivered a vicious kick backward, pushing her off me. I spun around. She was on the floor a few feet away from me.

"Who are you talking about?" I managed to ask before nausea doubled me over.

On her feet again, she darted forward and punched me in the jaw. *Son of a bitch!* Staggering back, I felt a wave of weakness wash through me. I did my best to ignore it then straightened and focused on her. I blocked her next strike and hit her with a right hook to the face and an uppercut to her chest. She snarled like an animal, crazed, unwilling to calm down or listen to me.

For her, it was kill first, ask questions later. Well, I wasn't ready to die yet. So we fought until I pulled my dagger out and drove it through her heart. She sank to her knees and fell forward on her face.

I pushed to my feet, and my vision blurred. God, I needed to rest. I tottered to the couch, put the bloodied dagger on the coffee table, and plopped down—for all of three seconds.

A shout came from the front door. "Melissa? Oh, no, Melissa!" A human woman ran to the maniac I'd just killed, wearing black pants and a dark blue jacket. Three female vampires followed her into the apartment, all dressed in attire identical to the dead vampire's.

Alarmed, I shot to my feet. What the hell was the deal with Lucas's apartment? Everybody had a sudden urge to pay it a visit tonight? Who were they?

The human cradled the dead body in her arms and trained her accusing stare on me. "She killed Melissa."

"I had no choice. I—"

The three vamps, whose Change appeared to have occurred in their early twenties, jumped me. I didn't have the strength to fight them, and within seconds, I was face down on the floor while one of the vampires cuffed my hands behind my back. Were they vampire cops?

"Take her to Pam," the human woman ordered, and they hauled me to my feet.

"No, you can't take me, I—goddamn it, listen to me. I'm sorry, but she was acting crazy." Ignoring my protests, they dragged me outside the apartment. Lucas's neighbors must have been used to loud noises because no one opened their door to see what was going on.

"Who's Pam? Where are you taking me?" I asked as they dragged me outside.

Instead of answering, they shoved me into the back seat of a black Audi waiting at the curb with the engine running. The vampires climbed in too, and I sat wedged between two of them. They duct-taped my mouth and jammed a burlap sack over my head. My pulse careened. The headache and nausea worsened.

"Where's Melissa?" asked a feminine voice from the front seat.

"With Trudy. Start driving," said the one on my left, and I felt the car lurch away from the curb. The windows were closed, I could tell by the lack of wind, but I was still cold due to the A/C pumping through the car. No one spoke during the long drive. It felt as if two hours had passed before the ride became bumpy, and it was everything I could do not to throw up into the burlap bag. Finally, the bouncing stopped, and a few minutes later, the car ground to a halt.

The doors clicked open, and I dreaded getting out of the Audi. I had no clue who they were, or what they were going to do to me. Tied up, I was powerless against them. My only hope was the cell phone in my jacket pocket. I had to find a way to reach it and call Gideon.

One of the vampires pulled me out of the freezing car. Outside, night insects chirruped. Even though a light wind was blowing, I thawed out and started to regain sensation in my feet and hands. Someone frisked me for weapons and took out my phone. I cursed inwardly. Great, there went Plan A. The bag over my head was pulled away, and I jerked my gaze around.

I stood in the circular driveway of an enormous Gothic, gray-stone castle. In the middle of the driveway sat a fountain featuring a marble statue of a woman in a flowing robe. I glanced back at the stone wall with its immense wrought-iron gate, trees looming beyond it. Great. Nothing said "peaceful, loving place" quite like a scary gothic vampire castle hidden in the woods.

"Don't bother plotting your escape," said the vampire nearest to me. "Our territory is heavily guarded—night and day. Strong magic keeps unwanted visitors out. No one can get in or out without our approval."

Of course it was. This night just kept getting better and better.

The car that brought me here sped away, and the two bloodsuckers from Lucas's apartment dragged me up to the massive wooden front door of the castle. They pulled it open, the hinges screeching in sharp protest, and forced me inside. The door closed behind me with the same unpleasant noise.

I studied the Gothic architecture around me, feeling as if I'd been transported back in time. An iron candle chandelier, strewn with spider webs, hung from the ceiling by a heavy chain, while flickering candles in the wall sconces cast eerie, dancing shadows. The boarded trefoil windows were stained glass, deep black to keep the sunlight away. The entrance hall had columns supporting the rib vaults above. A shiver ran down my spine as I looked around the spacious room. What was this place?

"What do we have here, warriors?" Observing me, a woman descended the curved staircase in front of us, her voice carrying authority. A red dress, not a uniform, clung to her model-like body. The click-clack of her black heels tapping the limestone floor reverberated off the walls as she reached the foyer and strutted toward us. She stopped before me, and I scanned her sultry features. Her skin was the color of dark obsidian, smooth, flawless... too flawless. Another freaking bloodsucker. Her walk, the way she held her body, and the expensive-looking clothes pointed to her being in charge.

"I killed one of you in self defen—" I started, but the leech next to me tightened her grip enough to drive me to my knees. The fast movement made my head spin. I coughed.

"Silence! Don't speak unless you are told to do so," the bloodsucker that held me down barked, and I was tempted to punch her in the face. However, conserving my energy was more important. Besides, starting a fight in my current physical condition would be pointless and stupid.

The vampire in front of me looked at the one who restrained me. "The mortal may rise."

The leech took her hand off my shoulder, and I got to my feet. The lady boss leaned in and sniffed the air. Her nose wrinkled in disgust.

Oh, I'm sorry, does my sick hurting soul disturb you? I moved my head a bit forward and coughed in her face.

"Oops, my bad," I said sarcastically. Her expression changed to one of annoyance. She reached up to her face and wiped away the tiny drops of my saliva. The vampire on my left raised her hand to slap me, but the lady boss stopped her before the back of her hand slammed into my cheekbone.

"No, don't. Not yet. Tell me what happened."

"My Ruler, she killed Melissa," the leech on my right said, bowing her head guiltily as if she was responsible for her death. "We've failed our duty to protect her."

"You have, warriors," their Ruler agreed. "Melissa was sick with the UV virus. However, it didn't alleviate your responsibility to protect her. In addition, you lied about the reason you needed to leave. You will bear the consequences. Guards," she called out, and four female vampires marched into the entrance hall. They wore the same uniforms as the ones next to me, but their leather vests were brown. "Take them to the Starvation Chamber."

Without arguing or putting up a fight, the vampires flanking me walked with two guards outside the hall.

The other two stayed in the room waiting for their Ruler's next command, which came a second later. "The mortal ended the existence of one of our own, and she'll be punished as well. Strip her of her clothes."

"What! No! Get away from me!" I yelled at them as I backed up.

"Then skin her alive," she added, her lips curling into a smile.

At her words, panic clawed through me, chilling my blood. *Run, my instincts screamed; fight, my mind contradicted. The likelihood of outrunning them was remote, so the latter option won out.*

Chapter 14

Fear pumped adrenaline through my veins as I punched, kicked, and struck the guards, but after a few moments, the lady boss lost her patience. With a snap of her wrist, she sent me hurtling to the ground. Pain exploded everywhere. She straddled me, her hand around my neck, anchoring me to the floor. She was way stronger than the guards. Her mouth opened, and she released a long threatening hiss, her lips drawing back, her fangs exposed. They were large and long. An Ancient. Crap. I wiggled beneath her, straining to push her off me, but to no avail.

She laughed at my useless attempts. "Such an ignorant mortal, thinking you can best me. At least you're not a coward like all of your kind. If you didn't reek of sickness and demons, I'd feast on every drop of your blood." Her face scrunched a bit, and she got back on her feet, as if she could no longer stand my stench.

I sat up. "You should be thankful for my sickness; it's the only reason I'm not enjoying kicking your ass right now. And by the way, you psycho leech, the last I checked, it's your kind who lives in the shadows, afraid to be discovered by us—the humans."

My big mouth earned me a painful kick to the stomach. She knew how to hit, I'd give her that. Her blow shut me up. Curled up in a fetal position, I gasped for air, coughing blood. The two guards stepped up to me. One restrained me while the other started to take off my clothes. I was too weak to resist them.

"Wait!" The leeches' boss stopped them when I was down to my bra and underwear. The stone floor was cold against my bare skin, and I quivered. Her cold touch didn't help when she took my left hand and inspected the tattoo.

"What in the name..." she whispered. "Who cast this on you, mortal?"

"Still trying to figure it out myself," I answered.

She dropped my hand and looked at the guards. "No one harms her. Take her upstairs and call the witch. She needs to come over. It's urgent."

A surge of relief coursed through me. I wasn't going to be tortured to death. Yet. The ink in my palm bought me time to think of a way to break free.

The guards threw my pants, undershirt, and sweater at me, but not my jacket. "Put them back on."

After I did, they grabbed my arms and steered me outside the entrance hall. We walked to another large room where we climbed a curving stone staircase. On the second level, we turned right and moved down a long, dimly lit hallway. At its end, they flung me into a small room.

They closed the wooden door behind me, and I heard the lock click into place. Alone, I surveyed my new surroundings. An arrow-slit window across from me let cold air and moonlight filter in. Without my jacket, my body trembled. I hugged my midriff to warm myself up and flinched at the pain. I grasped the hem of my undershirt and slowly lifted it. Examining the damage her kick had done was difficult because besides the moonlight, the only other source of light was a single candle on the floor. The room had no furniture, not even a chair to sit on. I let go of my shirt as my eyes caught the bust displayed on a pedestal near the window. I advanced on it, then scrutinized it. Her features were carved in exquisite detail, with delicate lines. Her hair was wavy, her lips full, and her eyes were pushed back under a dominant brow bone.

Who was she? Or more importantly, who were they? Where was I? Their leader called her minions "warriors", and now that I thought about it, I didn't recall seeing a single man around. Were they a vampire version of the Amazons? Someone unlocked the door and opened it.

A girl stepped inside. She wore the same uniform as the warriors, but I couldn't get a good look at her skin in the dim light, so it was hard to tell if she was a vampire. I presumed she was. I was even more convinced when the dim light didn't seem to give her any trouble as she looked me over from head to toe, shaking her head in horrified disbelief at my condition. She stepped closer and I realized there was something in her hand. A jacket. My jacket.

She held it out. "Here, wear it. The temperature in this room can get cold for humans." Her low voice was warm and kind, the complete opposite of the others'. A flicker of hope sprang up inside me. She could be my way out. I feigned a smile as I leaned forward to take my jacket from her. A drop of blood dripped from my chin and splashed on the floor. Two fangs popped out. She jolted back, away from the blood, startling me. Animalistic hunger flashed in her eyes as she looked at my neck. *Yeah, so much for her being my way out of here.*

Not planning on becoming her next meal, I reared back while my eyes darted around the room, searching for something I could use as a weapon. However, surprising me, she stayed in her place and closed her eyes, taking a deep breath and letting it out, clearly attempting to calm herself down. A few seconds passed before her fangs tucked back into her upper jaw.

"I'm sorry," she apologized, opening her eyes. "It's just that I'm a Newborn, and although your blood smells pretty foul, it's still challenging for me to handle my new urges."

"Um, okay, but seeing as it's important for your leader to keep me alive at the moment, I fail to grasp the logic of sending a *Newborn* to me while I have open wounds," I said.

"I heard the guards talking about you being sick, so I assumed the bad smell of your blood would assist me in resisting it. And they didn't send me. I'm not authorized to be here. If they find out, I'll be severely punished," she told me.

I frowned. "So why are you here? What do you want?"

A muffled noise came from outside the door.

She glanced back before looking at me again. "I must go before the warriors' training session is over. I'll return in a few minutes with human food," she promised and vanished from the room.

I stared at the door, wondering why she was being nice to me. Whatever her agenda was, it didn't matter right now. I had to concentrate on getting out of here. The way things were, I had two options: one, convince her to bring me my cell phone and then call Gideon. Or two, ask her to help me break free. The problem with plan number one was the strong magic protecting the castle. How would Gideon manage to sneak in and get me out? Since the Newborn vamp was probably more familiar with the security system in the castle, I chose option number two. I didn't trust her, but it wasn't as though I had better alternatives.

As I waited for her to come back, I sat on the chilly floor near the candle flame, which didn't do a thing against the cold creeping through my bones. I hugged my knees to my chest as I inhaled the scent of melting candle wax, watching the thin stream of moonlight slanting in through the slit-arrow window. An hour or so passed, and she was still a no-show. I dreaded to think what would happen to me if she didn't return and help me escape. My thoughts then wandered to the king of the fae. The last time I'd been in a similar shitty situation, he'd rescued me.

Feeling ridiculous, I said to the air, "Oberon, if you hear me, I could really use some of your Houdini power right now. Please, make me disappear from whatever this place is." I sighed. "Please be here." I waited for something magical to happen, but only silence followed my words. No voice spoke in my head, no fae king popped up out of thin air. Nothing. No one came.

The time ticked by, and the light of the dying candle started to fade away. Just when everything seemed hopeless, the door opened, and the Newborn vamp came in with food. In spite of not having an appetite, I took the sandwich she offered.

She sat across from me near the candle in the center of the room. "I've fed, so you shouldn't be scared of me, and we've got plenty of time before the guards return."

I forced myself to bite into the bread as my body needed energy. "Who are you? Why are you being nice to me?" I asked between chews.

The light from the flame touched her face, and I saw her features clearer. They were average, and she looked about eighteen years old. Her skin was a beautiful bronze, her dark brown hair pulled back in a tight ponytail, and her eyes were the same rich brown.

"I'm Alice, and I'm being nice to you because I don't approve of the way my fellow sisters treat humans. They have no compassion for humans. I'll help you escape, but I need something in return."

Of course she needed something in return; there was no such thing as a free lunch.

So what was it? My firstborn? "Okay, I'm listening."

"Drive a silver dagger through my heart before you sneak out of here," she said in a matter-of-fact voice.

With eerie timing, the yellow light in the room died, and darkness prevailed. The soft light returned when she lit a new candle and placed it on the floor.

From the short time I'd been exposed to the supernatural world, I'd learned that vampires were vicious monsters. Ruthless. While that was their fundamental nature, some weren't entirely bad. Gideon and Thomas, for instance. As I looked into Alice's sad eyes, something inside me told me she wasn't either.

"No, I'm sorry, I can't. I won't." My reply brought disappointment to her face. "Why do you want to die, anyway? I mean truly die."

"The Change ruined me," she replied. "My life is over. I'll never watch the sunrise or sunset, enjoy the taste of a delicious cake, or feel my heartbeat ever again. The idea of living in the shadows and feeding on human blood like an animal for eternity is unbearable to me. I'm not cut out to be a vampire. My mother promised me that I'd get used to it, but I don't see how.

"The day the Change took my human life, I promised myself I'd end my existence, but I don't have the courage to do it. I can't stab my own heart with a dagger, or go out into the sun and get the UV virus. I've seen what the disease does to my kind. It's a horrible way to die." She paused for a moment, then said, "I don't understand. You had no problem killing Melissa, so why won't you do the same to me?"

"I didn't kill her in cold blood. It was self-defense," I told her.

"You did her a favor. She was in great pain, dying from the UV virus."

That explained her aggression. "How did she get it?"

"Last year she contacted her son, which is punishable by Memphis law. She was sentenced to death and thrown into the Death Chamber, where there is no protection from the sun."

I was aghast. "She was sentenced to death just for talking to her son? What is this place? What's the Memphis law?"

She blinked with surprise. "You're new to our world? How much do you know about vampire history?"

"Close to nothing," I answered, rubbing my hands together near the candle's flame. "But please, educate me." The more I knew about the bloodsuckers, the better.

"Journals of vampires," she began, "have been passed down through families for centuries, recounting stories about loneliness, the UV virus, bloodlust, immortality, and more. But what obsessed vampires' minds the most was one question: where did we come from? There has been much speculation and conjecture over the years. Some believe paranormal beings were created by God along with humans; others think it was a mutation that created us. There are many more theories revolving around the creation of vampires. Which ones are correct? Sadly, we don't really know."

"Not even who was the progenitor of your race?" I said.

She shook her head. "No. What we do know about our history is that around 3,000 BC supernatural species lived out in the open among humankind. In ancient Egypt, vampires were believed to be gods on Earth while Daywalkers were thought to be humans.

"At first, Daywalkers left their homes to join the other vampires who lived away from humans only after they underwent the Change. When darkness fell, they'd come to farms, villages, and cities to feed. But with time, they started living with full-blown vampires before they went through the Change, and the vampire population began to grow. They were ruled by a king and his queen. Back then, females were considered equal to males. That, though, changed after the vampires obtained the Tera Stone."

"What is the Tera Stone?"

"It's a beautiful rock with great magical powers. The rumors—which later turned out to be false—claimed that it could cure a vampire from the UV virus. The king coveted it, and after the war, he got it."

"A war with who?"

"With the witches. In the beginning, the Tera Stone belonged to a tribe of witches called Tera, and the vampires went to war with them to procure it. The war lasted almost three months and resulted in bloodshed and many deaths on both sides. After the victory, the stone was squirreled away at the king's residence. Anen, one of the king's sons, found it, and at his touch, , something strange happened. The rock became red and whispered, 'You were born to rule.' Astonished, he ran to his father, who was with his council and shared his new discovery. They all heard the red stone whispering, 'You were born to rule.' The rock only responded to Anen's touch, and its color went back to white whenever he withdrew his hand.

"This made Anen, a Daywalker at the time, feel more powerful than his father and his older brothers, and he actually was. The stone reacted to the unique traits that differentiated him from the others. Anen was thirsty for more power and, after his Change, he killed his father, his two brothers, and his mother, then crowned himself the new king. However, the obstacles on the road to absolute power didn't end there.

"When his subjects learned about the Tera Stone, they wanted to touch it too, to see if they were special like him, but Anen forbade anyone to come near it. The angry mob would have none of it, and they swarmed his residence. The guards protected his consort and his two children while killing the rebels. Anen had to fight them too, but eventually, the rebels obtained the rock and put their hands on it in turns. To five only, the color turned red and the rock whispered. Anen knew he had no choice but to share power with them, and a new era began.

"He and the five other vampires ruled together. They were the Original Rulers, strong and powerful. Over the years, those who opposed them or attempted to topple them were ruthlessly suppressed. Every vampire had to swear fealty to them. The Rulers had absolute power over their subjects."

"What happens if one of the Rulers dies or is assassinated?" I asked. "Who succeeds him as the next Ruler? Who is permitted to touch the stone? Their children? How does it work?"

"If a Ruler dies, his sons are the first who may touch the Tera. If none of them is chosen, then this right is granted to the nobles, and after that to the high-level employees. If the rock still doesn't respond to any touch, all the Ancient noble vampires will fight each other. The winner will replace the dead Ruler."

"Only male vampires can be Rulers?" I asked, finishing the sandwich.

"Only males," she confirmed. "Even to this day. But at least today we have rights. There was a time when we didn't." Her expression darkened. "Anen considered us useless and stupid. He convinced the other Rulers to strip females of their rights. We lost our power and autonomy and were reduced to the status of slaves, including Anen's own consort and daughter. We became property to be owned."

"What a misogynistic pig," I blurted with out contempt.

She nodded. "Rape, beatings, and humiliation were the new reality for female vampires. Any rebellion was brutally crushed. Everyone feared the Rulers."

"Were they as cruel to humans?"

"Very. When Anen's father ruled as king, he enforced strict punishments for any vampire who harmed a human, but with the Rulers, it was different. Vampires were allowed to feed freely on humans and kill them even though we don't need to drink more than a pint of blood a day. Piles of bodies began to form everywhere, instilling panic and fear in your kind. There was chaos—until she came." Her stare moved to the statue in the room, and admiration filled her eyes.

I followed her gaze. "Who is she?"

"Our savior, Herit. All seemed doomed until a woman no one knew or had ever heard of asked to speak with the six Rulers. They were informed of her request. They were also told that she was not a vampire, a demon, or a human."

"She wasn't a vampire?" I asked, surprised.

Alice shook her head. "She wasn't. The Rulers' curiosity was piqued, enough for all of them to gather together in order to see who she was before they killed her. In the meeting, Herit ordered them to stop the slavery of female vampires and the slaughter of humans. They laughed, and Anen leaped at her, attempting to rip her head off. He failed. One by one, Herit fought off the six Rulers, vanquishing them and their guards."

"Wait a second." I raised a hand. "She defeated six Ancient vampires all by herself? What kind of supernatural creature was she? A witch with the ass-kicking abilities of a vampire?"

Alice got to her feet and stepped up to the statue, her eyes on Herit's face. "She wasn't a witch—even though she had magical powers and was an expert in witchcraft. And having no wings, she wasn't fae, either." Alice eyed the statue for several moments, as if the woman in it was a mystery she was trying to solve. "The truth is no one knows what or who Herit was. She possessed enormous powers nobody had ever witnessed before. Building temples for her, some believed she was a goddess, but that was just one of the many rumors about her."

I blew a warm breath into my hands. "After she overpowered the six Rulers, what happened?"

"They agreed to her three demands: one, to give female vampires their rights back. Two, to control the killing of humans. Three, to start hiding their race's existence from them. To live in secrecy among the humans. This she demanded from demons and witches, too. Herit expected that in a few generations, most of humankind would believe them to be fantasy creatures, made-up stories you tell before bed. Her third demand didn't sit well with the demons and witches.

"They were outraged that anyone would dare tell them how to live. She explained that it was essential to restore and maintain order. Then she added that as long as their existence was not common knowledge among humans, they were free to reveal their true nature to them. The demons and witches didn't accept it. As a result, the six Rulers broke their agreement with her. They formed a temporary alliance with the demons and witches to fight her, so she built a large army of rebels, and the Big War broke out.

"It took the lives of many, including humans, and ended with Herit's victory. Everything changed from then on. After her three demands were met, she created a system of justice protected by strong unbreakable magic, with laws that apply only to supernatural beings. Each race, though, was allowed to establish their own system of justice. She also constructed the Ice Prison."

Even with the dim light in the room, I detected a flicker of fear across her face when she uttered the last two words.

"Is it like a human prison?" I asked.

"Worse, much worse," she answered. "Whoever breaks Herit's laws, like practicing dark magic, would be sent there by the Watchers. They're magical beings created by her. Guardians of her laws. But like everything in life, they're not perfect. I've heard about supernatural beings who successfully concealed their criminal activities from them. However, it's not easy by far."

"Is Ice Prison inhabited solely by those who broke Herit's laws?" I asked.

"No. Demons, witches, and vampires send many of their criminals there too through the Watchers."

"Where is this Ice Prison?"

"It's in a pocket dimension attached to ours. The entrance is located in the Devil's Triangle." At my look, she said, "Yes, the same infamous Bermuda Triangle where ships and planes disappeared in the past. The magic in the triangle area is very strong. On rare occasions, its energy sucks things in the pocket dimension."

A cold breeze blew through the window. The candle flickered, and its light cast swinging shadows across the stone walls.

I rubbed my arms. "So all the people who vanished in the Bermuda Triangle ended up in Ice Prison?"

"Yes, but it's a price Herit was willing to pay to have order in the Hidden World," she replied.

Note to self: no more vacations near the Bermuda Triangle.

"What about the Memphis law you mentioned earlier? Are they the vampires' laws?" I asked.

"No, they are the laws of the Memphis Warriors," she said. "We are an Outsider organization of vampire warriors, consisting of females only. Our Founding Mothers fought alongside Herit in the Big War. When it ended, they settled in Memphis in ancient Egypt and vowed never to let the Rulers enslave them again. With time, more and more vampires joined them and were trained to fight. We grew bigger, having our own Ruler and a queen, and established our own laws."

My gaze slid from the candle flame to Alice. "Did you grow up here? Does your father live with you and your mother?"

"I grew up here, yes, and I've never met my father. All warriors are forbidden to have romantic relationships with anyone, but we're allowed to have sex. If a warrior is a Daywalker, and she conceived, her child will be adopted by a vampire couple who want children, unless the baby is a girl. In that case, she'll grow up here and be trained to become a warrior after her Change."

When she finished talking, a question struck me. "You said that the sick vampire I killed broke your laws by contacting her son. What's her son's name?"

"James."

"James? Not Lucas?"

"Lucas was his roommate and friend."

"Why did she come to his apartment tonight?"

"When she first met James, a year ago, she revealed to him she was his biological mother and gave him her phone number," Alice told me. "About a week ago, she received a call from him. He sounded scared. His human friend, Lucas, was in trouble, and so was he. Demons were following him, and he asked for her help. She drove to his home as soon as she could, but a human named Natalie refused to open the door. Tonight she went over there again. Her mother Trudy and her friends joined her."

"Did James say anything about a thumb drive?"

"A thumb drive? No, not that I recall."

I rose and moved toward her. She recoiled at my proximity, and I remembered I had bleeding cuts.

"Oh, sorry," I said.

"It's okay, but it's better if you don't come any closer."

I stepped back and looked at the statue. "Where is Herit today? You used the past tense when talking about her. Is she dead?"

"No one knows," she replied. "After the Big War, she vanished. The last time she was seen was in the New World. Two Ancient vampires recognized her. They said she looked very ill. Rumor has it she was poisoned with her known weakness—dark magic—and now she's no longer with us." Alice suddenly became alert. "Oh no, Karen and the guards. They're coming. I can hear them." With a blur of movement, she was at the door.

"Wait," I said. "Who's Karen?"

"A strong witch who works for the Memphis Warriors. She's mean; be careful with her. I'll come back as soon as it's possible for me, and help you even if you don't kill me," she promised and disappeared before I could thank her.

A minute later, the door opened, and two vampires in uniform entered the room. A woman followed them inside, carrying a lantern with a frame of wrought iron that held four glass panes. They closed the door behind them, the lantern's gleam brightening the room.

"Show me the dark magic," she instructed the vampires.

The leech on her right stepped up to me. Her face wore a stony expression, her platinum-blonde hair tied up in a tight ponytail. She grabbed my left hand, turning my palm up. The woman, who I presumed was the witch, came closer. A black dress, the same color as her hair, was draped over her body, the hem reaching mid-calf. She had several gray hairs and a few wrinkles at the corners of her eyes and mouth. She stared down at the number on my palm, awe on her face.

When she finally looked up, a smile formed on her lips. "I'm Karen and I'm a witch, not a vampire."

"Yeah, I figured that part out; the bad skin texture on your face kinda gave it away," I insulted her.

She chuckled. "Pam warned me you had a mouth on you. It makes it more fun to crush your spirit." She bent down and set the lantern on the floor, the shadows jumping and shifting with each swing.

She straightened and reached out to take my left hand from blondie. "Let me have a better look at it."

Her fingers ran over the number. She shook her head slowly in disbelief. "Marvelous. Absolutely marvelous. Pure dark." Her voice was low, her tone reverent. Then, her gaze moved up to my face. "How are you still alive and healthy with this inside you?"

"What can I say?" I shrugged. "I'm special." If she thought I'd spill all the details about how this damn thing had wreaked havoc on my body and made it sick with cancer, she was wrong.

"The human is not healthy, Karen. She reeks; her soul is sick, but it's from demons, not magic," blondie said.

"Who is the witch who branded you with the dark spell? Give me a name," Karen demanded.

"Wish I had one *not* to give you, but sorry, the man who kidnapped me and poisoned my body wasn't in a chatty mood," I said.

"A man with dark magic skills? Could be an illusionist," she murmured to herself and then looked at the tattoo, touching it again. Her eyes closed. After a short moment, she whispered, "Eternal gods."

Hearing those words, I jerked my hand back.

Blondie snatched my left palm. She took out a switchblade from her pocket, flipped the blade open, and looked at Karen. "Our Ruler said you must check the dark magic in your lab. To make it easier for you, I'll cut the tattoo out."

"What! No!" I panicked, trying to pull my hand away unsuccessfully.

Karen's eyes widened, seeming alarmed as well. "No! Don't!" she exclaimed when the point of the knife touched the tattoo.

As the vampire pressed the tip of the blade into my skin, I swiftly screwed my eyes shut, bracing myself for the pain, then waited. And waited. And waited, but there was no pain.

"What have you done?" Karen's voice trembled with fear.

I snapped my eyes open. My jaw slackened at the sight in front of me. "What. The. Hell?" I whispered.

Chapter 15

Everyone in the room fell silent. The brunette was standing next to Karen, whose face was drained of blood. Their attention was on the hand of the vampire holding the knife. Her fingers began to crumble into pieces as blackness slowly spread up from the tip of the blade. The small bits of her flesh floated around the room like dandelion fluff. Her mouth was opened as if she wanted to scream, but no sound came out. Crimson tears rolled down her cheeks. Her hand was gone, then her arm. It broke into pieces.

Starting to turn black, the knife stood straight up by itself in the center of the number on my palm. When it was completely black, it exploded into a million small fragments that fell to the floor.

My left arm became numb, and I lost control of it. I watched in terror as black, sand-like grains streamed from the tattoo and gradually assumed the shape of a giant snake—a pissed cobra with its mouth open. My heart pounded against my ribs. Sweat dampened my brow and the back of my neck while my stomach threatened to up-chuck its contents. What was that thing?

Karen started to mumble something that sounded like Latin, her voice unsteady, her body quivering. Blondie was long gone. The pieces of her body vanished from the room as the giant cobra's head dipped toward Karen. The other vampire hurried in front of her. The swaying snake studied the guard. Karen went on with her chanting even though her magic did nothing to harm it.

The vampire slid her sword out of the leather harness down her back. Two red dots, acting as eyes, examined her weapon. Then black fog poured out of the cobra's mouth, coiling around her body. Her sword clattered to the ground while her lips opened in a silent scream. When the color of her skin turned gray and she went motionless, the black fog moved back to the snake's mouth. She collapsed to the ground, dead.

Karen abandoned her spell and twirled around, rushing to the door. "Let me out! Let me out!" She banged on the wood with the side of her fists. The snake moved toward her and magically forced her to turn and face it. She seemed to be trying to move, but it looked like she was paralyzed in all her extremities. The snake's face was a few inches away from hers, her chest rising and falling in a rapid rhythm. The cobra's tongue whipped out, and when it touched her skin, the color of her eyes and hair gradually became white, skin wrinkling and shriveling. She dropped to the floor, lifeless, her body mummified.

And then that thing turned to look at me.

My heart almost leaped out of my chest. I swallowed hard and froze with fear. Its red eyes held mine. A chill rolled down my spine, and goosebumps erupted on my skin. At that moment, I knew it was pure evil. I felt its malevolence. The snake looked at me for a few long moments. I was certain I was about to meet my maker. To my surprise, however, it didn't kill me. The shape of the cobra started to fade and soon it returned to the black sand-like substance, streaming back into my palm. The number 650 reappeared on my skin, and I started to regain control over my arm until I felt it completely, as if nothing had happened.

I was still in shock when the door swung open a short while later. Pam waltzed into the room with four warriors. She stared at the bodies of Karen and the vampire.

"Jesus, they're dead," one warrior whispered.

"It was the dark magic. I sense its power in the room," Pam said, sounding a bit scared. "We ought to destroy it."

"I doubt you can." I gestured with my head to the corpses on the floor. "They wanted to cut it out with a knife and look at how they ended up."

"Of course it'll kill them. One must never remove dark magic from its host this way. It makes no sense the witch would do something so reckless," Pam told me.

"Then how do you plan to destroy it?" I asked.

"Although dark magic physically strengthens its host, it only protects itself—not the host," she replied. "Which means that you, mortal, can be killed. After you're dead, the new witch will seek a spell that can eliminate it." She looked at the vampire on her left. "Clean the room, contact the witch's cousin, and prepare the back courtyard for the mortal's execution. Our queen will be present too. Let your sisters know about her arrival."

She left the room, and I stared at the closed door. Oh my God, I was going to be executed. I had to figure a way out of here, with Alice's help or without. My head spun with thoughts of how to break free while the vampires dragged the bodies out. Before they left, they replaced the candle in the center of the room with a new one, lit it, and took the lantern with them.

Alone in the room, I paced nervously back and forth. I stabbed my fingers through my hair and felt a slight pain in my left palm. I glanced down at the number, and my fear mounted. If I made it out of here alive, what would happen when it reached zero? That thing was sinister. Diabolical. Its eyes had looked at me, and it was there—the evilness. I drew in a deep breath and rubbed my hands over my face to clear my mind. The door opened then, and Alice slipped inside.

"We don't have much time," she said. "In ten minutes, you're gonna be taken outside to the courtyard where we conduct our ceremonies and executions. Karen's cousin, a powerful witch too, is on her way here. When she arrives, they'll behead you."

"And what's the good news? Please tell me there is good news." My tone was pleading.

"There is good news. The protection spell Karen cast on our premises is not an illusion spell, so now that she's dead, it's down, at least until her replacement fixes it. Anyone can get in and out. Also, since Pam is afraid something will go wrong with the dark magic, she requested the attendance of almost all warriors at your execution. The gates will be less guarded."

"Yeah, but I don't think that's going to help me, because I'll be a little too busy getting beheaded to escape," I reminded her.

"Not if I issue an official challenge to the throne. All eyes would be on me. The last time a Memphis Warrior challenged Lucilla, our queen, for the throne was many centuries ago. Everyone will be shocked, and they won't pay attention to you while I combat my queen. It'll give you enough time to sneak out. Outside you—"

"No," I cut her off. "You won't do it, Alice. I don't know how good your fighting skills are, but no offense, I doubt a Newborn vampire can take out a..." My voice withered in my throat when realization dawned on me; winning was never part of her plan. "No, forget it. I'm not agreeing to this. I'm not letting you die."

"I'm already dead; I'm a vampire. And I do not wish to be one. Please, respect my decision. It's an honorable way for a Memphis Warrior to end her existence. I'd have challenged her before, but I just now thought about it," she said.

"No, Alice, you are not doing this, which means we have less than ten minutes to come up with a better plan, a plan where we both escape from here. You're coming with me." If by some miracle we did get out of the castle, I'd ask Gideon to help her deal with being a vampire.

"We have no time left. I hear the guards' footsteps. They'll be here in seconds," she said.

"Alice, please," I started, but she vanished from the room in a blink. Then, three vampires walked in. Without uttering a word, one of them grabbed me by the arm, and I was dragged outside the room. My terror escalated with each step as they forced me downstairs and down a few narrow corridors. After passing through three halls and making a few more turns, we reached the back courtyard of the castle. It was surrounded by a thick stone wall and lit by flaming torches.

The cold night air blew against my face while the guard pulled me across the lawn, toward a stage. I coughed, and a wave of dizziness passed through me as they tugged me up the makeshift stairs. Once we reached center stage, I looked out at the large crowd of about three hundred vampires, all in their uniforms. They were standing at attention in formation, facing the elevated platform I was on.

In heels and a short white dress, Pam stepped onto the stage too. Two vampires were at her sides, both of them in the same uniform: tight black pants, a warrior belt, leather armor, and leather gauntlets on their forearms. When the guard let go of my arm, Pam walked to me.

She stopped beside me and turned to the crowd like she was about to make some speech about my execution, and I was out of time and options. Across the courtyard, Alice strode with purpose toward the stage. She looked determined but scared out of her mind. So I did the only thing I could think to do. I stepped in front of Pam and said loudly, "I challenge your queen."

The odds were against me; I was sick and weak, and she was a queen of warriors, after all. But fighting her was the only option I had to try and save both Alice and me.

Pam laughed. "You? Challenging my queen?"

Her patronizing tone nettled me. I raised my chin. "If I win, I go free and choose one of your warriors to come with me."

She snarled at me. "You fool. The great queen of Memphis Warriors will never degrade herself by fighting a mere mortal." She turned to address the crowd. "It's time to..." Her voice died away as the vampires in the far back parted like the Red Sea for a shadowy figure passing through. Did their queen accept my challenge?

I caught a movement out of the corner of my eye and shifted to see one of Pam's vampires move to my side. Her eyes were trained on the crowd.

I returned my attention to the figure gliding through the warriors, then jumping into the air and levitating gracefully onto the stage. Light fell on the figure's face.

I blinked and sucked in a sharp breath.

Chapter 16

Gideon moved toward me and the vampires, wearing a knee-length, black leather coat and dark pants. What was he doing here? How did he find me?

Surprise flashed in the eyes of the vampire by my side before she said, "It's a great honor to have you here."

"It's not a social call, Lucilla. I'm here for the human. She is mine." Gideon's voice was stern.

Lucilla? *She* was the queen? I looked at her. Her brown skin shined in the bright moonlight, a braid of brown hair thrown over her shoulder.

Her welcoming expression fell into a serious countenance. "The human's blood doesn't smell marked."

He glanced at my face, which was probably in bad shape, and his jaw set.

His irises glowed bright gold as he looked back at her. "She is still mine. Release her, or blood will be shed." His tone dripped with venom.

There was a long silence before she finally said, "Very well, Gideon, I'll release her. But I do not appreciate being threatened. This is the last time you come here making demands." She gave him a long, hostile look. Then her focus switched to me. "You may leave."

Someone in the crowd approached the stage. It was Alice! After getting permission from Pam, she climbed the stairs to the stage.

I was about to make up a story about why I needed Alice to come with me when she said to me, "I'm glad you're free and don't need my help anymore." A crimson tear trickled down her cheek. Fear displayed on her face as her stare went toward Lucilla. "I challenge you for the throne."

"No, Alice, don't!" I pleaded, and one of the guards whooshed to Alice, plunging a dagger into her heart.

"Assisting a human? Traitor!" the guard spat out as Alice fell to the floor. She lay in a widening pool of blood, while her skin turned grayish. A smile spread across her lips before she died.

Without warning, a hot wave of nausea cramped my stomach. Unable to fight it off, I bent over and threw up. When I straightened, a spike of pain drove through my head, overwhelming me. I lost my balance, and two hands steadied me.

"We're leaving. Now." I heard Gideon's voice behind me. His hand took mine, guiding me out a back gate. A luxurious car sitting near a copse of pines came into view, a short distance ahead of us. We stepped next to it, and my body trembled with cold. He removed his coat and slung it over my shoulders, then helped me into the car. As he walked around it, I laid my head on the window glass, and in seconds sleep claimed me.

The next thing I knew, we were in Thomas's penthouse, and Gideon was carrying me in his arms to the guest room, where I'd slept for the past week.

He put me down on the bed. Standing next to it, he ran his fingers through his hair and shook his head in anger, his eyes flecked with bright gold. "What in God's name were you thinking, leaving here while you were still sick?"

"I got Lucas's address. I had to throw caution to the wind and go over there. If it hadn't been for those warriors, I'd have made it back to the penthouse safely." I recounted everything that had happened at Lucas's apartment. Gideon asked for the description of the illusionist who had stolen the thumb drive. I gave him something better: the private investigator's full name. He pulled out his phone. While he typed a text, I let my eyelids drift closed, just for a bit, but I went out of focus and dozed off.

When I woke up, I felt much better and like myself again.

"The doctor injected you with two doses of medicine and BFB," Gideon said. "This and the doses he gave you before you ran off have healed the bruises and cuts on your body and face. Your soul has fully recovered too." I pressed a hand into the mattress and pushed myself upright. The room lit up, and memories of recent events seeped into my head: the castle, the Memphis Warriors, me almost beheaded, Alice.

"Alice... she died," I breathed.

"She did, but it looks like it was her wish to end her existence," he said, perching on the bed next to me.

The image of her smile right before her soul had left her body surfaced in my mind. "She hated that she was a vampire." My eyes met his. "What is it like to be one?"

"Sometimes it's good, sometimes not."

"Do you miss being human?"

"Occasionally."

He didn't expand further, so I changed the subject. "How come the queen agreed to hand me over to you so easily? There were three hundred warriors there and only one of you; they could've taken you out without a problem."

"Yes, they'd have defeated me, eventually. However, I wouldn't say it'd have been done without a problem, and Lucilla knew that. She let you go because to her, you're a mere human, insignificant, and as such, you're not worth losing half of her warriors' lives over." He didn't supply any more details, like how Lucilla knew him, or what their history was. And it was clear he wouldn't.

I sighed. "How did you find me, anyway?"

"After I left here, I decided to drive out of the city to buy blood bags instead of going to a nearby vampire bar and ordering a Donor. Three hours later, I discovered you weren't in the bedroom, which didn't come as a surprise since you never listen. So I borrowed Thomas's car."

"Thomas's car? Isn't he blind?"

"His driver isn't. After he gave me the key, I compelled a human police officer to ping your cell phone. The wonder of modern technology."

"And compulsion," I added and glanced down at the tattoo. 649. Good, the number hadn't plummeted this time. I told him what had happened with the snake. When I finished, I asked, "Why would the tattoo turn me into a skilled fighter? The Ruler of the Memphis Warriors, Pam, claimed that dark magic didn't protect its host."

"Perhaps Pam was wrong," he said, and before I knew what had happened, his dagger was pressed across my neck while his left hand pulled my head back by my hair.

Alarmed and shocked, I was careful not to move. "Wh-what are you doing?"

"Testing the tattoo's reaction to your life being in danger." He withdrew the blade from my throat, pulling away from me.

"And what if it had reacted?" My voice rose, but I couldn't help it. What had he been thinking? "The snake could've sucked the life out of you."

"I'd have gotten a warning first," he said. "The snake was a warning, but the witch and warriors tried to fight it, so it killed them. The dark magic on your hand only kills when someone directly harms it, not when someone harms you." He pushed his weapon back in its place and updated me about Lucas's thumb drive.

I gulped air. "You have it? How'd you get your hands on it so fast?"

"Ian Robinson is a well-known PI in the Hidden World. It wasn't hard for Thomas to find his office and steal the flash drive back."

"Thomas is back?"

He got to his feet. "Yes, he's downstairs on the phone with Olivia. Now that you're fully recovered, I'll go down and join him. The flash drive is password-protected, and Thomas's tech guy will be here soon to crack it."

When he turned to the door, I looked over at the large window covered with a gray blind. "Wait. What time is it? How long have I been out?"

He stopped and glanced at his watch. "It's seven p.m. You slept for fifteen hours."

"Wow," I murmured. I kicked my way out of the covers and hopped off the bed, feeling no nausea or dizziness. "I'll go take a quick shower and then meet you downstairs."

He nodded and took off.

Not wasting time, I showered, dried off, dragged on a pair of jeans, a V-neck sweater, and my boots and headed downstairs. There, I followed the voices coming from the living room. The walls of windows gave a superb night view of the city. My eyes were glued to the skyline of Manhattan as I turned right and moved forward to the brightly lit living room.

"I reckon you feel better, Miss Newbern," Thomas said.

My gaze slid to the plush couch where Thomas, dressed in a pricey navy-blue suit, sat next to another dude with a computer in his lap.

Gideon stood in front of them, and I stopped next to him. "I'm better, thank you."

The stranger's gaze was fixed on the computer screen, his fingers flying over the keys.

"I take it he's the tech guy," I said.

The guy looked up. He was attractive, with a buzz cut, lean body, and sun-kissed skin.

The corners of his lips went up as his gaze took me in from head to toe. "Got that right, hot thing, and you look exactly like the girl who's gonna ride my cock later tonight."

His rude comment left me speechless. Gideon, however, wasn't. "Not if it's cut off," he said, the muscle ticking in his jaw betraying the calmness in his voice.

Gideon's threat erased the cockiness from the guy's face, and he stammered, "I-I didn't mean to... I'm sor—"

"You got on his wick. You'd be wise to shut up and get on with the job I paid you for, and quite handsomely I might add," Thomas advised him.

"Y-yeah, no worries, man. I'm already halfway to cracking the password," he said and returned his attention to his laptop.

Ten minutes later, he announced, "Done. You can access the file." He set the open computer on the black coffee table and got to his feet, telling Gideon, "Here, have a look." Gideon took his place on the couch, and I joined him.

Facing the computer, I leaned over and put my fingers on the touch pad to move the cursor. The thumb drive contained one file, a thumbnail image of a video named "Demons".

I said to Thomas, "He did it; everything's working."

The tech guy started toward the front door. "Okay, then, uh, I'll show myself out." Without waiting for a response, he left.

I hit play. Gideon and I watched the video. The footage was shaky, probably taken from a cell phone. The camera was trained on Lucas's face as he spoke in a low voice.

"Two days ago, I received an email from a woman who recently discovered my website, The Mysterious World of the Fae. She's certain her boss is a vampire. Yes, a real vampire. And I believe her. They exist, folks, and they are dangerous. If you find yourself around one, run. Run like hell. My sister didn't. She went out with someone who I think was a vampire. If you're a frequent visitor to my site, you already know I suspect something bad happened to her. Out of the blue, she decided to cut ties with us—her family. It's not like her. Since then, I've been searching for her." He was silent for a short moment, as if thinking about her before resuming his speech. "Anyway, the woman from the email started a new job as a secretary in a law firm six months ago, and she's overheard her boss mention vampires on several occasions.

"She thought he was crazy but out of curiosity searched the internet for the undead and supernatural beings. She came across my site and thought it was all nonsense. Then one night she saw her boss drinking from what appeared to be a bag of blood while on the phone, unaware that his secretary was peering at him through the cracked-open door.

"He was talking about some missing girls, then set up a meeting with the person on the other end of the line. The woman, who was familiar with my sister's story, sent me an e-mail telling me about the meeting. It's supposed to take place in this almost deserted parking lot tonight." The grainy footage spanned slowly as Lucas showed viewers his surroundings.

Lucas stood by a silver sedan, next to the driver's door. Aside from that car, there was a truck parked in the far corner of the lot, a Chevrolet beside the silver sedan, and a van opposite his car. The streetlamps in the almost empty parking lot cast gold light mixed with the bright moonlight. It was quiet. The occasional wail of the wind broke the silence. The camera showed the parking lot when he spoke again.

"My balls are freezing off out here, but I can't go back home. They're late—wait, someone's coming." Lucas ducked behind his car, judging by the change of the video feed. Then, the camera was carefully raised so it could film the new arrival: a black Mercedes. It parked near the van across from Lucas. A man climbed out of the Mercedes, rocking a suit and a trench coat. Because of the quality of the video, the features of his face were hard to make out, but somehow Gideon recognized him.

"Andrew Bassino," he murmured.

I hit pause. "You know him? Who is he?"

"He's a solicitor, a vampire, and a bastard who would sell his own mum for money," Thomas answered me.

"Let's see who he's meeting with," Gideon said and resumed the video. Andrew waited outside his car for about a minute before another car rolled in, a shiny Bentley. It stopped in front of him, blocking him from the camera's view. The front passenger door thrust open. A woman climbed out. A black coat covered her body.

"He's meeting with the royal demon that killed the human," Gideon told Thomas, who let out a curse.

Andrew hurried around the Bentley to greet her. She pulled something out of her purse and handed it to him. The camera zoomed in on her hand.

"It's a package," Lucas whispered. "Who is that woman? If anyone recog—" He stopped when Andrew turned to look in the sedan's direction. "Shit, he spotted me." The camera jerked up and down, and there was a sound of jangling keys. The door to the sedan opened, and Lucas got in, starting the car. The footage showed the car ceiling, as if the cell phone had been laid down on the passenger seat. "Phew, got away just in the nick of time. Jesus, this shit is beyond crazy. I need to find out who she was and what she was carrying in that package. And how it's connected to my sister," Lucas said, and then the video cut off. The battery of his phone seemed to have died.

I flipped the laptop closed and looked at Gideon. "He probably intended to post it to his site, but the demon murdered him before he had the chance."

"She didn't want anyone linking her to the missing girls," Gideon said.

"Or anyone to see her doing business with a vampire," Thomas added.

"Do you happen to know where we can find Andrew now?" I asked them.

"At his law firm, working," Gideon replied.

"Is it a vampiric law firm? Do they work during the overnight hours with clients living around the world?" I wondered out loud.

"No, they work in daylight hours as well. Their offices have tempered glass, which UV rays can't penetrate," Thomas told me.

Gideon stood up and headed for the door. "Let's have a chat with Andrew."

Chapter 17

After a thirty-minute ride, the three of us reached a high-rise office building in Midtown Manhattan. After we entered the spacious lobby through the revolving doors, Gideon compelled the security guard to let us pass, and we proceeded to the bank of elevators. We stepped inside one of them, Gideon pushed the button on the elevator panel, and the car began its ascent. The doors slid open on the thirtieth floor, revealing the firm's main lobby and a modern wood panel wall boasting the law firm's name in large silver letters. We got out and stepped up to the front desk. The reception area was empty. Something felt wrong. Standing beside Thomas, I looked around. Where was everyone?

"He knows we're here," Gideon said in a low voice. Just then, a dagger came hurtling through the air, aimed at Thomas's chest. He seemed oblivious to the weapon flashing toward him. My new fast instincts kicked in. Timing the knife's rotation, I caught it in midair by the handle, the silver blade a few inches shy of Thomas's heart. Then a vampire lunged in my direction.

"Gee, thanks for the new dagger. You shouldn't have," I told him as I kicked him in the stomach. He stayed upright, as if my blow didn't affect him at all. I scowled in annoyance. His fangs slid down, his eyes flashing silver. He took a swing at me. I dodged his fist, spun, and kicked his shin. Hard. He dropped to his knees.

"That's more like it," I said, then slammed a foot into his face, knocking him backward to the floor where he stayed for a second before leaping back to his feet. *Jesus, really?* As he attacked me again, I ducked to avoid his punch, twirled the knife in my hand with surprising expertise, and whipped the blade into his heart. He collapsed to the floor.

I looked down at the dead vampire, smirking. "Let's see you get up from that one."

"Nicely done," Gideon said, and I turned to Thomas. He stood motionless, looking like he was processing what had just happened, clearly not used to having his ass saved.

"Are you okay, Thomas?" I asked. He snapped out of his stupor and gave a curt nod. A corner of my lips quirked up. "You sure? 'Cause, you know, we don't have time to babysit." I threw his own words back at him.

A tiny smile spread across his mouth as he pushed his dark glasses up his nose. "Indeed, Miss Newbern, indeed," he said as his leg lashed out to aim a back kick at a vampire who appeared suddenly behind him. Then he spun around, pulled a silver stake from his suit jacket, and killed him with a single stab to the heart.

More bloodsuckers came out of hiding to fight us. After we finished them off, we moved down a hall, passing closed doors. It looked like no one, aside from the vampires who had assaulted us, occupied the place.

"Hey, guys, how do we even know Andrew is here?" I asked when we stopped at a corner office door labeled with the name Andrew Bassino.

"That weasel is here all right," Thomas said. The door was locked so he bashed it in with his foot, and we walked into a large suite with floor-to-ceiling windows covering two walls. The furniture was modern and dark. A two-seat couch, a low, glass-top coffee table, and a black floor lamp faced Andrew's desk. There was also a brown chaise lounge near the windows. To its left, a man in a suit sat behind a massive cherry-wood desk. His skin was white with the typical vampiric flawlessness, and he looked to be about thirty-five in human years, his hair blond, his eyes brown.

Gideon glided toward him. "Andrew!" he said in a theatrical voice. "There you are, hiding out and sending your guards to welcome us. Tsk tsk tsk, that's no way to greet old friends. I gotta say it does hurt my feelings." He pulled up a chair in front of the desk and settled in, kicking his feet up on the table, legs crossed at the ankles, hands clamped over his stomach. "And here I thought we were getting along so well. Oh, by the way, how's the eye I injected with rat poison doing? Still in pain?" A slow grin appeared on Gideon's face.

Andrew's nostrils flared, eyes flickering silver. His gaze then moved to me. "Who's the girl?"

"Who? Her?" Gideon nodded to me. "She's the one who will break your bones *one by one* if you don't tell her where her sister, Zoey, is."

Andrew's face creased in a scowl. "I don't know anything."

Thomas, who was standing next to me, became a blur of movement and then reappeared at Andrew's side. He slammed the lawyer's head into the desk and pressed his palm against the temple to hold him still. It'd happened so fast that when the sound of Andrew's skull crashing into the wood boomed in the room, I jumped. Gideon, on the other hand, didn't move a muscle, reminding me how inhuman he was.

"Andrew, you wanker, how does it feel to be a demon's little bitch?" Thomas growled.

"And this is Thomas, who I believe you already know," Gideon said, still in the same position.

"I can't give out any information," he told them. "If she knows I talked, she will end me, and then what?"

Thomas sneered at him. "And then the world would be a better place. My patience is running low. Spill everything you know. What was in that package the bitch demon gave you? Where are the missing girls?" He let go of Andrew but didn't move away from him.

Andrew touched his left cheek and hissed with pain. "You brute," he cursed. "I talk and Maura, the demon, will torture me to death. I don't, and you torture me to death, so I have nothing to lose. Do whatever you want with me."

Gideon relaxed in his seat as he looked at Andrew. "If you don't start talking, yes, I'll make you suffer, but I won't kill you. My goal is to extract information from you, and that's going to be hard if you're dead."

"Go ahead, torture away. Do your best. I won't break," Andrew said.

"I know you won't break under torture." Gideon smiled at him. "The beating part is just for my own amusement. After I'm done causing you pain, I'll make you talk."

Andrew snorted in contempt. "How? You have no leverage. Like I said, I've got nothing to lose."

"Wrong," Gideon corrected. "There is one thing you'd rather end your pathetic existence than lose." He swung his legs off the desk, stood up, slapped his palms flat on the table, then leaned forward until his face was close to Andrew's. "Money."

That single word made Andrew shift his weight in the chair while running his finger around his collar and loosening his tie. Gideon straightened and went on, "I bet your biggest client isn't going to like hearing about your dirty secret. How do you think he'll react when he discovers his two-hundred-year-old vampire lawyer is having a little too much fun with his precious fifteen-year-old human daughter? I'm curious, how much money does his business bring to your firm?"

Andrew gritted his teeth. "You wouldn't."

"Oh, but I will," Gideon promised. "However, unfortunately for me, the torturing part will have to wait until next time, but if you don't start talking now, Mr. Brown will get a call—"

"Okay," Andrew said. "What do you want to know?"

Gideon crossed his arms over his chest. "Everything. And for the sake of your firm, it better be useful."

Andrew leaned back in his seat. "I've been working for Maura for the past two years, doing small things for her."

Thomas snorted in derision.

"She's been paying good money. No one would've said no to that," Andrew told him.

"Speak for yourself," Thomas said.

Andrew ignored his comment and continued. "The last time I met with Maura was when she handed me the package you inquired about. She instructed me not to open the box and to keep it in my office until someone came to claim it. I have no clue what was inside it, but I heard her speaking on the phone before she took off. From what I gathered, the contents of the package have something to do with some human girls. That's all I know, I swear. My motto is as long as I get my money, I don't ask unnecessary questions."

"Did she mention the names Zoey or Kyla? Did she say where they were?" I asked.

His eyes met mine before returning to Gideon, as if I wasn't worth his attention.

"Answer her." Gideon's tone was annoyed.

"Never heard the names Zoey or Kyla, but when Maura got off the phone, she asked me if I happened to know any human girls between the ages of eighteen and twenty. I did, and she paid me generously for the girl's home address and phone numbers."

"That's it? That's all you got?" Anger laced my voice.

"That's all. My motto is—"

"Yeah, yeah, as long as you receive your damn money, you don't ask unnecessary questions," I finished for him.

"Who came to collect the demon's item?" Thomas asked.

"He was a male. Human. About six feet tall with dark hair and eyes, young, maybe nineteen years old. A week after meeting Maura, he waltzed into my office without an appointment, and I handed the box over to him. He went by the name Jupiter."

Jupiter... Jupiter... The unusual name was familiar. It took me a second to remember from where. The day I'd gone to Laurel's for the weekend, I'd visited Zoey in her college dorm room. She'd been on the phone when I walked in, flirting with a guy named Jupiter.

"I need a computer with an internet connection," I said. Andrew lifted his chin in the direction of a laptop that was on a nearby table. I moved to it and searched Jupiter's name on social media, starting with Facebook. I got just three hits: Jupiter Wilson, Jupiter Hill, and Jupiter Powell. I clicked on their photos, opening a new tab in the web browser for each account.

I carried the open laptop to Andrew and placed it on his table. "Take a look. Do you recognize any of them?"

He leaned forward and glanced at the laptop's screen. "The first picture, it's the same Jupiter who was in my office."

I checked his personal information, then looked up at Gideon. "He lives in New York and goes to college in New Haven. The last time I saw my sister was in her dorm room, and I think she was talking with this guy, Jupiter, on the phone. We gotta go back to New Haven and look for him."

"Or Maura. She might lead us to Zoey and Kyla, too," Thomas said.

"We should split up," Gideon proposed.

Thomas agreed. "Good idea. You two fly back to Connecticut. Look for Jupiter while I search for Maura. I'll arrange for the jet to take you." He pulled out his cell phone and issued a voice command to it.

"Okay," Gideon said, and we stepped out of the office, leaving Thomas with Andrew.

After hailing a cab, we drove to the airport. A surge of hope rose in me as I stared out the car window; Jupiter Wilson was our best chance of finding Zoey and the other missing girls.

Chapter 18

The new cell phone Gideon had bought me rang in my jeans pocket, surprising me. Who would call me? I dug it out and checked the display, then thumbed ignore. I shoved the device back into my jacket.

"It's Kelly. I'll call her back when we're done here," I said to Gideon as we stood in front of a two-story house, a fraternity banner hanging from the second-level balcony.

Most of Jupiter's posts and pictures on his social media were public. The names of his best friends, his hobbies, his daily schedule. But the most useful piece of data was his current whereabouts.

"And you're sure he's here because..." Gideon said.

"Because I've been reading his tweets since we landed."

"Tweets?" His brows wrinkled like I'd spoken in a foreign language. *To him, I might as well have. I keep forgetting the dude's old—like one hundred and sixty-five years old. He may have a cell phone and a laptop, but social media is not his area of expertise.*

"Twitter is like sending texts but to the whole world," I explained.

"I see. And Jupiter tweeted that he's at his frat house now?"

"He did."

We climbed the three steps to the porch, and I knocked on the front door. A guy with a bag of Doritos in his hand answered it. He welcomed me with a flirtatious smile, but it vanished when he noticed Gideon.

"Yo, not being disrespectful here, but when was the last time you saw the sun? Go to the beach sometime, work on your tan, bro."

Green colored Gideon's irises. "Where is Jupiter Wilson?"

"With the pledges in the basement."

"Go tell him to come up here," Gideon directed, and without a word, in a trance-like state, the guy turned around and walked away.

After a few minutes, Jupiter filled the doorway. He had the build of someone who spent hours at the gym. His eyes narrowed at Gideon, like he recognized the reason behind Gideon's pale, flawless complexion.

"Not here. Someone may hear us. Let's go upstairs. My bedroom is safer," Jupiter said.

We stepped inside a typical frat house, passing by a large living room where half a dozen empty beer bottles lay scattered across the floor. Two guys sat on a brown couch, laughing at something on the big-screen TV in front of them. When we walked by a pool table between the living room and dining room, the guys playing threw us a glance before returning to their business.

We went up the stairs to the second floor, trailing Jupiter to his bedroom, where he closed the door behind us. The medium-sized room contained an unmade bed, a nightstand, and a closet. A pair of jeans, socks, and a few T-shirts were strewn across the floor, waiting to be washed.

"Ever heard of a laundry hamper and a washing machine?" I said.

"You're welcome to do my laundry anytime you want, sweetheart, but first, I'd like to know who the fuck sent you two to me?" He cut right to the chase.

"You flew all the way to New York to pick up a package from a law firm in Manhattan. What was in it? Why was it sent to you?" I asked, ignoring his question.

He chuckled as if it amused him that I thought he'd answer me. "Listen carefully, sweet pea, I have powerful friends, so you better not piss me off. I ain't saying a word to you or to the vamp, so get your little ass out of my house."

I sighed. "Looks like we're gonna do it the hard way." I stepped in front of him and kicked his legs out from under him. He fell sideways, his shoulder and head hitting the floor. With a moan and a curse, he rolled onto his back and was about to rise when I planted a foot on his chest, pinning him down. He struggled to get free but failed. "You listen carefully. Call me sweetheart or sweet pea again, and your next sentence will be without your front teeth," I threatened as I applied pressure to his breastbone.

"What the fuck? What are you?" With the weight against his chest, his voice came out more throaty than the outraged shout he clearly meant it to be.

"Answers, Jupiter, I want answers," I told him.

His head turned to Gideon. "Get this crazy bitch off of me." He growled in pain.

One shoulder leaning against the doorjamb, hands in his front jeans pockets, legs crossed at the ankles, Gideon watched him, blue eyes twinkling with humor. "Crazy? Trust me, you have no idea. You should see her when she doesn't get her ice cream." He pulled his hands out of his pockets to mimic a mushroom explosion by spreading his hands and fingers apart, then advised, "I'd answer her questions if I were you."

My phone came to life in my pocket. I let it ring. "I'm waiting. Why was a package sent to you? What was in it?"

"I can't... fucking... breathe." Jupiter struggled to speak. He reached for the boot on his chest. "Get... your foot off of me."

I pressed down harder. "My foot will be off you only if you tell me what I want to know, so you better decide: putting oxygen into your body or answering my questions." My phone's tune signaled another call.

"Fine, I... I'll tell you."

I lifted my foot with a warning look and silenced my cell.

He sat up, coughing and rubbing his chest with one hand. Then he stood and went to sit down on his bed.

"The package wasn't for me. I was paid to go pick it up from a law firm in Manhattan, but I don't know what was in it. Could be blood, though. Look, I met this guy a year ago at a party my fraternity brothers threw. He offered to pay me a lot of cash to run some errands for him. Given that he comes from old money, I trusted he was good for it, so why the hell not, right?

"At first I sold weed for him. Then it was pills, MDMA. And then, it was blood bags. I was like, what the fuck, man? What kind of twisted shit did you get me into? He explained that vampires were real and warned me not to whisper a word about it to anyone. At the time, I was sure he was bullshitting me, or high on something strong, but the next day he showed me this real vamp chick, with fangs and all. Man, that was sick. Never seen anything so cool. I got all the proof I needed. The last errand he paid me for was that package in New York."

"And where's the package now? Did you deliver it to him?" I asked.

"I did, about a month ago."

"Is that guy a demon? Does he work for Maura?" I asked.

A quizzical expression crossed his face. "A demon? Demons exist too? Th—"

"What's the name of the man who paid you?" Gideon cut in.

Jupiter shook his head as if to clear his thoughts. "Uh, Brad Lauridsen. He's a senior at Yale and not a vamp, but not sure about the demon thing. And never heard the name Maura."

"William Lauridsen's son," Gideon said under his breath, his tone filled with scorn.

I blinked. "William Lauridsen? Who's he?"

"A powerful human with a lot of connections in your world, close friends with the governor," Gideon replied. "His ancestors worked for a US Ruler, Djar. For years William Lauridsen was in the business of human trafficking. Then, his older son, Noah, took over the business."

My heart dropped into my stomach. Human trafficking... All those missing girls. Oh God, Zoey... No, I couldn't even think about her being sold like a piece of meat.

I glared at Jupiter. "Where's Zoey? Zoey Newbern. You know her, I heard my sister talking on the phone with you. Where is she?"

His eyebrows shot up. "Zoey? Whoa, wait a second. She's your sister? Aren't you missing or something?"

"Where is she?" I repeated.

"I have no idea," he answered. "She wasn't picking up any of my calls, so I got worried and stopped by her dorm room. Her roommate told me she dropped out, just left town abruptly and took all of her stuff. Weird shit, if you ask me.

"There's something else you should know. Brad really had the hots for her, but she had a boyfriend, Philippe or something. I was surprised she didn't dump his ass for Brad, though. The dude is a babe magnet. I can't name a single chick who's said no to him, and here comes this super-hot babe and she turns him down. It drove him nuts. He became obsessed with her, then one day, poof. She was gone." He shrugged. "I don't know, could be related."

Yeah, it could be. Had Brad taken her? Was he working with his brother, who ran a human trafficking ring? The royal demon must be in the thick of it, but what was her role? Gideon brought up the same questions when we left Jupiter's frat house, then reminded me about the phone calls I'd gotten.

Pulling the cell out of my pocket, I looked at the display. Four missed calls, all from Kelly. *What the hell gives?* I dialed her number.

One ring. Two rings. "Oh my God, Sydney. Zoey was kidnapped, and I know who did it!" she shouted.

My eyes popped wide open. "Who?"

"Not on the phone. Where are you? We gotta meet—now." Her voice was urgent. I gave her Gideon's address before she hung up. After I filled Gideon in, we headed to his house.

There, I prowled around the living room. "Come on, come on, where is she?" I said, checking the time. Forty minutes had passed since I'd spoken with her.

"She just arrived," Gideon said, probably relying on his super hearing, and walked to the foyer. I did too. He opened the door as Kelly was about to knock on it.

She followed us into the living room and glanced around. "Where is the rest of the furniture? Are you moving out?"

"Kelly, is my sister safe? Who took her?" I asked when she sat down on the couch.

"Right, sorry. I don't know where he's keeping her. He wouldn't say."

"Who is 'he'? Brad? Noah?" I couldn't help the quiver of fear in my voice.

"It's Brad." She raised her eyebrows. "Wait, how do you know him?"

"What's your relationship with Brad?" Gideon interjected.

"A while back, Zoey introduced him to Izzy and me. He already knew, by the way, about the vampire world, and also that I was one. He was always by her side, so into her. It was totally obvious. I didn't like him. Yeah, he's incredibly hot, charismatic, and loaded, but my gut feeling told me something was off about him. I couldn't put my finger on what it was exactly. Zoey thought I was being overly suspicious, so I let it go.

"Anyway, a few hours ago, he called me, wanted to talk in person. I agreed, and he came over to my cousin's house, where I'm staying at the moment." Her stare slid to me. "He asked me about you. He knows you're Zoey's sister and that you've been looking for her."

My brows drew together. "How?"

"He didn't say. Maybe the people who work for him tipped him off. Anyway, he offered me a grand if I bring you with me alone—emphasizing the alone part—to a party he's having at his father's mansion. I refused, so he tried a different approach. He admitted to having Zoey and then threatened to kill her and the other girls with her if I didn't do it, or if I went to the cops."

Other girls? So Thomas's theory was right; they had been kidnapped and forced to call their parents. Brad was behind it, but what about the girls who had gone missing thirty years ago? Was it his brother's doing? Or his father's?

"Why does he want me there? To abduct me too?" I asked.

"I don't know," she said. "He wouldn't explain his reasons, just warned me not to say anything to you about Zoey. I had to, though. I called you the minute he was out of the house."

"Did he mention the name Kyla?" Gideon asked, and she shook her head.

"Or say what he was going to do to Zoey and the girls?" Dread dripped from my words. Another shake of her head.

I turned to Gideon. "He's probably working with his brother to sell them on the black market." My stomach churned at the thought of it.

"Sell them on the black market? Whoa, we're way over our heads here. We need to go to the cops," she said.

"No, we can't involve the police," I said firmly. "It's too risky; we don't know what Brad might do to the girls if he feels cornered. I can't gamble with their lives."

She looked as if she pondered my words for a moment before saying, "Yeah, you're right. He's crazy and unpredictable. So how are we going to save Zoey?"

"We do as he asked," I told her. "Go to the party in his father's mansion, just the two of us. If he—"

Gideon shot me a disapproving frown. "No. Absolutely not. It's dangerous. We don't have enough information about how Brad is connected to the royal demon. Maura may be there too. You're not doing this alone."

"It's not as if we have better options," I pointed out. "Zoey, and maybe Kyla too, are dead unless I show up—alone. If he wants to kidnap me, because maybe sisters are worth more on the black market, then I can find where he keeps her and the other girls and save them. Gideon, there's no other way."

"You don't have to let him take you; we'll force their location out of him," he insisted.

"No, because the minute he spots you with me, he might order whoever is guarding the girls to kill them. I won't risk Zoey's life," I told him.

His expression turned cold and grim. "And I won't risk yours. Going over there alone is dangerous. You'll be unprotected."

"I don't remember asking for permission. I'm going to the party and that's final," I said.

The room fell silent. "All right," he finally said. "If you insist on doing this alone, we'll put a tracker on you. I need to know where you are at all times. If he abducts you, Kelly will send me a text message. I'll come, and we'll rescue the girls together." To this, I nodded in agreement. He then turned to Kelly, "When is the party?"

The phone in her hand chimed, alerting her to a text. She glanced down at it, then stood and walked to the French doors. "Next week, on Saturday night," she answered, then said, "Sorry, but I gotta jet. My cousin needs me."

"Yeah, sure. We'll be in touch and meet up on Saturday. Call me if there are any new developments," I told her.

After she walked out, Gideon informed me that during the next week I'd be honing my fighting skills, and by that, he'd apparently meant having my ass kicked more times than I could count. His strength was equal to an Ancient's, and he was an expert in martial arts—with about a hundred years of practice under his belt. Knowing who took Zoey and doing nothing about it for a week was hard too, but I had to sit tight and be patient if I wanted to save her.

When Saturday night finally came, I was ready to face whatever was waiting for me at Brad's party, including demons. I opened the closet door in my bedroom and pulled out a knee-length, black dress with a touch of peacock blue. Under it, I wore a thigh holster strapped around my leg. Next, I twisted my hair into a knot, slid into a pair of black heels, swallowed a BFB pill, took a jacket, and stepped out of the bedroom, the watch with the tracker already around my wrist.

In the living room, I found Gideon sitting on the couch. His gaze met mine. He was anxious about tonight; it was written all over his face.

"I'll be fine. I have a GPS chip in the watch you bought me and a silver dagger under my dress. No need to worry."

Expression stern, he padded to me. He reached for the jacket in my hand and helped me into it.

"Remember the plan," he finally said. "Call or text me if he doesn't kidnap you, so I know you're safe. If he does take you to Zoey, Kelly will alert me and I'll track your location using the signal from your tracker. Then you and I will rescue Zoey, Kyla, and the girls. If I don't hear from you or Kelly by midnight, I'll search for you at the mansion. Whatever happens, keep the watch on."

"I will," I said. Then I remembered I still had to deliver on my end of our deal. "Listen, I know you won't need my blood until after you kill Djar, but I think you should take it now and keep it in the fridge. You know, in case I don't make—"

His eyes wavered between blue and gold, and a muscle in his jaw ticked. "Don't." His voice was rough, stopping me from finishing the sentence.

The room was quiet until the cell in my purse rang. I fished it out and spoke to Kelly. She was waiting for me at her cousin's house. Gideon ordered me a cab and checked the tracker in my watch before reminding me to text him as soon as we got there. As I slipped into the cab, I waved goodbye and prayed that everything would go as planned.

Chapter 19

In a lavender dress and black stilettos with rhinestones, Kelly was waiting outside her cousin's house when the cab pulled up. Her hair hung down over her shoulders. She slid into the car, and I gave the driver the address of Brad's father's mansion. Worry registered on her features as she asked me if I remembered to drink a BFB pill and bring weapons with me. I calmed her down, but when we were a few minutes away from the mansion, her nervousness came back.

"Everything's gonna be okay," I told her as a cluster of security men stopped the car at an ornate gate.

One of them approached and bent over to glance inside, pointing a flashlight at us. We were waved on through. As we drove down the long, tree-lined driveway, I texted Gideon, updating him about our arrival. When the driver pulled in front of a huge house, we paid him and got out. The mansion was massive and surrounded by lush gardens and illuminated fountains. We climbed five steps leading up to a wide porch framed by four tall, white columns. There was lighting behind each pillar. At the big front doors, Kelly pulled out her cell, putting it to her ear.

"Calling Brad?" I asked.

She nodded and said into her phone, "Brad? Yeah, it's m—hello? Brad? Can you hear me? Yeah... it's Kelly... hello? Oh, okay." There was a short pause, then, "Yeah, now it's much quieter. Okay, uh, so, I'm here at the front door with Zoey's sister." The last two words dropped to a whisper. "With Zoey's sister," she repeated louder and ended the call with, "Fine, I'll wait."

She put her phone back into her bag and told me Brad had sent his friend to come and get us.

The front doors opened a few moments later, and a shirtless, barefoot guy in shorts and damp hair told us to follow him. We passed a bunch of orchids and lilies sitting gracefully on a round glass table in the center of the foyer. As we crossed the marble floor toward the west wing of the mansion, I took in the wealth oozing everywhere. A wide staircase with gold balustrades wound its way to the upper floors. We also passed an enormous living room, two libraries, and a dining room with a long mahogany table and thirty chairs.

The house was empty. Where was the party? I received an answer when Brad's friend opened the door to a brightly lit hallway. At its end, there was an elegant spiral staircase leading downward. The muffled music turned to a full blare. As we stepped down the stairs, the smell of chlorine reached my nose, and the air became heavy with moisture.

At the bottom of the stairs, I was welcomed with yet another room, but in this one, there was a rectangular, indoor pool with a cascading waterfall. Two separate hot tubs were located in the corners. The room wasn't packed, but by the look of it, the party was in full swing. Bikini-clad girls splashed in the pool. Those without swimsuits enjoyed themselves outside the pool, drinking, dancing, or both. Brad's friend led us toward the bar tucked in the back of the room. My dress adhered to my sweaty skin as we moved forward. I shook off my jacket.

"Sit at the bar. I'll go look for Brad," the guy said and walked away. After we hoisted ourselves onto barstools, I placed my jacket on the bar top.

"Gosh, I'm so nervous," Kelly said.

"Don't be. Our plan won't fall through. Just contact Gideon if Brad takes me." I calmed her down, but she was right to be on edge. I had no idea what he was up to. What if he didn't abduct me? I had to—

"Get you anything, girls? Maybe two cherry cocktails?" the bartender asked over the music. Vampires didn't get drunk on alcohol; nonetheless, Kelly ordered a martini, and I said yes to the cherry cocktail. He returned with our drinks after a short moment. I sipped from it so that I'd have the smell of alcohol on my breath. I needed Brad to think I was drunk. Easy prey.

With the glass in my hand, I scanned the room until my gaze fell on a gorgeous guy in a magazine-model type of way, relaxing with his friends against the hot tub jets. A blonde girl in a blue bikini cuddled up to him in the hot tub, her body molded to his while everybody's focus was on him. He was the center of attention. As he laughed at something someone had said, our eyes met.

He observed me before his eyes went to Kelly. His mouth moved close to the blonde's ear. He seemed to excuse himself then got out of the water. After grabbing a towel from a nearby chair and draping it around his neck, he strutted in our direction, carrying himself with ease and confidence. By the way he moved, looked, and behaved, I guessed his identity even before Kelly whispered it to me. Brad Lauridsen, a narcissistic egomaniac who liked to kidnap girls in his spare time.

When he reached the bar, he stood in front of me, wearing just a pair of longish black swim trunks. He smoothed his sandy-blond hair behind his ears and got rid of the towel around his neck, tossing it on the chair next to me. He grinned at me, revealing a set of perfect white teeth. On the outside, he was lovely; on the inside, hideous.

"Hi, I'm Brad."

"Sydney," I said, giggling while pretending to be wasted. I put a hand on his chest. "Wow, you're working out a lot, aren't you? Dig the abs." I forced my fingers to trail down his six-pack as I tittered some more.

"Glad you like the results," he said.

I dropped my hand and glanced up at him. "I love your," a giggle, "your house too. Why don't youuuuuu take me someplace more," another chuckle, "private?" I slurred.

His lips curled into a satisfied smile. Oh, he liked the idea of having a helpless drunk girl alone with him. *Attaboy. Now, be the little psychopath that you are and kidnap me.*

He took the glass from my hand and set it on the bar top behind me, then threaded his fingers through mine and brought my hand to his lips for a soft kiss. I almost recoiled from his touch. Luckily, I was able to feign excitement as I slid off the barstool. With my hand in his, he steered me toward the stairs leading to the main floor.

I heard Kelly's voice saying behind me, "I'll stay here." I glanced back, nodding to her purse to remind her to text Gideon, and weaved through the crowd with Brad. We went upstairs as I deliberately staggered, wondering where he was taking me while we crossed the living room, turned left, then right to a long hallway. When he came to a halt, he unlocked a door, and we stepped inside a dark room.

He turned on the light, and I surveyed an office with cherry wood paneling and a coffered ceiling. An Aubusson rug covered the floor, and bookshelves stuffed with old books lined one wall. Everything was tidy, no paper scattered across the antique oak English desk facing a leather chair and built-in window seat, nor on the burled walnut desk in the corner. He closed the door, hand still holding mine, guiding me to two wingback chairs situated against the wall across from the bookshelves.

"Sit," he said, and I obeyed. A loose strand of hair tickled my cheek. I twirled it around my index finger until I spotted a long lock of dark hair poking out from behind the desk near my chair. Oh my God, I sucked in a gulp of air and shot to my feet. An unconscious girl in a miniskirt and heels was tucked behind the table, the modesty panel partly concealing her.

"Did you kill her, you bastard?" Crouching next to her sprawled body, I checked for a pulse and sighed with relief when I felt it under my fingers.

He barked out a laugh. "Not so falling-down drunk anymore, huh? I had a feeling Kelly wouldn't keep her mouth shut. She told you everything, didn't she?"

I straightened and looked over at him. My concern for my sister's well-being must have been evident on my face since he said next, "Zoey's safe. Kelly defied me, but your sister is still alive. For now. So long as you play ball, she'll live, and you may be reunited with her."

I let out a breath I hadn't realized I'd been holding. "Yes, of course. Anything." *Just take me to Zoey already!*

A vampire opened the door, holding Kelly by her upper arm. She squirmed to get out of his grasp, but his big body was too much for her to overpower.

"I did what Brad wanted, he's with Sydney. Let me go!" she yelled at him.

"But you had to blab everything to her, didn't you?" Brad sounded angry.

Her head whipped to him. Surprise showed on her face, as if just noticing we were in the room.

"Candace and Jenny are next," Brad told his vampire. "They should arrive at the mansion soon. Tell Jacob to drug them before they get into the party." His employee nodded as he took out his cell phone and dialed.

"What about me? You gonna sell me too?" Kelly asked in an alarmed voice.

"Shut up," Brad said to her and stepped toward me. His blue eyes scrutinized me from head to toe. "So you're Zoey's sister..." A mean smile tugged at his lips. "Not nearly as hot as her, but you're still worth a fuck."

He turned and walked to the desk facing the window, opened a drawer, and pulled out a piece of fabric and a small glass medicine bottle. The label on it read: Chloroform. I watched as he saturated the cloth with the liquid in the bottle. He then came closer to me with the drenched fabric. The sweet odor of chloroform reached my nose.

I backed up until my legs hit a chair. "You don't need to do this. I already said I won't fight you. I'll do whatever you want." I tried to reason with him, my voice calm even though I was on the verge of shouting at him.

He kept advancing toward me. "Prove it." I was about to argue before he added, "You wish to see your sister again, don't you?"

Ah, the magic words. What a jerk. I was itching to draw my dagger out and strong-arm the bastard into bringing me to Zoey, but it was too risky. Her life was in his hands, and his vampire might issue the order to kill her if I did anything to his boss.

"Are we gonna have trouble here or not?" he asked, standing close to me. I reluctantly shook my head, biting back a string of curses. His smug expression made me want to punch him in his face, but I resisted the urge as he pressed the piece of cloth to my nose and mouth.

The sweet smell engulfed my senses, and I began to feel woozy. My vision started to blur, my feet became heavy, my head spun, and my eyes fluttered closed. Everything turned black.

Chapter 20

Something cold was attached to my legs and wrists. What was it? Disoriented, I blinked a few times then squinted against the bright white light, which caused me a headache. I moaned, hearing soft sobs.

When my mind came into focus, I remembered I'd been drugged. How long had I been out? I tried to move my legs and my hands, which were behind my back, but couldn't. Fear slammed into me. Lying on a cold tile floor, I gazed down at my body.

A metal chain was wrapped around my ankles, double looped, and secured with a U-shaped padlock. I struggled to my feet. With the metal wound tightly around my lower legs, it was hard to keep my balance. Another chain snaked around my wrists at my back. From what I could see, it seemed that it was double-looped and secured with a U-shaped padlock too. Still wearing my short black dress, I noticed my daggers and watch weren't on me. Crap.

"Don't scream," someone whispered. I swiveled my head to the source of the voice. It was the blonde girl who had cuddled Brad in the hot tub. She was standing next to me, still wearing her blue bikini from the party, her hands and legs bound just as mine were. To her right, eleven scared girls were lined up in a row. They were tied up with metal links affixed to padlocks too, the same way we were. To my left stood the brunette who had been sprawled unconscious in the office. Her legs and hands were bound too.

I counted fourteen girls, including me. We'd been positioned in a straight line, standing barefoot. Six were in bikinis, five in dresses, and three in skirts and bikini tops. It seemed we had all been abducted from the party. None of the terrified faces belonged to Zoey or Kyla. Where were they? My confusion deepened as I studied my surroundings.

We were in a huge room with a digital clock on the wall, fluorescent lights mounted above a suspended ceiling, no windows. There were two doors on the wall to my right, white and red. The white one was in the corner; the other, ten feet away from it. Six feet in front of us sat a row of large, open glass tanks filled with water. I counted fourteen. One for each girl. All of the tanks were about twenty feet high and ten feet wide. A platform elevator, at the floor level, was attached to the side of every one of them.

"Let me out of here! Please," shouted the third girl from the right, crying. "Brad, if you hear me, please! Ple—aaaaaaaaaaaagh!!" Her pleas turned into a scream of pain as her face contorted. She fell to the floor, curling into a ball.

"What happened to her?" I asked the girl who had warned me not to raise my voice, but terror filled her expression and she refused to answer.

The white door opened. Brad, in jeans and a T-shirt, entered the room with a man holding a gun.

"What happened to her?" Brad echoed as he walked up to me. "This." He pressed a button on a small device he was holding. A burning sensation ripped through me. It was as if fire was devouring me from the inside, destroying my body. I screamed. He pushed another button on the device, and the burning feeling ceased.

He grinned at the black box in his hand, which had names on it, mine included. "Worth every penny."

"You bastard. What are the water tanks for? Why are we here? Where's Zoey?" I said through clenched teeth.

"I'd watch my tongue if I were you, Sydney. Like every slut in here, you have an electronic patch on your arm, and it connects you to this amazing device I'm holding. It won't kill you, but it'll deliver enough pain that you'll wish you were dead. So no more questions—or name-calling. I expect complete obedience. Am I clear?"

I glared at him and forced a curt nod. He smiled. "Oh, come on, I'm not all that bad. You see, I'm giving you bitches the chance to walk out of here alive, that's how awesome I am. All you have to do is pass several challenges—and you'll be free to leave."

As he moved to the row of water tanks, thoughts raced through my head. What was going on? Were these challenges for his personal enjoyment? Or were we being watched by other sadists who paid for the entertainment? Had Zoey gone through the same sick game?

"In this challenge," he continued, "you have ten minutes to dive into the water tank in front of you and unlock the padlocks on your legs and wrists. Then you go stand at the red door on your left. How will you open the padlocks, you wonder? On the floor of every container, there are two keys: red and gray. The gray key is fastened to a ten-inch-long rope bolted to the floor. The padlocks on your wrists and legs can be opened with it.

"For those of you who can swim with your hands and legs tied up, like you, Shailene and Jenny"—he glanced at two girls—"you have an advantage. But don't waste your time and energy trying to tear the rope off the floor and swim back up to the surface to open the locks there. The rope cannot be ripped off. Another thing you should all know: the elevator platforms are automatic. They'll deliver you up and down, triggered by the weight of your body.

"Now for the second key. If you look closely, you'll notice it's encased in a cube-shaped glass. Its base is the tank's floor, so you can't lift it. To unlock the red door, you're gonna need the red key, so I suggest you find a quick way to obtain it. You're allowed to use whatever you want in order to get it out of the box.

"There are some rules you must follow, break them and Roger here"—he pointed at the man standing by the wall to our left—"will shoot you in the head. Here are the rules: you're not allowed to talk or help one another. And you can only use the keys from your tank—which is the one in front of you.

"If ten minutes have passed and you're not standing with a red key next to the red door, Roger will shoot you. When you hear the buzz, the clock on the wall will start counting down. Good luck." He moved to the white door and exited the room.

A loud horn announced the beginning of the challenge. The digital clock on the wall facing us read 10:00. My pulse exploded into a gallop while I stared at the tank of water ahead of me. The words "drowning" and "die" forced their way into my mind. I'd never operated well under pressure.

"Don't panic, don't panic, don't panic," I chanted, calming myself down.

Then, my father's words came to my mind. When Zoey and I had been little and camping, he used to say to us, "Girls, if you ever find yourselves in danger, always control your panic. Panicking is the number-one enemy of survival. It leads to hyperventilation and consequently damages one's clear mind."

I closed my eyes and concentrated on one thing: my breathing. I inhaled and exhaled a few times slowly, then opened my eyes. Calmer, I started to plan my next moves. I had three minutes—the time I could hold my breath underwater—to dive to the bottom, unlock the padlocks, and rise back to the surface. After that, I had to figure out a way to break the glass and get the second key.

I hopped over to the tank. To stay focused, I did my best to ignore the sounds that surrounded me: splashing water, sobs, chains rattling, the clock ticking down. I stepped onto the platform elevator. My heartbeat thundered in my ears when the metal platform started to move upward. Unlike Jenny and Shailene, I couldn't swim with my legs and hands tied up, so I had one shot. If I failed, I'd suffocate. I'd drown. I'd die.

"No, don't go there. Block the negative," I murmured to myself.

Once the platform reached the top of the container, I took a deep breath and plunged into the water. I reached the key tied to the rope and, with my fingers, awkwardly maneuvered it into the hole of the padlock attached to my wrists. Four times the damn thing fell from my hands. The cells in my body began to demand oxygen. The urge to breathe was strong. I resisted it as I kept trying, hearing a muffled shotgun blast and terrified screams. I mentally blocked the noise out and continued with my efforts to free myself.

On my fifth attempt, I succeeded. The chain loosened, and I disengaged it from my hands. The three minutes were almost up, and my lungs ached for air. Legs still bound together, I used only my arms as I swam upward like a mermaid. I shot out of the water and inhaled sharply. As I brought oxygen into my lungs, my eyes caught the red liquid on the floor. Horrified, I glanced at the dead girl on the floor, her hands and legs wrapped up in chains. Blood pooled around her head. I started panicking again. Not because of the dead body but because of the seven girls standing by the red door, holding a key. I checked the timer. Four minutes left. I dived back in and opened the second padlock without trouble, releasing myself from the chain around my legs.

Now, I had to get the second key and fast! I returned to the surface and crawled onto the platform elevator that took me down. I looked at the water tanks that the girls by the door had taken the keys from. How had they broken the cube of glass? The water in their containers was pink-ish, and their elbows and feet were injured, which meant that they'd smashed the box with their bodies.

I searched the room with my eyes, looking for a better way to break the cube until I registered a fire extinguisher in a glass case in the back corner of the room. I ran to it and tore off the small metal hammer hanging from a thin chain. My eyes darted to the clock. Two minutes left. I dashed to the tank, got on the platform, jumped into the water, broke the glass box with the hammer, grabbed the key, and got out of the container. The sound of a loud buzz indicating that time was up caught me just when I reached the other girls standing by the door.

We were eight. Eight out of fourteen had made it. Six didn't. The sight of five dead bodies floating in the water tanks and another one lying on the floor sent a shudder down my spine.

Brad's voice came through a speaker in a corner of the room. "Congratulations on passing this challenge. Well done. Unfortunately, six of you have failed. I'm sad to say that Lucy was shot in the head since she broke the rules. Didn't I specifically tell you not to ask for help? Well, shit happens, I guess. To start your next and final challenge, please use your key to open the red door. Do it one at a time."

As he'd ordered us, we exited the room one at a time. The door automatically shut behind each girl. When it was my turn, I unlocked it and stepped into another room, my face twisting at the foul, fishy smell. Standing near the door, I scanned the room. Its size was similar to the one I'd just left. They both looked alike but with a few differences. Across from the red door, there was a black one. A short, brown line had been drawn on the floor in front of it. On my left, a row of fourteen water tanks sat by the wall, identical to the ones we'd just escaped. Except these contained fish. Dozens of them. And at the bottom of each tank, an object I couldn't quite make out. Like before, a platform elevator was attached to every tank's side. Unlike before, there was a bucket and a knife next to each container.

After the last girl was inside, Brad and Roger entered the room from the red door too. When it closed behind them, Brad told us to put our red keys near the red door and follow him to the black one on the opposite side of the room. Roger and his gun came too. As we walked with them, some girls started to wail.

"For God's sake, I got the point, you're scared, now lay off the crying. You're giving me a headache," Brad barked at them, then rolled his eyes. "Ugh, never mind."

He and Roger stopped near the brown line on the floor, and the eight of us huddled together in front of them. Brad pulled eight label stickers out of his jeans pocket then handed each girl the one with her name on it.

"A new room, a new challenge. Listen up and pay close attention to what I am saying," he told us. "On your left, you have a row of fourteen tanks. Inside each of them, there is a black key lying at the bottom, and it's not tied to anything. There are thirty-two flesh-eating piranhas in every container. They're extremely aggressive, mind you. Next to the tanks, you'll find some stuff that can be of assistance to you: a bucket full of gutted fish and a knife. As in the first room, all the elevator platforms are automatic. Now, behind Roger and me stands a black door—your only way out of here. It leads outside the building. In this final challenge, there can be just one survivor who gets to live and walk out the black door. Or no one, in case all of you fail.

"Okay, let's move on to the instructions. You have fifteen minutes to pick a tank, put your sticker on it, and get the key lying at the bottom of that tank. Then with the key, you come over here and stand on the brown line. The first girl whose foot touches it is free to leave. The rest will be shot to death." He paused, observing our reactions, then a grin spread across his face. Bastard. "During this challenge, you're permitted to do or use anything you want—as long as it doesn't fall under the restrictions I'm about to list.

"Here is what you are not allowed to do, I repeat, not allowed to do: use more than one bucket of fish or more than one knife. Help each other. Force a girl to do your challenge in your place. Threaten Roger or me with the knife in order to escape. Do any of this, and you get a bullet in your skull. One more thing." He turned to look at Roger, and his man approached us, pulling a knife from his jacket. "Roger will cut those of you who aren't bleeding. Just to make things more interesting." He checked our bodies for injuries, nicking the arms of three girls and me. "Okay, that's it. Good luck."

This time, when the buzzer went off, my mind went blank. Frozen, I stared at the piranhas. They appeared restless, swimming from side to side. The girl next to me was in the same state, motionless and shocked. The rest had already claimed a tank with their stickers.

I jerked nervously when screams pierced the air. Then I noticed with horror that Jenny had slashed another girl's throat. Her blood spurted out in a stream and splattered everywhere.

"What have you done? You can't do that. Are you insane?" someone shouted at Jenny, and she dropped the dead body, shaking.

Her head whipped to Brad, who was near the black door, fear on her face. "It was not forbidden to do that, right? Y-you didn't say it was against the rules to kill another girl."

He crossed his arms over his chest, looking amused. "No, I didn't say it's forbidden to kill one another, so yes, it's okay."

She sighed with relief and dragged the corpse to the platform elevator. On it, she put her bucket, her knife, and the dead body. When she reached the top of the container, she rolled the lifeless girl over and dropped her into the water, then emptied the bucket full of dead fish inside the tank.

Smelling blood, the piranhas rushed their food, and she quickly jumped into the container with the knife. The dead body and fish were a good distraction but not enough. There were too many piranhas in the water. The ones who weren't feasting on the dead girl darted to Jenny the moment she plunged into the water. Unable to fend off all the piranhas with her knife, she drowned as they tore, ripped, and gnawed at her flesh.

"No, no, no, I can't do that. I'm giving up," the girl beside me, Marie, mumbled, shaking her head frantically. Her gaze shifted to Brad. "Why are you doing this to us? Why?" Tears welled up in her eyes.

He ignored her, laughing at Candace's unsuccessful attempts at breaking the thick glass of her tank with a hammer taken from a fire extinguisher.

"You know what? Screw you! I won't be part of this crazy-ass shit. Kill me now." Her tone was a mix of anger and desperation.

Roger started toward us with his gun.

Marie backed up a few steps. "No, no, no, w-w-what are you—no, don't. I didn't mean to say that. It was her!" She stabbed a finger at me. "She forced me to say it. It's her fault. Shoot her, not me." She moved behind me and shoved me in Roger's direction.

Brad's voice kept his man from advancing any farther. "I know she's giving you a migraine, but it's not against the rules to be hysterical or lie like a stupid bitch. You'll get your chance to shoot her when she fails. Which will be in five minutes."

Five minutes? My head snapped to the timer. Shit!

I had to clear my mind and somehow manage to get the key without being eaten alive by piranhas. For a few moments, I gazed over at the eight unmarked tanks and the deadly fish inside them.

"Tick-tock-tick-tock, the clock is ticking. Three minutes until your time is up. It doesn't look good for you two, Sydney and Marie," Brad said, a spark of enjoyment in his eyes.

Think! Think! I urged myself. *Focus.* In my head, I went over everything he'd said about the challenge: what was allowed, what was not. And then I realized something.

I rushed to an unmarked container and took the knife placed next to it. With it, I ran to the red door and picked up one of the keys on the floor. I got into the first room, chose the nearest water tank, and slapped my sticker on it. I used its platform elevator to jump inside and dive to the bottom. I sliced away at the rope with the knife, freeing the gray key and taking it with me up to the surface.

When I was outside the container, drenched in water, I ran back toward the red door just as Marie opened it. She pushed me aside. I lost my balance but managed to steady myself before the door closed. I sped to the brown line with the gray key in my hand. Forty seconds were left. I ran like crazy. Twenty seconds, fifteen seconds, ten seconds. I increased my speed. Five seconds, two seconds. My feet touched the brown line, and the clock ticked down.

Brad stepped to me. His expression was surprised, confused maybe. Staring at me, he didn't utter a word. The door across from us opened, and Marie came in, her voice breaking the silence.

"Why do none of the elevators work anymore? Why'd you permit her to take the key from the other room and not me?"

He dropped his head forward and pinched the bridge of his nose, squinting his eyes shut, as if he couldn't bear to hear her anymore.

"Because the challenge is over," he said. When he opened his eyes, he looked at Roger. "Now you may shoot her."

Roger drew his gun and fired. With a bullet in her head, she died instantly, collapsing to the floor. All the others were dead too. So much blood, smeared everywhere, spread everywhere, in the water, on the walls, on the ground. The room looked like a scene from a horror movie.

"You sadistic son of a bitch." I glared at Brad, and I didn't care about the stupid stick-on electronic patch he'd put on me. *Go ahead, press the button, you asshole.* God, I despised him.

Unmoved, he asked, "Why'd you take the key from the water tank in the first room? Your freedom depends on your answer."

"Your instructions were, and I quote, 'Pick a tank, put your sticker on it, and get the key lying at the bottom of that tank.' You never said that the key had to come from a tank in this room. As you well know, there were fourteen of them lying at the bottom of the tanks in the other room. Taking a key from there doesn't fall under any of your restrictions," I said.

"But the key in your hand is gray. Why do you think it will match the black door behind you?"

"I don't. In fact, I'm pretty sure it won't, but whether or not it matches is not relevant for this challenge. Unlike the first one, your instructions did not stipulate that we must have a black key, or any key for that matter, to unlock this door."

He slow-clapped. "Well done." He pulled out the black device from his pocket and put it on my arm to remove the patch from my skin.

"I finished your twisted game. Now tell me, where is Zoey? Where's Kyla? Did they go through the same thing? Are they..." I swallowed. "Dead?"

He laughed. "Dead? Aren't you the pessimistic one? Think more positively. I hear it's good for the soul." The black door opened, and he motioned to it. "You're free to go. Goodbye, Sydney." He turned and walked away.

"Wait! I need to know; where's my sister? Where's Zoey?" I called out at his retreating back. I strode toward him, but Roger grabbed my arm, pulled me back, and threw me outside the room.

The door slammed in my face. I pounded on it. "No! Tell me where Zoey is!" I shouted until I got tired, then rested my forehead against the door. I had to contact Gideon, but how? I had no money, no phone, and no watch with a tracker in it. I wondered if Kelly had texted him. What if Brad had done something to her or taken her too?

I drew my eyebrows together when a warm wind caressed my body. It was winter, but the temperature was high. With a wet dress and no shoes, I should be freezing. I whirled around. What the hell?

Ten feet away from me, a wide river with a high boardwalk led to a vast expanse of nature, where tropical trees created a thick wall of greenery. Where was I? I jerked back to look at the building I'd been thrown from a moment ago, but it was gone. Stunned, I closed my eyes, rubbed my face, then opened them again. Rubber trees, jungle ferns, and wild ginger stood where the building was supposed to be. I reached out, touching air. It couldn't be an illusion. I was immune to it. Since objects didn't disappear into thin air, it had to be some kind of magic.

Great, Brad had witches working for him.

I sighed. How was I going to reach Gideon or Kelly in the middle of freaking nowhere?

I moved toward the bridge and stopped at the beginning of it when I spotted a glowing butterfly. It danced and fluttered around me, leaving a long trail of tiny sparkly gold particles. My lips parted as my gaze was glued to the magical glittery light, which looked like translucent fairy dust. While I gawked at it, I felt a sudden shift in the air's texture.

There was a nuclear flash, and a great-shaking explosion followed it. The clap of thunder startled me and apparently the butterfly as well. It flitted away, disappearing into the jungle, and the trail of glowing particles behind it faded. A few seconds later, red raindrops began to splash my skin. I gazed down at my hands and the ground. Was it raining... blood? Sweet. Baby. Jesus. What was this place?

Chapter 21

Covered with blood, I searched for shelter and hurried to a broad-leafed tree not far away, and waited out the weird storm. Standing on a dry spot, I watched the downpour of red rain splattering the ground. Eventually, it let up and then stopped altogether. The strong scent of fresh blood hung in the air. I breathed through my mouth and trod lightly on the blood-slicked ground, heading back to the bridge. Careful not to slip, I crossed the boardwalk over a pink-tinged river and examined the place. Was I even still on Earth?

Other than the glowing butterfly and blood falling from the sky, the landscape looked like an ordinary tropical jungle teeming with buzzing and climbing insects. I gazed up and found one moon over my head, not two, or three. Stars dotted the black sky, some covered by clouds. The moonlight was bright, casting a soft light. On the other side of the river, I discovered a thatch umbrella. It was positioned at the entrance of the jungle. Two objects were under it.

I approached them with caution. Two duffel bags. I looked right and left, but there was no one around. Who did those bags belong to? Had Brad brought his men here? I unzipped the first bag and slipped my hand inside. I dragged a folded sheet of paper and a flashlight out. I turned on the flashlight and unfolded the paper. It was a note. I shined a light on the words.

Hello Sydney,

Congratulations on your win. These bags are for you. Inside you'll find brand-new clothes in your size. Body measurements of all the girls were taken when you were unconscious by a female employee of mine. In one bag, there are also toiletries, food, and water, and in the other, weapons. Guard the weapons well, especially the gun with the silver bullets, as it's essential for your survival.

This is where our ways part now. I wish you the best of luck out there. You'll be needing it. Ice Prison is a tough, cruel place inhabited by dangerous creatures. Not to mention the prisoners, most of whom haven't had human blood in a very, very long time. Hope you make it more than an hour or two. Again, best of luck to you.

Brad.

I blinked at the paper, and my jaw almost hit the floor. Ice Prison? I was in Ice Prison? Oh. My. God. Why would that psycho bring me out here? Probably just for the fun of it. I unzipped the second bag and sagged with relief. He hadn't lied. It contained weapons: a machete, a silver dagger, and a handgun. At least I had something I could use to protect myself.

My stomach growled as I rifled through the other bag. There was bottled water and canned food, enough to last me about three weeks, and a sandwich with cheese and bacon. I dug it out. Saliva gathered in my mouth at the smell. I wiped my hands against the wet, dirty dress. Then I bit into the sandwich, chewing savagely. I was famished; I didn't even care about the taste of blood my hands left on the bread. Once I calmed my hunger, I had the energy to plan my next steps.

At the Memphis Warriors' castle, Alice had told me the portal to Ice Prison was in the Devil's Triangle, a.k.a the Bermuda Triangle, so I was in another dimension. Crap. The second thing I knew about Ice Prison was that a powerful being named Herit had built it to lock away supernatural criminals—not humans. This was helpful information, but it wasn't enough. If I intended to survive—and I did—I had to learn everything I could about this place. Like the kinds of danger it probably held: wildlife, deadly insects, poisonous plants, and inhuman prisoners. And then, search for a miracle way back to my universe.

A gust of breath left me. To let despair take root inside me was tempting. Returning home sounded impossible; however, I refused to give Brad the satisfaction of breaking me. Somehow, I'd find a way back to my universe. *I will.* Thanks to my father, I wasn't scared of being in a harsh environment like the jungle—even if it was in another dimension. I had wilderness survival skills training. In addition, when I'd honed my martial arts skills, practicing with Gideon, I'd learned that I knew how to use almost any weapon because of the dark magic on my hand.

A bright blue thunderbolt lit the dark sky, drawing my attention. When the crashing boom arrived milliseconds later, I expected another red shower. Instead, clean water splashed against the umbrella and dripped off its edges. I took out a bottle of shampoo, a bar of soap, and the dagger, then stepped into the rain. I freed my hair from its elastic band and stripped naked. I kept the knife close to me while I scrubbed my body and hair with the shampoo and soap, letting the rain wash the stink and dirt off.

When I was clean, I ducked back under the umbrella. The warm wind touched my bare wet skin as I pulled all the clothes and a pair of shoes out of the bag: a leather belt with holsters, underwear, bras, a black shirt, a black ribbed tank top, hiking boots, and cream knit socks. I put them on and wore the belt with the holster ends strapped to each thigh. Then I emptied the weapon bag, shoved the dagger and gun into the holsters, and calculated my next moves. First things first. I had to find a somewhat safe place to camp for the night, preferably on a high hill overlooking potential threats. Then I'd set booby traps around it, so I wouldn't be ambushed while I slept.

When the rain stopped, I started into the jungle, leaving the second bag, which I'd emptied, behind. The combined scent of wet soil, decaying leaves, and damp moss reached my nose as I cut a path into the foliage using the machete. Although it was no longer raining, drops of water continued to fall from the leaves and branches of the canopy, trickling to the uneven forest floor. Twigs and ferns crunched under my boots as I kept going.

A symphony of sounds surrounded me. There were screeching monkeys, croaking frogs, millions of buzzing insects, flowing water and, from time to time, crashing branches falling through the tropical trees. Just when I thought everything looked like a regular jungle, a giant creature with the appearance of a wide snake with three heads slithered over the buttress roots of a nearby tree.

I came to a halt and slowly backed up. A twig snapped under my feet. I screwed up my face when the creature spotted me. Three of its heads hissed at me, showing sharp fangs.

"Hey, there." I took another step back. "All the, uh, hissing and fangs thing is not by any chance your way of giving a friendly welcome greeting, right?" I asked it, as if the creature could understand me, or maybe in this dimension, monsters taken right out of a nightmare could. The head in the middle opened its jaws and ejected a yellow substance that smelled like a rotten egg. Having fast reflexes, I dodged the smelly substance in time.

"No? Okay, just checking."

The fuming liquid, which had missed my feet by a few inches, ate away at leaves and branches. I looked up to the creature. It was slithering in my direction, and it was fast. Outrunning it over a gnarled jungle floor of roots and moss would be a tad tricky, so I dropped the bag on the ground and raised the machete. At that exact moment, its vast body froze. All three heads held terror in their eyes.

At first, puzzlement filled me, but then relief replaced it. My spine straightened as I bragged, "Yeah, that's right. You better be scared." I sliced the air with the blade. Instead of fleeing in screams from my mighty machete, the three of them ignored me and looked up at the sky through the canopy. My gaze went up too.

One by one, the stars disappeared. When the moon vanished as well and the sky started to brighten, the jungle went silent. Even the insects held their breath. A wail like an air-raid siren erupted, painfully loud. The creature in front of me slithered away. Well that couldn't be good. I grabbed the bag and hoisted it onto my shoulder. As my gaze flicked around, searching for a place to hide from whatever was coming, a hand landed on my upper arm. Gripping the machete tighter, I jerked away as I turned, ready to attack whoever—or whatever—it was, then gasped with shock.

Kelly?

Chapter 22

"Whoa, whoa, careful." She backed away from my weapon. Barefoot, she was still wearing the lavender dress from the party. Her hair was messed up. "Sydney, we gotta hurry! We don't have time. Follow me."

I snapped out of my shock and ran behind her. I couldn't see anything except leaves slapping my face, vines, and gray mist rising from the uneven floor. Branches hit me in the ribs, and I almost tripped a few times, the weight of the bag on my shoulder only adding to the difficulties.

As we ran, the siren stopped, and the night just... ended. One moment it was dark, the next, rays of sunlight broke through the canopy of the forest. Kelly screamed in pain. Having BFB in my system, the sun hurt me as well, but we both kept moving. To where? I had no idea. A jolt of terror streaked through me when screeches began echoing in the jungle, sounding eerie and ghoulish. I ran faster.

Kelly finally halted and motioned me to climb a rope ladder leading to a tree house twenty feet above our heads. I quickly scampered up the ladder and crawled inside a single rectangular room made of wood. Its roof was slanted, and there was no furniture of any kind or windows. Being a vampire with super speed, Kelly was inside too in seconds, closing the door behind her. Everything went black.

The sound of my panting filled the small space before I spoke. "Kelly, what—"

"Shh, don't talk. Don't move," she said in a low voice. But her warning came through loud and clear.

Sitting on the floor, I zipped my mouth shut and went motionless. The demonic howls in the jungle made my blood run cold, and a knot of fear grew in my guts. Not knowing what was roaming free out there rendered the situation even scarier, yet I tried not to panic as I sat in the dark. What felt like a few hours passed, and the sinister howls outside stopped.

"They're gone," Kelly finally said in a normal volume.

I let out a deep sigh and stretched my arms and legs while she opened the door. Soft moonlight—not sunlight—filtered into the room.

Surprised, I stood and peered outside. "It's night again. How is that possible?"

"We're in another dimension; things work a bit differently here. Don't freak out, but we're in Ice Prison, a prison for supernatural beings," she answered.

"I know, but it's a jungle. Why is it called Ice Prison?"

"'Cause when supernatural beings die here, hey turn to ice. Each race has its own section in Ice Prison. The vampire area is called the Jungle. Kill or be killed," she explained. "Here it's night most of the time. The sun comes out once or twice a week for three or four hours. That's when the gargoyles leave their caves to hunt—anything that comes their way."

My eyebrows soared. "Gargoyles?"

"Yeah. They can fly, they're ugly as hell, and their saliva prevents their victims from turning into ice after they kill them. My father used to tell me many stories about them. A gargoyle was once a vampire prisoner." She looked outside the door. "The Jungle's air messes with the vampires' DNA. Our fast-healing ability protects us from it, but not forever.

"If we breathe oxygen here for more than ten years straight, the damage becomes too much for our body to handle, and we gradually mutate into an animal. We could turn into a frog, a butterfly, an alligator, or even an animal that doesn't exist on Earth. It all depends on the vampire's strength, age, and DNA. Those who were strong, like Ancients, will transform into gargoyles. Once a vampire fully mutates, there's no coming back to Earth. The mutation is a slow process that takes years. After about ten years of breathing the Jungle's air, a vampire will start to lose his or her memories while the body slowly changes. In the end, you'll have no memory of who you once were, and you'll become an animal."

Thousands of questions piled up in my mind, and they came out in a flurry. "All the animals in the Jungle were once vampires? Why do the gargoyles get out only when the sun's up? Who set off the alarm? What about the green trees? Don't they need sunlight to grow? You know, photosynthesis and all that... and what about humans? What happens to us here?"

"All the animals you've encountered and will encounter in the Jungle were once vampires. The gargoyles differ from the others in that their eyes and legs don't work in the dark. The sunlight helps them see, and it fuels their bodies with energy. About twice a week, they eat, and when the night returns, they go back into their caves to sleep until the next time the sunlight wakes them up." She raised a hand. "Hold on a second."

She vanished and reappeared in front of me two seconds later with something in her hand.

"The smell of your blood is driving me nuts. I'm starving. I gotta feed before I sink my teeth into you."

I stared down at my body. From the run earlier, I had a few new open cuts on my arms and legs. Thank God she had bags of blood with her. Had Brad given them to her? "How'd you end up here? Was it Brad?"

She gulped blood and sat down on the floor. "Yeah, that jerk took me too. After you passed out, he searched you for trackers and weapons. He found your silver dagger and tortured me until I couldn't take it anymore. I'm so sorry, I had to tell him about the tracker in the watch... He was hurting me and was so mad I hadn't kept my mouth shut.

"As a punishment, he ordered a witch to open a portal to Ice Prison. He forced me into the Jungle, and because I brought you to the party alone as he'd asked, he gave me ten bags of blood." She took a long sip before continuing. "Then I spotted you from afar. The three-headed snake was about to eat you. I rushed in your direction, and the siren blared. I don't get it, though. Why would he throw you in here?"

"I have no clue. Only God knows what's going on in his crazy head," I said, and my gaze swept over her. She seemed to be in bad shape, mainly emotionally. "I'm sorry I dragged you into all this, Kelly." Because of me, she was in Ice Prison. I felt terrible.

Her tongue darted out and licked the blood off her lips. "Don't be. I wanted to help find Zoey. Did you see her?"

I shook my head. "No, I woke up in a room with thirteen girls who had been taken from the party too. We were tied with chains and had to go through some cruel challenges. They all died. I survived, so he let me go, but turns out the door was actually a portal to Ice Prison, and then the building vanished."

Wide-eyed, she said, "Seriously? He made you do challenges? Gosh, that's really messed up. You think he did the same to Zoey?"

That would be the rational conclusion. Zoey could be in the Jungle too, breathing this air.

"You didn't answer my question from before. Is the oxygen here fatal to humans too?" Silence. "Kelly?"

"Yes, they'll die within a week," she finally answered. "The air is highly toxic to regular humans."

"Regular humans?" I echoed.

"Yeah, not Gifted. Some humans are born with a supernatural gift, like fortune-tellers and tea readers. The body of a Gifted human can sustain the toxic environment of the Jungle longer. They have about a month before it shuts down."

My stare moved down to the tattoo on my palm, and she said, "Gifted humans cannot contain such powerful dark magic. They'll die instantly. But apparently you can, so it may indicate that you're some kind of super Gifted human."

"Too bad the only way I can know whether I am super Gifted is if I don't croak in the next few days." The bitterness in my tone was sharp. "Say I am. What about Zoey? Is being Gifted genetic?"

She shrugged apologetically. "I don't know."

The thought of Zoey dead made my stomach hurt. If she was here, she'd already breathed the toxic air in—wait.

I cast Kelly a questioning look. "How come there's oxygen in the vampire's section of Ice Prison? You don't need it to survive."

"We don't, but mutated vampires do. Their heart returns to beat once they transform fully into an animal. Though, they don't lose their immortality," she replied.

"Where does your detailed knowledge of Ice Prison come from? Your father?" I wondered.

"Not just him. Everything about Ice Prison is common knowledge in the Hidden World."

A bright yellow bird flew inside the tree house. I watched its unique color with fascination while it hovered above our heads before it fluttered out.

"It's beautiful," I commented.

"It was a Yellow Dreamer, a harmless bird," she said. "Watch out for the glowing butterflies, though. They're gorgeous, but one touch of their sparkle trail and you're paralyzed. Once you fall to the ground, it slips into your body through your nose or mouth then eats your liver, your colon, and your kidneys while you're still alive. After that, they'll eat the lungs and then the entire head. It's a painful way to die."

I sucked in a breath. While I'd been admiring the beautiful butterfly back at the river, that little monster had its eyes on its next meal—me.

"Yeah, they're really nasty," she continued. "Keep in mind that they're drawn to blood and can sense when someone is unable to move because of illness or an injury. They'll exploit it and enter their body to eat them, so be careful around them."

"Don't worry, duly noted," I told her and changed the subject. "What's the deal with the siren? Who sets it off?"

"Not who. What. Magic," she answered. "Ice Prison was sculpted and designed by Herit. Ever heard of her?"

"I have. She's supposed to be some sort of bad-ass warrior, super strong and powerful. Yet no one knows what she is."

She nodded. "Herit was very powerful; even the Original Rulers were brought to their knees by her, begging for mercy." She paused, as if imagining the event in her head. "Anyway," she went on, "Herit built Ice Prison in another dimension, so things work differently around here. The night and the moon dominate this area. On Earth, twenty-four hours count as one day. If we follow this time measurement unit here, I can say that the sun appears in the sky once or twice a week at random times. That's when the moon and stars vanish for three or four hours, and the hunt begins.

"Herit thought it'd be wise to give the prisoners a heads-up before the gargoyles come out. Otherwise, they would eventually slaughter everyone in the Jungle—where they're at the top of the food chain. They have no predators, so she cast a spell that functions as an alarm. It goes off whenever the sun is approaching."

"The three-headed snake knew the siren was about to go off a few seconds before it actually did," I said.

She swatted a buzzing insect off her face. After slapping at it and crushing the little mutated vampire, which turned into ice as it fell to the floor, she shifted her attention back to me.

"Yeah, some animals can sense the energy of the sun when it's about to come, and that gives them a few seconds of advantage. Oh, and about the green trees and photosynthesis you brought up earlier. The trees have adapted to the harsh environment, and now they can tolerate low light levels. Keep in mind that there's plenty of Herit's magic surrounding the place, so lots of stuff in the Jungle won't make sense to you."

A warm breeze blew in through the open door. Sweating, I fanned myself with one hand. "Like having one-hundred-degree heat even though the sun shows up only twice a week for a short period?"

"Exactly. Most vampires hate the heat, and this being a prison, it's not supposed to be comfortable for us."

"Then why does it rain blood here?" I asked.

"Herit was against starvation. Since the food sources for vampires here are limited, with her magic, she made sure that blood rain would occasionally fall in the Jungle," she answered and got up to throw the empty bag of blood in a corner.

My eyes traveled across the room. "Whose tree house is it?"

"I don't know. I found it empty a week ago, and no one has come to it since then."

"A week?" My voice rose in confusion. "Brad's party was only several hours ago." Had I been unconscious longer than that?

She returned and sat down in front of me again. "It was, but I've been sleeping in this tree house for a week now according to my calculation. The time in Ice Prison moves much faster than in our dimension. An hour on Earth is twenty-four hours in the Jungle."

"Great, so for you and me, it'll take Gideon forever until he discovers Brad trapped us in Ice Prison. I don't understand; he's not a Watcher, so how the hell does he have access to this place?"

"He doesn't. The demon king, Damon, does. Brad paid him lots of money to get his help. I saw the demon in his father's mansion with a witch when Brad threw me in here. To open a gate to this dimension, you need a Watcher. Or a skilled witch and a powerful supernatural being who contains strong energy inside of him or her, like Damon. The witch has to draw her power from this energy to be able to open a portal.

"Anyway, don't count on Gideon to save us. I don't think he has the resources to create a gate. The good news, though, is that we're not real prisoners, which means the magic in Ice Prison doesn't know we exist, so it won't block our way as we cross through the portal to our dimension."

"What portal? The ones we came through to get here are closed."

"Not the temporary gates, I'm talking about the main gate. Which leads to the Bermuda Triangle," she said.

"But won't we find ourselves in the sea once we've passed through? And is the portal even visible?" I asked.

"It's supposed to be, and we'll build a log raft. It's not ideal, but at least we'll be back on Earth," she told me.

A rickety log raft in the middle of the ocean was too dangerous. "I don't know, Kelly. It's not safe. Besides, without tools, it'll take us forever to make a raft."

"Being in Ice Prison is a lot less safe," she pointed out and nodded at the weapon on my thigh. "We have a dagger and a machete. They'll be useful. If not, we'll figure out everything at the portal. But first, we have to find it."

"And hope for more empty tree houses on our way over there in case the sun goes up again," I said.

"There must be more shelters throughout the Jungle. Don't forget that I'm not the only vampire here," she told me.

Somehow, that was not reassuring.

"Okay, so now all we have to do is track down the main portal, which is somewhere in a forest full of dangerous mutated vampires, before the toxic air kills me." I sounded hopeless.

"Pinpointing the main gate's location won't be a problem—because of you."

I lifted an eyebrow. "Me?"

"Yeah, you. Humans are naturally drawn to it since Ice Prison was not built for them. Unlike vampires."

"Are you positive about that? I don't feel anything."

"And you won't until the BFB leaves your system."

"I see," I said, and hope flickered inside of me. "If Zoey ended up in Ice Prison, she might've found the gate and gotten out of here."

"Unless Brad kidnapped her again, keeping her locked away. He was obsessed with her. Maybe he never threw her in Ice Prison in the first place," she said.

"Yeah, you're right."

After I found Zoey, I'd deal with Brad. Preferably, I'd tie him up and drop him into a tank full of leeches and make him search for a goddamn key in all the colors of the rainbow, giving him a taste of his own medicine.

Rage consumed my body at the thought of his evil smile, so I shoved him out of my mind and looked down at the tattoo, wondering how it would react in this dimension. Time would tell.

I sighed and returned my gaze to Kelly. "We're gonna leave the tree house as soon as the BFB wears off and go search for the main portal. Until then, we get some shut-eye. We need our strength to face whatever is waiting for us out there."

"Sounds like a good plan. I'm exhausted." She went to a corner and sat down as I stood up and closed the door.

The room turned black. "Sleep tight," I heard Kelly say.

I lay down across the entrance, so if someone tried to get in, it'd wake me up. Then I put my head on the bag, using it as a pillow.

"You too," I said and fell asleep.

Chapter 23

Dream images faded away as I felt a gentle shake on my shoulder. "Sydney, wake up."

I opened my eyes to Kelly's face looking down at me. It took me a few seconds to remember where I was. I sat up, feeling refreshed, rested, and hungry.

I checked the number on my hand. It'd decreased by one. Good, the dark magic didn't behave differently here.

"Have any idea how long we've been sleeping?" I asked.

"My body clock says seven hours, maybe eight."

I got to my feet. Sweat trickled down my chest as I opened the door. My skin was sticky with the increased humidity of the air. It was night outside, and everything looked like before. Something was different, though. I felt some sort of compulsion to get down and start walking west.

"Do you feel drawn to the portal? Did the BFB wear off?" Kelly said.

I went to the bag and pulled out a can of food. "Yes, but first I gotta eat. What about you? Aren't you hungry?"

She vanished into a dark corner and then moved back to the door, a duffel bag on her shoulder. "I've been here longer than you, and I'm running low on the blood bags. I need to conserve my food as much as possible and feed on the next red rain."

I nodded, and after I finished eating, we climbed down the ladder and walked into the dense forest. We had to stop several times to drag away fallen branches blocking our path. The terrain was hilly, never flat, making the hike more challenging. The heat and the clothes sticking to my damp body didn't help.

Taking a break, I gave the machete to Kelly and drank water, trying to cool myself off. I inhaled the damp, slithery rotten smell of the forest into my lungs as I put the bottle back in the bag. That's when I noticed the small insects nipping on my arms. Alarmed, I slapped at them and checked my legs. "Jesus," I said with horror. They were covered in a mountain range of red bites.

Kelly stepped close to me, examining my legs with her eyes. "Ooh, doesn't look good, but don't worry; they're not life-threatening bites."

I glanced at her skin. It was smooth and perfect—not a single bite or cut. "God, I wish I was a vampire right now."

"Bugs feed on the undead too," she corrected my assumption. "I'm not immune to insect bites, but vampires heal fast, so I don't even feel it."

"Being a vampire does have its perks," I said, wiping the sweat off my face with the hem of the shirt before taking the knife back and continuing with our journey. We brushed elbows and hips against encroaching foliage as we walked along little streams that weaved through the forest and many clusters of mushrooms. We followed the direction I kept being drawn to like a magnet.

For my human eyes, Kelly strode after me with a flashlight, illuminating our surroundings while I hacked a trail through the mass of vegetation. As we walked through the forest, I admired the beautiful sight of glowing funguses perched on the sides of rocks and trees along the way. A loud clap of thunder rumbled, and a few seconds later, the rain began. At some point, the rain cranked up, yet we didn't get too wet since the forest's canopy kept most of the water from hitting the ground.

As time ticked by, weakness suffused through my limbs, and we took another break.

"Eat something. You look weak," Kelly said.

I sat down on the rocky floor and followed her advice, opening the bag and taking out a food can. When I was done, I hauled myself to my feet, and a wave of dizziness swept through me. I swayed and quickly put my hand on the bark of a towering tree to steady myself.

"Whoa, you okay?" Kelly shot to my side, ready to catch me if I fell.

"Yeah, it must be the heat." Or the toxic air. "It'll pass," I said, not wanting to worry her. As I glanced around, a thought occurred to me. "We've been plodding through the forest for what feels like forever, but we haven't run into any prisoners. Where are they? Those who haven't mutated? Not that I'm complaining, just wondering."

"The Jungle is a lot like human prisons," she told me. "Vampires here live in groups. Gangs that mark their own turf. Rarely will you see a prisoner wandering alone. It's not easy to survive on your own here. The inmates usually remain on their own turf most of the time. They don't roam freely in the Jungle unless they have to."

"Well, let's hope we don't encounter any vampire gangs on our way to the portal," I said. Although my body was still drained of energy, we resumed our hiking, bent on getting to the gate.

As we proceeded, I became overwhelmed by the ineffable beauty around us. Enchanted gleaming flowers and fireflies surrounded the place. Many balls of light danced among the trees, creating a magical spectacle, and when we passed a pond, I watched in awe at the clear reflection of the stars on the water. It was as if they were there.

My attention focused on the stupendous views, and Kelly reminded me to watch my steps. The rain had long since ceased, but the forest floor was ankle-deep mud, which hid tree roots and rocks. Almost tripping a few times, I tore my gaze from the gorgeous view and watched my steps.

After we trundled up a hill and moved through some dense undergrowth, we reached a small lake. Ten feet from the water's edge, I came to a sudden halt.

"Oh, good, another body of water. I'll go wash the mud off my feet," Kelly said behind me.

When she moved forward toward the lake, I whispered sharply, "Don't take another step."

She froze and stared over at the lake and then at me in bewilderment. "Why?"

"Do you feel any wind?" My voice was low. She shook her head, her brow furrowed. "Look out at the water again," I told her.

Her gaze turned to the lake once more. A dreadful expression of dawning realization appeared on her face. "It's not flat," she murmured.

Ripples gave way to small waves moving at different speeds and different directions across the pond. Something was in there. And it was not friendly.

My eyes were on the shore. "Now look at the bank." I waited for her to notice the broken teeth, skulls, and pieces of bones lying along the waterline.

"Jesus, that was not done by fish," she whispered.

"Nope, and I don't know if whatever is in the water can hear noises from..." I trailed off when she squatted, snatched a stone, and threw it into the lake.

There was a sharp movement in the water, and an octopus-like head the size of a wrecking ball rose to the surface. We jerked back as one wide tentacle emerged from the black water and smacked the muddy bank, two feet away from us. To close the gap, the sucker-bearing arm extended in our direction. We jumped aside, and the long tentacle reached the vegetation instead, tearing whatever it touched: grass, roots, leaves.

As the creature searched for us, I put my index finger across my lips, motioning Kelly to stay quiet. That thing seemed to be blind and relied on its sense of hearing. I preferred not to use the machete to cut it since the creature's skin looked too thick, so I thought of another solution. Gaze fixed on the octopus-like head, I slowly bent down and grabbed the first stone my hand touched.

Holding it, I inched toward Kelly, leaning to her ear. "When I throw it, run. We'll meet on the other side of the lake, away from its bank." She nodded, and I tossed the stone.

It sailed through the air in an arc and fell onto the mud. A bushy stream of misty air and vapor exploded from the creature's head as it swam toward the sound the stone had caused. I raced in the opposite direction, and Kelly disappeared. The noise my feet made drew the creature's attention, and its arms moved after me. I kept running, speeding up.

Finally reaching the other side of the lake, a safe distance from the creature, I stopped and dropped the knife to the ground. I leaned over, my hands on my knees, panting. My body shook, and I felt weaker.

"You made it," Kelly said, her voice relieved.

"Yeah, but I think we'll call it a day, or night, whatever," I told her when I caught my breath.

"Sure, but we gotta find a safer place to sleep, somewhere I won't be exposed in the event the sun comes up. We need to search for a tree house. Can you walk a bit longer?"

"I can, but you think we're gonna run into one soon?"

"Just a sec, let me check." Like Spiderman, she climbed up a tree and was back on the ground a minute later. "There's a hut, that way." She nodded to our left. "We'll go put our stuff in there and get some rest."

"We're not alone in the Jungle, Kelly. We may be welcomed by dangerous vampires," I said.

"I know, but the area seemed abandoned. We'll be careful. Turn off the flashlight until we're sure no one is nearby."

"Okay, after you." I gestured with my hand to the left.

We toiled through the forest again. Fortunately, it wasn't long until she announced, "We're getting closer. I can see it."

My eyes, though, saw only curved vines dangling from trees, trunks covered with moss, and grass—not a hut. She led the way with the machete, and as we moved forward, the forest became darker. Its canopy closed over us like a shroud. Here and there, a shaft of moonlight crept through the leafy branches, preventing absolute darkness. When Kelly stopped cutting vines, the chatters and growls of the animals sounded louder, echoing through the forest.

"There it is." She pointed forward, and I caught sight of a single bamboo hut not far away, camouflaged under the greenery.

We cautiously approached the small shelter. Its palm-thatch roof was rotting, and no one appeared to be inside. Nonetheless, I drew out a dagger as I nudged the door open with my foot.

It was pitch black inside, but Kelly said with confidence, "The room's empty, not even furniture, just a wooden beam in the middle. Like I told you, it's deserted."

I trusted her super vampire senses and stepped inside. I returned the dagger to its place, put down the bag, took out the flashlight, and turned it on. Then, I reached up to massage my shoulder blades. My back hurt like hell, my head felt ready to explode, and my body screamed for rest. I sat down on the thatched floor. It'd be hard to sleep on it, but now was not exactly the time to be picky.

After we ate, we put the heavy wood beam across the steel bars at the sides of the door to secure it and went to sleep.

Chapter 24

My body didn't renew its energy after my sleep. If anything, I was weaker. My appetite was gone too, and I suffered from a debilitating headache. According to Kelly, we had slept for six hours, give or take; however, the number on my palm had declined by three. My sickness seemed to affect the dark magic.

I was tired and wished I had a few more hours to sleep, but time was not on our side. The Jungle air was clearly starting to take a toll on me. We had to get out of this dimension. And fast.

Red rain began to fall outside, so I told Kelly, "Go feed on the blood rain. I'll eat here, then we'll leave."

She nodded and stepped to the hut doorway. Careful not to dirty her dress, she reached out and cupped her hands together. Blood pooled within, and she drank it. As she fed, I went to my bag and pulled out food. After I finished eating, I felt a bit better. We waited out a regular storm following the red rain and then resumed our hike.

The ground of the forest was sticky and the air heavy. I fought off the buzzing, biting mosquitoes as we strode through the endless maze of towering trees and small plants. After what felt like a few hours, we stumbled upon three separate hot springs in a row. I hurried to one of them and filled my empty bottles with water before we jumped into another spring to wash ourselves. Then, refreshed and rested, we resumed our walk, hoping the portal was getting closer.

A short distance ahead, I registered something big stuck up in the trees. I shined my flashlight on it and gasped. A plane crash. A small jet, broken into two sections, hung in the branches of a tree, thirty-ish feet above the ground. Engine parts, gnawed aluminum, and chunks of sheet metal littered the floor. A dead man was sprawled on his back near the debris, a long object protruding from his belly.

"A human," Kelly said.

"You think he got here from the Bermuda Triangle?"

"He must have. That means the portal is close."

The man I had presumed was dead moaned. "Help... please, help, help... I have a first-aid box..." He wheezed, his voice a thin thread of whisper.

"Oh, my God, he's still alive. You stay here. You're Newborn, and he's bleeding," I said and dashed to him. I knelt beside his body. It was bad. His jeans and shirt were torn. Blood streamed down his face, and his left leg was most likely broken. It seemed he'd impaled himself on a sharp piece of debris during the crash, and now it was stuck deep in his abdomen. He was in critical condition and needed a hospital, not a first-aid box. Still, my gaze darted around, searching for it.

"Sir, how did the crash happen? Did you fly into the Bermuda Triangle?" Kelly asked from where I'd left her, raising her voice so he'd hear her.

"Yes, I was flying above the ocean," he said, then coughed up blood.

"Don't speak," I said. "Let me look for the—"

"There was a grayish cloud of electromagnetic fields," he cut in. "And a tunnel-shaped vortex of sorts... we... we hit a big... huge beast, scary... it looked," a cough, "it looked like a giant..." His breathing became heavy.

"Gargoyle," Kelly completed the sentence for him. "Sydney, his plane crashed the day the gargoyles last came out to hunt."

God, he'd been like this since then? But why hadn't the gargoyle eaten him?

As if reading my thoughts, she said, "The smell of oil probably kept them away. Sir, you said 'we'. Who else was with you?"

"Buster," he answered. His voice was weak, and his eyelids drifted shut.

I glanced back. "Kelly, please search for the first-aid kit. Hurry up."

"No, wait." He opened his eyes. "I don't have much time left but my dog, Buster," a long cough, "he... ran... he was scared and didn't come back. I heard him barking, please... find..." His eyes closed again. "Please... find Buster." His breathing slowed until it stopped altogether.

"Sir? Sir?" I nudged his shoulder with my hand. He didn't respond. "No, stay with me, sir!" I shook him again.

"Sydney, he's dead. I don't hear his heartbeat anymore. I'm sorry." Kelly stepped to me, a first-aid kit in her hand.

"You found it," I said.

"Yes, but... too late now."

"You think his dog is still alive?"

"I don't know," she said. "And as harsh as it may sound, we can't go looking for—"

The sound of a dog barking rang from the trees.

"It's the dog! Come on, let's get him." I shot to my feet, taking the flashlight with me and running toward the source of the sound.

When I reached the edge of a clearing lit with the moonlight and stars, I stopped cold and swiftly turned off the flashlight. The dog, a black, adult Labrador retriever, stood in the middle of a circle of vampires. I counted thirteen of them, four females and nine males, spread out around Buster, harassing him and laughing at his distress and confusion.

"Stop playing with the food. I'm hungry," said one of them.

A tall vampire near him drew a knife. "I vote we play with him a bit before feeding on him." He cut the dog's rear leg. Buster cried out and tried to escape, but they didn't let him.

I gritted my teeth. My blood boiled. I was about to step into the clearing when Kelly's hand latched onto my shoulder, holding me in place.

"Are you insane?" she whispered harshly. "There are thirteen of them and only two of us. Do the math. Rescuing the dog is a suicide mission. I'm sorry, but we gotta go before they spot us and we're dead along with the dog."

I shook her hand off my arm. "I'm not leaving Buster here with them. They're torturing him. Look at him; he's helpless and bewildered. He survived a plane crash, and he's terrified."

"Me too," she said. "I don't wanna die. How are we gonna fight them, huh? It's just us—a Newborn and a sick human."

I understood her fear. She was right; the odds were against us even with my weapons. However, there was no way I was letting those monsters kill Buster. I was more angry than sick, and my rage charged my body with energy, causing an adrenaline rush.

"Give me the machete," I told her, and she handed it over. "You hide here behind this tree while I go over there. If they kill me, run and save yourself."

She opened her mouth to argue, then closed it when I shot her a don't-bother-to-talk-me-out-of-it look.

I stepped out into the clearing, and she remained behind the tree blocking her from the prisoners' view. My fingers flexed around the machete's hilt as I looked over at them. The bloodsuckers were too busy abusing Buster to notice me. Fury coursed through my veins.

I put two fingers in my mouth and emitted a high, shrill whistle. "Hey, dickheads, want fresh meat?" All eyes turned to me. "Come and get it," I said under my breath as I rolled my shoulders and rocked my head from side to side, ready to kill.

The first two vampires who charged me managed to knock my knife out of my fist. When I turned to glance at the machete, a powerful kick to my belly knocked me to the ground, an agonizing pain ripping through my body. I winced and growled.

Laughter filled the air, and then a female voice said, "Christ, you smell this? She's human! I can't believe we're gonna feast on pure human blood."

A vampire built with heavy muscles, about six feet tall, leaped on top of me. "First let me enjoy her a little bit." I felt his erection against my thigh as he caged me between his arms. His friends assembled around us.

"Hurry up, Adam. We're hungry," someone told him.

Buster barked at them and then yelped with pain after the vampire holding him by the collar viciously hit him.

My stare moved from the dog back to the leech on top of me. "Sorry to disappoint, but the only thing you're about to feel is my knee smashing into your balls. Then nothing, because you'll be dead." My voice was calm even though I was pissed.

He barked a loud laugh, fangs drawing down. "You're a feisty one, aren't you? I've got a little confession," he said, dismissing my threat as if I wasn't capable of following through with it. His face inched closer to mine, and his sewer breath touched my nose.

I grimaced and averted my gaze. "Don't tell me, you don't believe in tooth brushing."

Before he could respond, my knee shot up, and I kicked his groin with full force, then swiftly plucked the silver dagger from the holster on my thigh and plunged it deep into his heart. His features froze in an expression of astounded disbelief as his face started to turn into ice.

"Hey, can't say I didn't warn you." I pushed his body off me, taking the dagger with me. I rolled over and leaped to my feet, glancing around at my angry opponents. "Which one of you dickheads is next?"

Three sprang at me. I stabbed the chest of the first vamp, icing him while my foot whipped out to kick the second bloodsucker. The blow propelled his body into the third leech. They both stumbled back and landed on the ground, but got up in a blink. With battle cries, they lunged at me again. A fist caught my jaw. Grunting, I leaned to the side and dodged the next punch, and the next, and the next until vampire number three captured me from behind and wrapped his hands around my neck. Almost out of breath, I snapped a back kick right between his legs and slammed my head back, cracking into his forehead. Breaking loose, I pivoted and faced him.

Bent over, he howled with pain, then bellowed, "You cunt! You bitch! You are de—" My dagger silenced him after I swiftly closed our distance and sliced his throat. Blood sprayed all over me. I didn't care. I thrust the blade into his heart, then released my grip from his hair. The body dropped to the floor as it became ice.

I turned to vampire number two, one eyebrow quirked up in question. "Got any *charming* last words, too?"

Face flushing red, he darted toward me, his movement a blur of speed. I failed to block his fast blow, which cracked into my hip bone and knocked the knife from my hand. Ignoring the pain, I spun in place and hook-kicked him in the face. It sent him off balance, and he lurched backward. Exploiting his disoriented state, I rushed to him, seized his head by the hair, and smashed his face with my knee. When he hit the ground, I picked up my dagger, crouched, and drove it into his heart.

Back on my feet, I assessed my progress. *Four down, nine to go, three females and six males.* A few wore alarmed expressions while the rest looked surprised. Obviously, they had anticipated a different outcome. Seeing me as a real threat now, they bothered themselves to deal with me. Luckily, none of them were armed, except the one holding Buster.

I dropped the dagger to the ground and wrenched the gun out of its holster as five vamps charged at me. Brad hadn't provided me with an extra magazine, so I had to make sure every shot counted. I raised the gun and fired, hitting them in the chest. As five of them turned to ice, three other leeches lined up in front of me. They loped in my direction. I flipped around and sprinted toward the tree twenty feet ahead of me. I sped up as I neared it, then ran up its trunk and did a backflip over them. When I landed on my feet, they were all with their backs to me. Perfect. I held up my gun and fired before they could turn around. Three shots, three dead vamps.

There was one leech left—the monster who had cut Buster in the leg and then hit him. And for that, he'd get special treatment. Squatting, he was holding him by his collar.

The bloodsucker bared his fangs at me. "I'm gonna drink you dry, breather," he spat out and then lobbed the knife in his hand toward me.

I jolted to the side before the blade whooshed past my ear and stuck in the trunk of a tree behind me. I put my gun back into the holster and went to pull his knife out.

With it in my hand, I gazed over at him. "Has no one ever taught you how to aim properly? Here, let me show you how it's done."

His knife flew back at him, landing right in his eye socket. The blade wasn't silver—which was why it was my weapon of choice and not a silver bullet. I didn't want him dead, not right away, anyway. He'd suffer before he died.

Screaming with agony, he shot to his feet, and the dog got free of his hold. Bemused, scared, and injured, Buster limped away from his abuser as I marched toward the vampire. He was struggling to pull the knife out without causing more pain.

"Need some help with that?" I offered and reached out to tug the knife out of his face, flicking the eyeball off the blade. His screams echoed through the forest.

"Sucks to be the one who's getting the abuse, doesn't it?" I said and stuck the knife into his other eye socket. "Now you know how it feels to be helpless," I added over his curses and screams.

He tried to hit me, but without his eyesight, he failed. Again and again and again until I broke his legs with two hard kicks to his knees. Then with a blow to the chest, I sent him flying backward. His body slammed into a tree. He collapsed at its base, screaming in pain, his face a crimson mess.

"Kill him. What are you waiting for?" Kelly asked, standing next to me.

I turned to her. "How long before his legs heal?"

"In his current condition, uh... about three hours."

"Excellent, it'll give them enough time to get to his body and eat him from the inside." I gestured at the four glowing butterflies fluttering not far away from the tree he was slumped against.

I glanced around, searching for Buster. He was outside the clearing, and he looked exhausted. I started toward him.

He shrank back, so I stopped moving, holding my hands up by my shoulders. "Hey, it's okay. I won't hurt you."

He stayed in his place as I sidled toward him again. When I was near him, I noticed he had scratches on his face from the plane crash. I patted his back. He allowed it, letting his guard down. After I gained his trust, I checked his bad leg. Blood seeped from the cut the vampire had given him. I rinsed it, using the water from my bag. Kelly handed me the first-aid box, and I took out a small bottle of hydrogen peroxide and a roll of gauze.

"Okay, Buster, this might burn a bit but only for a short time," I promised him, stroking his head. He didn't move the entire time I treated his wound.

When I was done, I rubbed behind his ear. "That's a good boy."

"No, no, no, God, noooo! Get 'em out of me!" the vampire I'd left at the tree hollered.

"It's not safe here with the butterflies nearby. We gotta keep going," Kelly said over the vampire's shouts of pain, giving me the machete and the dagger. "I'll carry the dog until we come across someplace we can rest. I won't even feel his weight. Come on, let's go."

Buster permitted her to take him into her arms, and we began to walk. It wasn't long before we came upon another deserted hut. Inside, Kelly set Buster back on his feet, and after we secured the door, I flopped down on the ground, my body weak, my muscles aching.

"My gosh, you look so pale," she said, turning on the flashlight.

I hurt everywhere, and not just from the fight. "I feel lousy. It's the air."

"Probably. We need to locate the portal as soon as possible—or you'll die."

I glanced at Buster. "What does the Jungle's air do to an animal from our dimension?"

"I'm not sure, but probably the same thing it does to humans," she replied and then suggested, "You should get some rest before we continue hiking."

I put my head down on the floor. "Rest sounds good," I mumbled.

Buster limped in my direction and lay down next to me. I smiled at him. I patted his head until my eyes drifted closed, and I fell asleep.

Chapter 25

Violent weather forced us to stay inside the hut for the next five days, at least according to Kelly's calculation. While we'd stayed away from the heavy rain and wind, I'd been nursing Buster's leg and sharing my food with him. Kelly had reproached me for splitting it with him. She also hadn't liked the idea that he was coming with us back to our dimension, claiming he'd slow us down and become a liability. Her arguments against taking him with us didn't matter, though; leaving Buster in Ice Prison was out of the question.

When the storms finally ended and Buster's leg had improved, we returned to hiking. As we progressed through the forest, I became weaker and sicker. At some point, I wasn't sure I'd be able to climb a slope, but eventually, I did. I stopped at the top of the hill, my hands trembling as pain racked my body. Sweat trickled along my brow, my damp hair plastered against my face. Something was wrong with me. Very wrong.

"Kelly, I... I..." Everything around me spun into a whirl. I collapsed to the ground, my knees too weak to support my weight. The magic pulling me toward the portal grew stronger, urging me to keep going. Every fiber of my being screamed to move toward the gate. I rose on unsteady legs. They wobbled, then gave way, and I fell again.

Looking worried, Kelly said, "You have to drink to keep yourself hydrated." She grabbed my bag and unzipped it, pulling out a bottle of water. "Then we'll continue."

My brain ordered my hand to take the bottle from her. However, it just wouldn't respond. Neither would my legs. It was more than exhaustion. "I can't move. I'm paralyzed from the neck down. What the hell is happening to me?" I panicked.

She knelt beside me. "Calm down. Stress will make things worse. You shouldn't have shared your food with the dog; now you don't have enough energy. We can't afford to stop, Sydney. We gotta keep moving. You're getting sicker. We have to locate the portal—like now, before it's too late. I'll carry you, just tell me where to..." Her voice died away as her face twisted with exertion when she tried to sweep me into her arms.

"What in the name of God? I can't lift you. It's like you weigh tons." She gazed down at me, confusion on her face. "Your skin, something's happening to it." Her eyes went to my hand. "And the dark magic. Look at it." I moved the only part I could, my head.

Glued to the ground, I stared down. The number on my palm glowed white on and off while spidery black veins started to run under my skin, spreading throughout my body and coloring my arms and legs black.

I shook my head with shock. "Oh my God, what is that thing doing to me?"

Just when I thought things couldn't get any worse, an air-raid siren blared. Kelly's face froze in an expression of horror before she frantically tried to pull me up once more but with no success.

On her third attempt, I stopped her. "No, don't. Leave me here. Run and look for a place to hide. Take Buster with you."

"Wait, give me a second. There must be a way to pick you up." Her stare moved around, seeking something that might help.

"You don't have a second. The sun's coming up. Take Buster with you and go, hurry." I raised my voice over the siren. "I'll be fine. The tattoo will protect me," I lied. The dark magic protected only itself and my left palm. Somehow, I doubted my hand would be the first part of my body that the gargoyles would tear apart.

"You don't have much time," I said. Being in a clearing, I had a full view of the sky. It became brighter. If she didn't rush off, she'd die and so would Buster. Getting to her feet, she hesitated. I urged, "Kelly, you gotta go with Buster. Now!"

She stomped her foot. "Damn it! This can't be happening." Her stare went to the sky, and then she turned and ran into the trees.

Buster edged over, grabbing my tank top with his teeth and pulling back, attempting to drag me after Kelly had gone.

"No, Buster, I can't be moved. Go, follow Kelly."

The siren stopped, and the sun was in the sky. We were in the center of a large clearing, exposed to the gargoyles.

"It's an order. Leave!" The sunlight touched us, and loud bloodcurdling howls filled the Jungle. Shit! "Listen to me, you have to hide. Bad creatures are coming here. Please, go," I pleaded, hoping he understood me. He didn't move.

My heart hammered against my ribs as the screeching of the gargoyles became louder—closer.

The tattoo ceased to glow, and the blackness in my veins faded away until the color of my skin returned. I gave another try at getting up, but I couldn't. I was still paralyzed. Powerless. We were about to meet our deaths. Never had I experienced such a terrifying moment as this. I was drowning in helplessness, scared for Buster and me.

The wind shook the leaves in the trees. The sound mingled with the eerie animalistic screams approaching us. I turned my head to look at Buster. His head rested between his front legs, his gaze on me. I blinked, and a tear escaped my eye, falling on the ground. He inched closer and put his head on my shoulder as if to comfort me. Then he pulled his gaze up and jumped to his feet. Looking at the sky, he snarled and barked furiously. My attention shifted from him to the ten-foot gargoyle flying in circles high above us. Scary as hell, it had leathery wings and alligator-like skin in an ashy gray color. Its legs were plump and ended in cloven hooves, eyes fixed on us.

"Buster, it's an order, you hear me? Run! RUN! RUN! NOW!" Screaming from the bottom of my lungs was pointless, he just kept barking at the gargoyle. I tried to force my hand to move and pull out my gun to shoot at the creature. Another useless thing to try to do. Like Buster, my body wouldn't obey.

An icy wave of terror rolled over me as the creature dove toward us. That was when Buster finally listened to me. He turned around and sprinted toward the trees. A mix of relief and fear tangled in my belly until he made a U-turn at the edge of the clearing. Perplexity dominated my emotions. What was he doing? He raced back toward me. His speed picked up, and when he came closer, he leaped over me, and something incredible happened.

In midair, his fur melted away, first from his head then from the rest of his body, which grew longer and into a different shape. His skin became scaly and blue. Wings sprang from his back, several times longer than his body. When his new deadly razor-sharp teeth sunk deep into the gargoyle, whose hand was a second from slashing my chest with its talon, Buster was fully transformed into a magnificent blue dragon—the size of an airplane. His glittering golden eyes peeked down at me from above before he took the screeching creature with him and flew upward. A strong gust of wind from Buster's wings blasted my hair, air whistling past my body. Far away from me, he threw the beast in the air and breathed a jet of flame, burning the gargoyle alive. Its corpse fell from a height of about three-hundred feet and crashed somewhere in the forest.

While Buster killed another one in the sky, eight gargoyles, having the same appearance as their dead friends, emerged into the clearing. They drew closer and surrounded me. Still paralyzed, I couldn't run away. Buster quickly dove toward me. When he landed next to me, his wings expanded around my body, covering me protectively. He heaved a gut-wrenching roar that made the ground shake, then snorted. A puff of dark smoke rose from his nostrils. He lowered his head to the gargoyles' eye level and looked at them one by one as if to warn them: come any closer, and you'll die.

The gargoyles had just lost their title. They were no longer the king of the Jungle. And not being stupid, they acknowledged it too, retreating outside the clearing. Yet Buster was still in full combat mode, maybe waiting to see if they'd return to attack. When it was a safe bet that they wouldn't, he relaxed and pulled his wings into his sides, and I had a better view of his glory.

The scales were deep blue, including his horns, and gleamed in the sunlight. A line of spikes ran down his spine, from the base of his head to the tip of his coiled tail. The word "terrifying" came to mind as I watched him, feeling like a tiny ant next to him. His long neck curved as he brought his head close to mine. Heat caressed the skin of my face. Was I dreaming? Was I hallucinating? Was I dead?

I remembered Audrey had told me that dragons were soul rippers.

My brow knitted at the giant beast next to me. "Did I die?" I whispered.

His tail moved to touch my leg. With the connection, the word "no" suddenly materialized in the air, right before my eyes.

"Whoa! You talk, sort of. What's going on? Why were you in a dog's body?"

The black letters in front of me dissolved, and others appeared: *a human aircraft entered this dimension. It crashed into me while I was flying in my true form. The severity of the impact caused my life energy to leave my body. Without this energy, the dragon's body cannot exist. It burst into flames in the black sky while the plane plummeted. On the ground, I used the dead body of the canine as a temporary vessel because our life energy must be contained inside a body.*

"What are you doing in Ice Prison?" I asked.

All the words faded away like smoke evaporating into the air, only to be replaced by new ones: *to keep the ratio between evil and good on Earth, we sometimes collect evil or good souls from other places. Places where the balance of good and evil is not essential. Then, we import them to Earth. Without memory, a tabula rasa, their souls are inserted into fetuses.*

"I don't get it; if all this time you could've transformed back into a dragon, why didn't you do it sooner? Why did you allow the vampires to hurt you?"

Two new paragraphs formed in the air: *the evil souls attacked my vessel a few moments before my life energy had revived it. Giving life can gravely weaken my kind. It renders us confused for a certain amount of time. Therefore, I was unable to create my true form from the dead canine at that time.*

After you healed the vessel, my energy regained its strength, and I could transform back into my real form. However, I did not wish to leave you unprotected in a place full of evil souls.

"Thank you for that. I'd have been dead if it wasn't for you," I said, then wondered, "Are you fully healed now?"

The words in front of me dissolved into the air, and his answer replaced them: *some of my abilities are temporarily gone. I cannot see if a soul is evil or good. I can only guess it.*

His massive head snapped up to the sky, and he suddenly spread his wings, flying upward. The force from his wings sent out a strong wind and erased his words in front of me.

Lying on my back, unable to move, I squinted against the sun's glare. Three gargoyles were circling above, ready to attack. Killing them took the dragon mere minutes, and then he fluttered down to me.

His tail touched my leg again, and the next message in the air was: *we have limited time, little human. My brothers have already sensed my life energy because I am in my true form. They are coming for me. I must leave with them and face my punishment for breaking the law.*

"What law?" I asked.

The sentences in front of my eyes disappeared before his new words appeared.

My kind's laws. Two of them, I have broken: I am forbidden to save or reap souls that are not on my list. And I must let my life energy block my emotions. After you eliminated the evil souls who attacked my new vessel, I prevented the emotions in my life energy from being blocked. I was grateful to you, and I wanted to protect you.

The words vanished from the air at once, and my stare followed his. In the sky, six dragons came into view. They were about the same size as the dragon next to me. One after the other, they flew down toward us and hit the floor, filling the large clearing and folding their wings at their sides. There was a series of thuds. The ground vibrated on impact and shuddered like an earthquake. The trees around us swayed and leaves rained down.

Each beautiful scaly beast had a different color: red, gray, gold, purple, black, and white. The red dragon moved toward us.

The one who used to be Buster curled a wing protectively over my body. No words materialized in the air. The communication between the two dragons seemed to be telepathic. In the next few minutes, all I heard was the screeches of creatures in the forest. After the silent conversation ended, the red dragon turned, opened its wings, batted them to regain altitude, and flew away. The others followed suit, but not the blue dragon near me. He lifted his wing from me.

"What happened?"

The answer to my question appeared in the air: *Garil allowed me to remain with you until the sun disappeared. Then I will face the consequences of my actions.*

Garil? So they had names, and Garil belonged to the red dragon. "What's your name?"

I read the new words that were forming in front of me: *I am called Vakan.*

"Vakan, I really hope they don't punish you because of me. It's not fair; you don't deserve—" Suddenly, a pins-and-needles sensation crept into my arms. I tried to flex my fingers into fists and succeeded. "Oh my God, I can move my hands again."

I lifted an arm, then twisted my torso. I tried to move my legs next, but they didn't work yet.

The air was empty of words until I moved upright with a groan.

The dark magic on your palm is the reason behind your temporary paralysis. It was not your sickness. You are unwell because of your soul. It is sick.

I guessed he was right. Despite partly regaining the feeling in my body, the weakness was still there, and the simple act of sitting upright hurt like hell. Was the environment in the Jungle making my soul sick? Unfortunately, Vakan didn't have an answer for that or for why the tattoo had acted the way it had. Millions of other questions flooded my mind, but a severe headache forced me to stop talking and lay down.

Rest, little human. Vakan's words formed in front of me. Then, I closed my eyes and dozed off.

A loud thump interrupted my sleep. The ground shook beneath me, and when I opened my eyes, I saw a silver dragon tucking its wings against its back in the clearing. I sat up and looked at Vakan next to me, then up at the sky. It was night. The gargoyles were back in their caves, and the silver dragon was here to take Vakan with him, but until Kelly emerged from the trees, he wouldn't take off.

When she stepped into the clearing, he created in the air the words: *goodbye, little human.* And they both flew away.

I watched Vakan while I got to my feet. My body was functioning again. Gazing down, I checked the tattoo. The number had dropped to 620. But at least it was not glowing or painting my veins black.

The burning desire to walk toward the portal rushed back, almost as intense as the pain in my body. Would I manage to reach the gate? I'd better as I had to get out of this nightmarish place.

Chapter 26

"**I** repeat, those things, those huge things that just took off were Soul Rippers, Sydney. Dragons." Kelly's voice was almost a shout, her expression asking, "Why aren't you shocked like me?"

"I know they're Soul Rippers." I was short on words. The need to reach the gate was stronger than the need to talk. Although my body had no energy, I picked up my bag and headed into the trees.

"What were they doing here? And what happened with the tattoo? You were paralyzed, and now, you're not. I mean I'm glad you're okay, but to tell you the truth, when it got dark again and I left the tree house, I thought for sure you were dead." She paused and swept her eyes around the clearing. "The dog, where is it? Was it eaten?"

"No, Buster was the Soul Ripper. It's complicated, but long story short, the plane crashed into Vakan, the blue dragon. The dog died, and Vakan entered his dead body. Then, when the gargoyles were out, he had to reveal his true form to me in order to save me," I answered as I hiked toward the portal.

"The Soul Ripper was in the dog's body the whole time? And it stayed to keep you safe? The dragon actually communicated with you? How?" she asked, coming after me.

I explained how while we strode through the forest. Every time my body told me to take a break, something inside me forced me to continue.

My legs kept moving until a feminine voice whispered in my head, "I'm here, human. I can feel you... so close."

"Whoa, someone just said something in my head." My words brought a smile and excitement to Kelly's face—not the reaction I'd expected.

"You heard her. At last! It's right here!" Kelly's voice changed. It suddenly had an accent I couldn't place.

She grabbed my arm, holding me in place.

"Kelly? What the hell? Let me go!" I tried to jerk away, but her grip was an iron shackle.

"My apologies, Sydney, but I have to give you to Serena." The accent got thicker.

"Serena? What are you talking about?" Alarmed and befuddled, I fought against her hold. Her incredible strength was equivalent to Gideon's. She was not a Newborn. *What gives?*

"Don't resist. It will only make it more painful for you."

I stopped struggling against her grip. "What's going on? Let go of my arm."

"I can't do that."

"Why not? And what's the deal with the accent?"

"I'm Mayet, daughter of Anen, one of The Original Rulers. His son, Djar, is my brother."

"Djar? The US Ruler?" I couldn't contain my shock.

"He is not the real Ruler. I am," she corrected and explained, "Before females of my kind lost their rights and became slaves, I lived with my brother in the same house where the Tara Stone was stored. One night, young and curious, we sneaked into my father's chamber and found the stone. It didn't react to Djar's touch, but to mine, it came to life, glowing and whispering to me, 'You were born to rule.'

"My father was behind us when it occurred and was furious that the rock would dare to choose a female to be a Ruler. He couldn't bear the notion that his son would not succeed him, and out of rage, he ordered vampire females stripped of their rights. Then he sold my mother and me, turning us into slaves. He announced to the other Rulers that the stone glowed at Djar's touch, and they didn't even ask to see it happen. Anen had a lot of power, and they believed him.

"My mother and I were treated like we were animals. We were humiliated and tortured until Herit freed us. She spared my father's life, but I didn't. For years I planned his death—dreamed of it. After I decapitated him, Djar was declared the next Ruler. But I didn't fight the decision. It'd have been foolish of me to do so. Despite the fact female vampires received their rights back, we were still considered inferior to male vampires, even to this day. It is unacceptable to have a female Ruler. No vampire would accept me as a leader."

"So Djar ruled instead of you?" The new revelation dazed me.

"Djar has never really ruled," she said. "He doesn't know how to lead. He does anything I tell him. I have been behind his every decision since he replaced my father. I control his every move."

"Okay, so you're the real Ruler, but what does that have to do with me?" My face twisted in puzzlement. "Why am I here? What do you want with me? Who's Serena?"

"A powerful demon. She's extremely dangerous, so her security level is classified as maximum, which is why she's held in an invisible cell. It changes location every month or so, around the three sections of Ice Prison. High-security prisoners are separated from their bodies, and their souls are locked in an invisible box for eternity. Magic becomes their only food source, not human food, human souls, or blood."

"Wait, you want her to feed on my soul? Have real food? Is that it?" My voice rose with anger.

"Not exactly. It's your body she wants," Kelly said.

"What! No, don't do it. Why are you helping her? She's a demon, your enemy!" I pulled back.

She yanked me to her and answered, "Yes, but things changed when thirty years ago it came to my attention that the king of demons was searching for the location of Serena in Ice Prison to free her. Because supernatural beings can't touch, feel, or sense inmates that are in boxes, he asked his witch to pinpoint Serena's cell for him. Though, all her magic was able to find was in which section of Ice Prison her box was located."

"Why is Damon interested in getting her out of Ice Prison?" I was afraid of the answer. He was a demon, so his reasons had to be evil.

"Many years ago," she started, "there was a vampire named Edwin, a brilliant thief. His daughter contracted the UV virus, and he sought a cure. He was willing to do anything to save her, even steal the red dragon's blood for Ferdinand, who was a US Ruler before he was killed. Ferdinand lied to Edwin about having a cure for the UV virus and promised to give it to his daughter in exchange for a few drops of the red dragon's blood. Edwin agreed, and he did the impossible: stealing a small amount of the red dragon's blood. To never be on the Soul Reapers' death list, the four Rulers of the US drank it, including me. Edwin realized then that Ferdinand had deceived him. There was no cure.

"After his daughter died, feeling betrayed by Ferdinand and the Rulers, Edwin stole the vial containing the dragon's blood from my brother. Furious at the Rulers, he didn't want them to have it. Since dragon blood is indestructible, he hid it before he committed suicide to join his daughter. Now, Damon is after the hidden vial, and Serena can help him find it because she possesses unique abilities, one of which is the power to phase through solid objects. Damon was desperate and willing to try anything to get her out of Ice Prison, and I saw an opportunity.

"Serena can sense a human's soul from many miles away and draw her victim to her as she eats their soul. However, Damon can't use humans to locate her since they don't survive in Ice Prison. The moment regular humans set foot here, their bodies shut down, and they die. Serena doesn't eat dying souls or ones that are in severely injured or sick bodies.

"So, thirty years ago, I came to Damon with a solution: put a Gifted human in the section where Serena's cell could be found. In Ice Prison, the victim's soul doesn't get sick for a month—sufficient time to locate Serena. I have the Tera Stone in my possession, and I offered to help him find Gifted humans with the help of the rock, which glows when near them.

"Damon asked me what was in it for me. I told him I wanted Dr. Johnson, a genius scientist who works for him. He's an epidemiologist who specializes in demon and vampire diseases and is very loyal to Damon. I need him to work on a cure for the UV virus. Many vampires have tried before me to find an antidote but all have failed. If I'm the one who makes this cure a reality, I'd gain respect from the other Rulers. I'd be accepted as a Ruler—no vampire would question my leadership. My authority.

"Damon acquiesced to my terms and had a few demands of his own. The Gifted human must be a female between the ages of eighteen and twenty. Serena is going to take over the human body, and she'll want it to be in that age range. His second request was that the Gifted human would be smart enough to survive Ice Prison. Like any other demon, if Serena begins to feed on a human's soul, she must complete the feeding before her victim dies, or she will die as well."

"The challenges," I whispered, thunderstruck. It hadn't been Brad who ran everything, after all.

Reading my expression, she said in a placid tone, "Yes, I lied. Brad didn't pay Damon to help him. It's the other way around. He works for the demons too. The challenges were Damon's idea, and he was the one who planned them. Twenty girls each time. He believed a human's probability of surviving in Ice Prison would be higher if they knew how to pay attention to the small details while under pressure. I concurred with him on that. Throwing the first person the stone detected into the Jungle, a place where there are many traps, without checking the human's suitability beforehand, would be unwise. If the Gifted human doesn't survive until she reaches Serena, Serena will die too.

"After he explained the importance of the challenges, he moved on to his third and final request. Selecting a Gifted human who had never been compelled. Compulsion by an Ancient may sometimes leave a permanent odor on the human soul and body. Only demons smell it, and to some, it can be extremely repulsive. Damon was afraid Serena wouldn't want to take over a body that had been touched by an Ancient.

"Understanding that, I agreed to his terms and started the search. To blend in, in a span of a few months, I studied the way young humans speak and act. Then, I melted a piece of the Tera Stone and made a pearl necklace out of it. Wearing it on my neck, I looked for Gifted humans, girls between eighteen and twenty. As my Change happened when I was twenty, I pretended to be a college student. Unthreatening, weak, and naive. I targeted human females who weren't rich or from prominent families, spending my time in universities, bars, and nightclubs, waiting for the stone to react."

I snorted in anger, shaking my head. "God, I can't believe it. It was you all along. You kidnapped all those girls."

"No, not me personally. The chosen Gifted human had to think I was a victim as well since I was supposed to join her in Ice prison," she explained.

"Right, so you asked Brad to do your dirty work."

"Not at first. Brad was not born yet at the time, but his family has been working for my brother for a long time, many generations back, so I contacted Brad's father, William. Our arrangement was simple. He took care of the abduction part, making it look as if the girls had decided to leave everything because they needed a new start. That way, the human police wouldn't get involved. Every time the stone located a Gifted human, I gave him her name, her description, and her home address. He handled the abduction and forced the girl to call her parents and the people who were close to her. Then he kept them locked up in his basement for months—even years—until I had twenty girls. Detecting Gifted human females could take a lot of time. He was paid handsomely for his trouble, however.

"Years later, Noah, Brad's brother, replaced him. Then, two years ago, Brad took over and did things differently. He preferred to woo the girls and make them fall in love with him, then lied. He told each girl a different story, but the most common lie was that he was going to another country and asked them to leave their lives behind to join him. He did it because he wanted the girls to sound convincing when they called their parents."

A clap of thunder cracked the sky, and I said, "But I don't understand; why did you spy after that vampire who broke into your apartment, and what were you doing at Philippe's home that night? You looked scared... and you..." I trailed off, my thoughts jumping from one place to another.

At my confusion, she told me, "The vampire who Izzy saw in my apartment works for me. His name is Daniel, and he didn't tear it up. It was Philippe, suspecting I had something to do with Zoey's disappearance. He broke into my apartment. I knew it was him; I lied about hiring a private detective to find the identity of the culprit, of course. The night following the break-in, I sent Daniel to my trashed apartment to collect the Tera necklace. I prayed Philippe hadn't gotten his hands on it. Izzy was there, snooping around. I didn't have time for that human. Twenty Gifted humans had just failed the challenges, so I had to start the search all over again. Izzy annoyed me to no end. I tolerated her only because she introduced me to many female humans who were her age.

"After the failure of the twenty Gifted girls, I was tired and frustrated. Fortunately, my brother gave me some good news. He came across an Ancient vampire with a rare ability. Lucius, the Ancient, can sense Gifted humans and lure them toward him, which meant I didn't need Izzy anymore, and I didn't need to spend my time in bars and nightclubs.

"I'd have forgotten about Izzy if she hadn't gotten you involved. When Daniel was on his way to meet me, he spotted the two of you trailing his car, and he updated me about it over the phone. I ordered him to pull over and shove the two of you into his back seat, then bring you fools to me. With you two in his car, he parked in the woods, where I was in the middle of a meeting with my brother and Lucius. Daniel sent me a text message. After I paid Lucius to find me Gifted humans, I went to Daniel. Izzy was shocked to see me. She—"

"What? What are you talking about? That's not how it went down." I cut her off. Rain started to pelt us. "He didn't shove us into his car, and we weren't in the woods. We were in a factory area."

A slow smile formed on her lips as if my bewilderment amused her. "Back then, you weren't immune to compulsion, and I'm an Ancient vampire. I wiped the memory of this event and put in a new one to replace it. Then I compelled you to tell me everything about yourself. I learned that Zoey was your sister and that you have a strong vampire named Gideon by your side. When I noticed the powerful dark magic on your palm, I knew immediately that you were Gifted even before the stone glowed. Never in my many many years of existence have I ever witnessed such rare dark magic. It's tremendously powerful. I was stupefied that a mere human was capable of carrying it in her fragile body. I knew you must be exceptional and was sure that you'd pass the challenges. I decided right then and there you'd be one of the twenty Gifted humans."

"But you have a problem now. You compelled me, and Serena won't take my body. You didn't follow Damon's third demand. You're gonna have to let me go." A sliver of hope slid into my words.

"Demons love dark magic more than anything," she said. "When I told Damon about what you have on your palm, he was fascinated. He didn't even care that I'd compelled you. He agreed that the smell of the dark magic would excite Serena more than the odor of my compulsion.

"After I ended my call with Damon, I contacted Brad. I informed him that I had a faster way to find Gifted humans and that he'd be getting the next twenty names in a matter of weeks, not years. He wasn't pleased to hear that because it didn't give him enough time to court each girl and make her fall in love with him. Later that night, he called and suggested assembling all the girls in one place, at his father's mansion. He'd fake an interest in them by inviting each girl to his party, then like his brother and father, force them to call their parents and say they would not be coming back. But with you, things had to be done differently, so I told him I'd deal with you myself. Of course, I could've just kidnapped you in the woods, but I didn't because of Gideon. I had to make sure he wouldn't cause trouble if you disappeared, so I killed Izzy and drove you to your vampire's house to see who he was."

I gasped in horror. "Izzy is dead?"

"Yes. I compelled you to think she was driving, but it was me. I had to learn more about Gideon. And I was right to be cautious; my sources informed me he had many connections in the Hidden World. I waited until I'd gathered more information on him before I took you. I had to be certain I could handle him in case he didn't believe me when I told him that Brad killed you at the party.

"My original plan was to separate you from Gideon, then compel you to do the challenges and take me to Serena's cell, if you passed them. However, I had to change everything when I discovered that Gideon had taught you how to resist compulsion, and then Brad called me, telling me that you and Gideon were in New York City, talking to Andrew, the lawyer."

My eyes widened, rain soaking me to the bone. "The package was for you? What was in it?"

Not seeming bothered by the weather, she answered, "It was for me, yes. Since I have no way of knowing if a Gifted girl smells bad to demons, Damon supplied small bottles of a potion that reveals whether a human has been compelled in the past. If the human consumes a few drops of it, he or she can't be compelled by Ancients for a year. A few months back, the supply ran low, and I notified Damon. He ordered Maura, a royal demon, to give me more bottles. Not wanting to deal with it, she paid the vampire lawyer to take care of it, as I did with Brad.

"By then, I had only fourteen names of Gifted humans. There was no time to search for more since you were getting closer to the truth about me. That's why I had to act fast and instructed Brad to host the party at the mansion in a week, giving him the names of the girls he needed to seduce. After I explained the situation to Damon, he agreed to let fourteen girls, instead of the usual twenty, do the challenges. And then I called you, making up a story about being at my cousin's house."

I glared at her. "It was all a lie. You saying that Brad had come over and offered to pay you to bring me to his party, you acting scared at the mansion and at Philippe's house—wait. Jesus, you were the one who killed Philippe, weren't you?"

"I had to. I couldn't risk you querying him about Daniel. He'd have known I lied, and he already suspected me. I didn't want him to plant doubts in your head about me. I had to eliminate any possible threat to my plan. When my men informed me he'd returned to that dirty alley he referred to as home, I rushed over to kill him. As he ran from me, he managed to call his cop friend before I daggered him.

"Then, I heard your voices outside his basement. I quickly hid in the living room. When you and your vampire came inside Philippe's office, I headed to the front door. My phone slipped out of my hands to the floor, so I had to show myself. I improvised a story about why I was there."

I huffed in contempt. "And played the perfect role of a skittish Newborn vampire, so you could kidnap and force me to do those damn challenges. You know what I don't get, though? Why go to all this trouble with them if your poor victim has you—an Ancient vampire? Isn't your protection in the Jungle enough?"

"How can I really protect her if I'm supposed to act as a weak Newborn vampire? For my plan to work, the Gifted human's cooperation is mandatory. She can't know about my real motives. She needs to lead me to Serena without rebelling," she answered.

"If it's so crucial to keep the Gifted human alive for Serena, why didn't you help me with the vampires abusing Buster?" I asked.

The rain finally stopped, and she tucked her wet hair behind her ear. "When you were overpowered by them, I almost did. I was about to reveal myself as an Ancient to kill them, but then you fought back, and to my surprise, you turned out to be an excellent warrior. After the fight, I was sure the worst was behind us until the dark magic on your palm pinned you to the ground, and I had to decide fast. Trying to save you meant I could die from the UV virus or from the gargoyles, but leaving you in the clearing meant you'd die, and I'd suffer Damon's fury because I'd failed. In the end, my existence was more important."

I thinned my lips with anger before my face twisted with pain. My headache escalated, and my weakness intensified.

"It's Serena. She's feeding on your soul to get stronger," Kelly told me.

I thought about everything she'd revealed, and then about Zoey. "My sister, is she..." My voice wobbled. Since the first moment I'd searched for her, I refused to consider the possibility she was dead, even when everything had pointed to that conclusion. I could not deny the obvious anymore, though. And it hurt more than Serena's feeding.

"I am sorry. She's no longer with us. Neither is Kyla," she replied.

Hearing it out loud made something inside me snap. Seething with anger, I punched her with my free hand. The blow caught her by surprise and shoved her backward. I was free of her hold, and in a semicircular motion, I swung my leg around and struck her. As she staggered sideways, I pulled the dagger from its holster. She regained her balance, fangs popping out of their sheaths, long and wide.

I scoffed at her. "And to think I trusted you. You killed Zoey!"

"But I'm not a monster. I didn't want to hurt her," she said. In a flash, she was a few inches away from me. I was quickly disarmed and in her grip again.

"Not a monster? You've been murdering innocent girls for thirty years! You psycho bitch!"

"I didn't enjoy doing it, but the end justifies the means. You must know it was not easy for me, especially with Zoey. She was as brave as you are. I respected her." Her expression softened as her mind seemed to travel back in time. "I met her after months of searching for the twentieth Gifted human. By then, I was tired. Tired of spending my time where young humans were, pretending I was one of them. When the stone finally glowed after Izzy introduced me to Zoey at Asgard's club, I was thrilled. Brad, at the time, had in his basement nineteen humans, and he was dating Kyla, the girl's name I'd given him three months before."

"That bastard dated Kyla?" Olivia had mentioned her daughter was secretly seeing someone. So it was Brad.

"He did," she confirmed. "And she fell in love with him like the other Gifted humans. When I gave him Zoey's name, I warned him that her heart belonged to someone else. She already had a lover."

"Philippe."

"Yes, Philippe. Brad insisted on wooing her despite that. However, she didn't want him. Not only because of Philippe but also because her mind was occupied with you. Most of her time was spent looking for you. One night, she and I talked, and she revealed that a blind vampire with a scar on his face was helping her. Running a background check on him, I learned that he was an assassin. Zoey was not you; she wasn't worth the trouble of having Thomas snooping around my business. I told Brad not to take Zoey, but it was too late; he'd already kidnapped her. The damage was already done, so I proceeded with the plan and ordered him to prepare the rooms for the challenges."

"I watched the girls through a small camera installed in the rooms. Kyla died during the first challenge, but Zoey passed it and hid a piece of glass in her clothes. In the second room, she stayed in her place, and when the time ended, Roger pulled out his gun to shoot her. She was not a warrior like you, but she managed to distract Roger and press the piece of glass to Brad's neck. She directed Roger to unlock the black door. Brad told him to do as she said while my brother and I dashed to the room to stop her, but the idiots let her escape, not willing to enter the Jungle."

"Are you saying Zoey escaped?" My voice filled with surprise. A flicker of hope rose in my heart. Maybe Zoey had found a way out of the Jungle and back to our dimension after all.

"She did," Kelly answered. "Not knowing whether Serena had already started to feed on Zoey, I had to search for her to keep her alive at all costs. The problem was that I didn't bring the bag of human food with me, and the temporary gate had already closed. Zoey could have starved to death without it."

"What about Damon's witch? Why didn't Brad ask her to teleport the bag to the Jungle?" I asked.

"Magic that isn't Herit's doesn't work in Ice Prison."

"But opening a portal requires magic."

"It stays on the border of Ice Prison. It doesn't enter the Jungle. It can't. I was the one who brought your bags here. After the challenges, I got into Ice Prison through a different portal. Damon's witch created two temporary entrances, one for me, one for the chosen Gifted human," she explained.

"Did you track Zoey down in the Jungle?" I needed to know what had happened to her.

"Eventually, yes. My brother and I followed her screams as she tried to get a prisoner off her. I killed him and the three others who heard her and came. In doing so, I exposed myself as an Ancient. She was shocked to know the truth about me and my real motives. After that, not only did she decline to lead me to Serena, but she also tried to kill herself with the piece of glass she'd kept, so the demon would die too. My brother stopped her in time and found a solution to our problem.

"Since Serena is searching for a body to accommodate, she'll draw any healthy human soul toward her by eating it slowly. If her victim doesn't move to her over an extended period of time, she'll feed on the soul in one suck, killing him or her instantly. Djar suggested we tie Zoey up in a tree house. When Serena realized that your sister was not moving in her direction, she'd eat up her whole soul at once.

"I was satisfied with that solution. Later on, Damon's witch pulled me out of the Jungle, so I gave my brother the bag of human food, and he remained with your sister, protecting her until Serena was done feeding on her."

I closed my eyes. Zoey was dead. Despair tore through my chest until it was hard to breathe.

"I was sad too, Sydney. I hated doing it."

I opened my eyes, and red colored my vision. "Will you shut up? You don't get to ta—ahhhhgh!" A sharp pain exploded near the crown of my head.

My surroundings blurred. I blinked a few times, but everything around me became more unfocused.

"I'm afraid our time has come to an end. Your eyes are turning black, a sign that Serena has eaten fifty percent of your soul. Now she's ready to enter your body," she said matter-of-factly.

Panicking, I tried to yank my arm from her iron grip, but I wasn't able to break loose. With her free hand, she reached into her cleavage and pulled out something. I squinted at what looked like a small container, the size of a mini-alcohol bottle. She drew out the cork with her teeth and threw its contents to the ground a few feet away from us. The smell of sulfur hit my nose.

"What the hell is that?"

"Serena's blood. Damon's witch magic can't free the demon from her cell. That's why he gave me her blood. If it comes in contact with the ground near her presence, the smell of her blood will restore her power to pass through solid objects. She'll be able to free herself from her box. And then Brad will ask Damon's witch to open a temporary portal close to us."

"How does he know where you are?" God, I hoped he didn't, and she and her demon would rot in here for eternity.

"I have a tracker on me. It can locate anything anywhere, even in another dimension."

My vision continued to deteriorate; objects around me ceased to have distinct outlines. One last time, I tried to get free with the little strength I had left. Then, complete darkness surrounded me. I was blind. Heat touched my body, almost burning me. Something crashed into me, and it felt like being hit with endless electric shocks.

"I succeeded, Serena. You're free," Kelly's voice announced, exhilaration in her tone.

Chapter 27

I woke up drenched in a cold sweat, gasping and panting. It took a few seconds before awareness settled in. I sat up and glanced around, realizing I was in a familiar setting—my dorm room. I looked down at my palm. No tattoo, no countdown number, no dark magic. My eyes darted around the room. No sign of Serena, Kelly, or the Jungle. I let out a deep exhale as I shook my head and rubbed my hands over my face. It was all just a dream—an extremely vivid one, but still a dream. God, what a nightmare!

Rays of sunlight slanted through the window. I glanced over at the clock on the nightstand. Nine a.m. Shit! I was going to be late for class. Why the hell hadn't the alarm gone off? I threw back the covers, jumped out of bed, brushed my teeth, then rushed to my closet. I pulled out a pair of washed-out jeans and a shirt. Laurel was sleeping in her bed across from mine, and she was very much alive, if her loud snoring was any indication.

I half-smiled to myself as I quickly dressed and stuffed everything I needed for school today into my backpack. Then I hitched it onto my shoulder, put my sunglasses on, slid into my sneakers, and hurried outside, skipping breakfast. It was a sunny day with a cloudless blue sky. I smiled. Finally, a break from the rain. The campus was already buzzing with activity, students bustling in all directions.

"Hey Syd, wait up." I heard June's voice behind me as I hurried to the philosophy building.

I turned and walked backward. "Sorry, June, I'm seriously late for class. Talk to you later."

She stopped moving toward me and waved a hand in the air. "Yeah, no prob. I'll see you."

A few minutes later, I reached the lecture hall. Professor Reed had just rolled in too, so I rushed to my seat and slipped into the chair.

"Morning, sunshine. Glad you made it. Hot date last night?" Ethan whispered from the seat next to me as Professor Reed started his lecture.

My eyes moved to Ethan. He looked a bit sad.

"I wish, but no. Just overslept. Even Laurel's snoring didn't wake me up, and my stupid alarm decided not to work this morning. Where were you yesterday? Laurel was waiting for you."

"Yeah, sorry. 'Bout that. Kimberly called..."

I gave him a sympathetic look. "Talking to exes you still have feelings for is a big no-no. You gotta meet someone new. Heal your heart. Oh, by the way, Josie, you know, my neighbor across the hall, has a major crush on you. She thinks you're cute. You should totally ask her out." This drew an offended look from him.

"Cute? What am I, a puppy? Thanks, but it's gonna be a hard pass for me. Besides, I'm kinda dating Cheryl now."

My lips parted with surprise. "Cheryl? Really?" Was she his type?

A guy in the row ahead of us turned to shush me, so I pulled out my notebook, opened it, and wrote down: are you coming to Laurel's this weekend? If you are, bring Cheryl with you.

"I haven't decided yet," he whispered and received a glare from the student who had silenced me. We kept quiet, and our focus went to Professor Reed's lecture.

When it was over, Ethan walked me outside the philosophy building, and he got a call from Cheryl. When he answered, I texted Zoey, telling her about my possible hiking plans with Laurel and asking whether she wanted me to stop by her college if I went to Laurel's.

She texted back, saying she was busy studying for an exam and maybe next time. I put my phone back in my jeans pocket. Strangely, any desire to go hiking with Laurel on Friday vanished, and I decided to spend the weekend at home instead. Ethan finished talking on the phone, and we headed to the cafeteria.

The sun disappeared behind the clouds, and I pushed my sunglasses to the top of my hair. The air suddenly took on a chill, the wind picking up. I looked up. The clouds had turned gray. Weird. A loud rumble of thunder pierced the sky. I halted and crossed my arms over my chest, gripping my biceps and hunching over, the wind blowing my hair into my face.

"Why are we stopping?" Ethan sounded confused.

"It's about to rain, but literally a second ago it was sunny and warm. Don't you find it a bit odd?"

His brow wrinkled with puzzlement. "No. What's going on with you today? You seem off."

"I don't know. Something suddenly doesn't feel right. I have—" My words stuck in my throat when my gaze fell on a man emerging from the building across from us.

He wore black leather pants and a tight white T-shirt showcasing his toned muscles. He was marching toward me, his intense stare gluing mine to his. My jaw dropped at his gorgeousness. Unutterably beautiful. Utterly stunning. A fallen angel.

He stopped in front of me, well over six feet tall, broad shoulders, a square jaw, a symmetrical face with clear turquoise eyes and flawless skin. His straight, silky hair was silvery-blond and reached his shoulders, tips of pointed ears poking out from it. A stern expression covered his stunning features.

Ethan said something to me, but I didn't hear it. The gorgeous stranger took my undivided attention. He looked mysterious and dangerous. I was curious. Who was he?

Rain began to fall on my face, shaking me out of my trance.

The man extended his arm to me. "Come with me."

Despite my better judgment, I reached out, but before my hand could touch his, Ethan shouted, "Are you crazy? What are you doing? The dude is a total stranger."

Yes, he was. I didn't know him. Where did he want to take me?

"No." I snapped my arm back to my side. "My friend's right. Who are you? What do you want with me?"

"Don't listen to him. Take my hand. Trust me." That voice... I'd heard it before. When? Where?

"He could go all Ted Bundy on you. Don't go with him. C'mon, let's go. I'm starving," Ethan said, and another clap of thunder tore through the sky.

I took a few steps away from the man, and a frown of worry creased his brow.

"You must take my hand. Now. I cannot force you. You have to do it willingly. We don't have much time." There was an urgency in his tone.

Ethan tugged at my arm. "He's mental. Come on, let's go. It's raining, and I'm getting soaked here."

"Wait," I told Ethan. "Look at him. Something's wrong. We're both wet, but he's dry. Why isn't he wet?"

Ethan grabbed my arm again. "You're tired, forget about him." He steered me away from him. The distance between us grew. Ethan's hand fell from mine. My eyes widened with horror when his fingers started to crumble into ash, then his arm, his shoulder, his face. As Ethan disappeared, shocked, I glanced around me. Buildings, cars, people, and trees turned into pieces of ash and blew away in the wind. Then, in a blink, night fell, and the moon and stars decorated the sky.

What the hell? What was going on? While objects vanished around me, a large crack opened in the ground under my feet, and I plunged into it. I screamed, terrified. The gorgeous stranger appeared from above, standing on the edge of the hole, watching me as I fell. Magnificent white, feathered angel wings spread from his back, tearing his shirt to shreds. He dove to me and caught my body in midair. Holding on to him, I wrapped my arms around his neck as he flew upward, back to the edge of the hole. He landed on solid ground and put me down. His wings folded to his sides. Was I dreaming?

He stuck his arm out for me once more. "Sydney, come with me before it's too late."

"You know my name." I stared at his extended hand, hesitating as chaos churned around us, the wind whipping my hair into my face.

"I do. You must trust me."

For some reason, I suddenly did. I took his hand. The second our skin touched, a door popped into existence behind him. He led me to it.

Before opening it, he turned to warn me. "After you pass through, don't look at me."

I nodded and stepped through the open door. On the other side, a jungle welcomed me. It was night, and the ground was wet from a recent rain. As I looked around, it all came rushing back. I was in Ice Prison where Kelly had held me against my will.

"Oh my God, Serena," I said with panic.

"I ended the demon's existence, but I had to let the night creature escape in order to save your life. Time was running out, and you were dying," a deep velvet voice said from behind me. I recognized it. Oberon, the king of the fae, was here with me. I felt his strong presence.

I resisted the urge to flip around and look at him. "Where was I?" Why did I relive the day I'd told Laurel I'd come to that hiking trip?

"To insert herself into your body without resistance, the demon temporarily locked your soul inside your subconscious, where you wouldn't be able to fight her. After I pulled her out of your body and eliminated her, you were trapped inside your subconscious, creating your own reality."

Made sense that my subconscious would choose that day to relive. If only I had changed my mind and said no, I wouldn't be in this nightmare.

"Why did you wait for my permission to take me out the door?" I asked.

"Forcing you out of your subconscious is dangerous. It might have killed you. It had to be your choice to step out and regain control of your body," he explained.

Feeling no pain, no more headaches or weakness, I glanced down at my palm. The dark magic was still there, and the number had jumped to 700. "I'm not sick anymore."

"I was able to heal your soul in this pocket dimension as it doesn't require using magic. It is now whole again," he said.

My mind was still hazy, but I remembered I hadn't died from a heart attack when my eyes had been on Oberon. "How come I could look at you earlier without dying?"

"I am a royal fae. My body contains an immense amount of magic, which your human eyes are incapable of translating. They perceive it as a tremendous fear. A fear that stops a human heart from beating. In your subconscious, your soul was looking at me, not your eyes," he answered.

I sighed, shaking my head in disbelief. "I can't believe you're here. You are actually here. Have you any idea how many times I've tried to contact you? You left me with no explanations. Why did you save me back then and now? How did you know I was in danger? Oh, and the tattoo, do you know who did this to me? Who ruined my—"

"Sydney!" Gideon's distant voice called out.

"Gideon?" I whispered in shock. What was he doing in the Jungle? How had he entered Ice Prison?

I opened my mouth to call back to him when Oberon spoke. "You should hear what I have to say before the night creature arrives here."

Confusion roiled through me as I wondered what that was about. "Okay, uh, I'm listening."

"Since the demon prisoner didn't have a body, she was too weak to completely digest the last soul she'd fed on."

"The last soul?" I repeated.

"Zoey's soul. I healed and freed it when I ended the demon's existence. However, without her body, it will soon be gone from this world. If you wish Zoey to live again, you must cast the night creature called Gideon out of your life.

"You'll be allowed to honor the deal you've made with him. Return to your dimension and give him your blood as you promised, but then you'd have to say your goodbyes. Should you accept my offer, I'll take Zoey's bones and soul to Earth, and with my magic, restore her body and put her soul inside. She will be returned safely to your parents. The memories of her recent ordeal will be erased. She won't remember the Ice Prison or the Hidden World."

"Sydney, where are you?" Gideon's voice was getting closer.

My head was swimming with questions, but only two came out of my mouth. "Why do I have to stay away from Gideon? And why are you helping me?"

"Decide quickly; time is of the essence." He ignored my questions, and it was clear he wouldn't answer them even if I asked again, so I dropped it. *Maybe the next time he shows up to save my life, I'll get more from him.*

"Well?" he said, and my mind went to his proposition. I didn't need to mull it over. Zoey would live, and it was all that mattered. Happy tears ran down my cheeks.

"Yes, okay. Please, hurry."

When I didn't feel Oberon's presence anymore, I shouted, "Gideon! I'm over here!"

A few moments passed before he emerged from the trees, his blue shirt covered with blood. On his face, he had many severe cuts, which had already started to heal.

"What happened to you? Are you okay?" I asked.

He closed the gap between us in a blink, and his gaze swept over me as if to check whether I was harmed.

Looking relieved, he answered, "I'm fine. But Kelly, not so much. I ran into her in the Jungle."

"Gideon, she's the real Ruler."

"I know. Djar is her brother."

At my surprised look, he said, "After you went to the party and I lost the signal from your tracker, I drove to the mansion, but I was too late. You, Kelly, and Brad were gone. I compelled Brad's men, and they told me that Kelly was behind the abductions of the girls and also the true Ruler. I got your location too.

"I took the bike and rode to the building where Brad kept you. There were dead bodies in water tanks and on the floor around the rooms. I didn't see you or Brad, so I returned to the mansion, killed the guards, and searched for Brad. He heard me coming and somehow decided it would be a good idea to play hide-and-seek with me. Doors were broken down, windows were shattered, and eventually he got the message that I wasn't in a mood for games.

"That filthy piece of a human came out of hiding. He willingly told me what he'd done to you and where I could find you in the Jungle. But before I left the mansion, I drank him dry, making sure the experience would be painful for him. After he died, I drove to Lydia, one of the few witches powerful enough to open a temporary gate to Ice Prison by using my energy.

"In the Jungle, I was searching for you when I encountered Kelly. She was running from something and reluctant to answer my questions about your whereabouts, so it got messy"—he nodded at his bloodied shirt—"and she eventually revealed everything before I drove a silver stake through her heart. Now we need to get to the portal before it closes."

I followed him through the forest, and after a few moments, we arrived at a gate to our dimension. To me, the gate was invisible; to him, though, it wasn't. He took my hand and led me through the portal. His living room gradually replaced the green of the forest until nothing remained of it—no towering trees, no moist air, no sound of animals. Ice Prison was gone, and I was back home.

Chapter 28

After we returned from Ice Prison, Gideon updated Thomas about Kyla. Seeking retribution against everyone responsible for her death, Thomas flew out to New Haven. They looked for Djar. After his sister died, he came out of his hiding place to search for her, so it only took Gideon and Thomas a few hours to track him down. While they went out there to kill him, I stayed at Gideon's house.

When Gideon got back, there was sorrow in his eyes. I told him how sorry I was about Kyla's death. He acknowledged it with a nod and retreated to his bedroom. I respected his wish to be left alone and went to my room. Feeling my eyes drifting closed, I lay down on the bed.

I slept more than ten hours, yet I still felt tired. To stay in bed was tempting, but I had things to do, promises to keep. With a deep sigh, I willed myself out of bed and went to the bathroom. While under the stream of hot water, I mused over what I was going to do next. Happiness flooded me at the thought of Zoey, alive. But it was mixed with another emotion. An unexpected emotion. After Gideon drew my blood, I'd have to leave his house and never see him again. Because of Oberon, and because that was our deal from the beginning. So why was I sad? It was not as if we were friends. And he was a vampire.

Well, it didn't matter. It had to be done. Then, I'd find a job and a place to live since I couldn't return home. A maniac was still watching my family, and I had dangerous dark magic on my hand. I wanted my family to live a normal life, a life where the supernatural world was just a fantasy.

Back in the bedroom, I dried myself off and put on jeans and a V-neck, long-sleeved shirt. I glanced at the time. It was eight p.m., and Gideon should be awake by now. It was time to uphold my end of our deal.

The smell of tomato and omelet caused my stomach to rumble as I climbed down the stairs. In the living room, Gideon held a plate of food as he walked out of the kitchen, his mood improved.

"I apologize for my lack of cooking skills. Obviously, human food is much more complicated than... well, vampires.'"

I took the plate from him and put it on the coffee table. "Thanks, but we need to talk."

"First, eat. Your body is weak, and I heard your stomach rumble." A short pause and a smile. "And don't worry, there are plenty of Ben & Jerry's waiting for you in the freezer."

"About our deal... It's time for me to give you my blood."

He picked up the plate from the coffee table and handed it back to me. "Not before you've eaten."

My empty stomach protested again, the sound loud and demanding. "Okay," I said and sat on the couch. Joining me, he drank blood from a glass that had been on the coffee table.

He eyed me while I ate, silent. When I finished, he chugged the rest of the red liquid. These were my final moments with him, and I needed to get more information.

"Gideon, I want to know, what is my blood for? And why did you kill all the US Rulers?"

He hesitated. "What do you know about the red dragon's blood?"

"Not much. Audrey said that if someone drinks it, he or she will never be on the dragons' list."

"With a magical vial, the red dragon's blood can be extracted from the person who drank it after he or she dies," he said. "The dragons are responsible for keeping the balance between good and evil. Without it, chaos will rule the streets. The four US Rulers endangered this balance, so I killed them to pull the dragon blood out. Contrary to popular belief, it can be destroyed. To cast a powerful spell that will make the red dragon blood disappear, Lydia needs two things. One, a sufficient amount of it—like the quantity the four Rulers consumed. Two, something powerful to draw on. Unfortunately, my energy wouldn't be enough."

"But my blood, which has strong dark magic in it, will be," I concluded.

"Blended with mine inside my body. This will provide Lydia the power and energy to do the spell."

"But what about the vial that Edwin hid? Damon is searching for it." I assumed Gideon knew the story about Edwin, the thief.

"He is," he replied. "Once he finds Edwin's vial, he's planning to drink from it and then duplicate the blood, risking the balance. I can't let that happen. I have to find the vial before he does, so Lydia can destroy the blood."

"Is it even possible to duplicate the red dragon's blood?"

"As far as I know, no," he said. "But I'm certain that Damon will somehow find a way. If he succeeds, it'd give him power and money. He could get whatever he wishes from any supernatural beings who would want to buy the blood."

Silence fell on the room as I had no more questions on this matter. Now it was time to give him my blood. I stared at him as I tucked my hair behind my ear and exposed my neck to him.

"It's all yours." I tried to keep my voice steady, my mouth dry. Would it hurt? What if it was painful? What if—

"Relax," he crooned, inching closer. His hand cupped my cheek before it trailed down along my neck. He cupped the back of my neck and tilted my head to one side, and his fangs came down. My heart raced when his mouth lowered to my throat. He licked my pulse point, and his teeth grazed my skin. I shuddered and gasped with anticipation before his fangs sank into my throat. I closed my eyes, bracing for pain. There was none.

If anything, waves of passion began to build inside me, and spirals of pleasurable warmth spread through my body as my blood spilled into his mouth. My insides curled and tingled with every pull of his mouth. I moaned. He tightened his grip and drank deeper. A jolt of heat seared through my body, a shiver of pleasure racing over my skin. *God, don't stop!* I begged in my head, but soon after, he did, and I almost groaned with protest. His tongue ran over the spot he'd drunk from. Then he pulled away from my neck.

"You taste delicious," he said, licking the trace of my blood from his lips. "I have to go to Lydia now before my body digests your blood." He must have seen the look of disappointment on my face, because a corner of his mouth lifted. "When I return, I'll finish what I've started," he added, brushing his fingers over my cheeks.

The next thing I knew, the French doors opened and closed, and he was gone. On the couch, I reached up to my neck and caressed the spot he had bitten. My skin was not broken or sore. There weren't any fang marks. His saliva had probably healed it.

A knock at the front door pulled me from my musings. Who could it be? I stood up and went to it.

"Who is it?" I said through the door.

"Miss Newbern?" a male voice asked.

"Who is it?" I repeated.

"Oberon sent me. I'm here to pick you up and take you to the airport."

Airport? I looked through the peephole. A man in his thirties wearing jeans, a sweater, and a coat, stood by the door.

I opened it with caution. He didn't seem as if he was about to attack me. My muscles eased.

"Oberon sent you?" I was surprised. "How do I know you really work for him?"

He raked a hand over his bright brown hair, and I noticed he didn't have pointed ears. His tired face grew impatient as I scanned him.

"Look, pretty face, I don't know the man, all right? A hot chick hopped into my cab an hour ago. Blonde, big boobs. She whispered some kind of mumbo-jumbo gibberish and boom—I can't fucking do anything other than drive over here and take you to the damn airport. I'm supposed to inform you that a cab driver will be waiting for you when you land in New York. He'll drive you home where you'll see your sister reunited with your parents."

Oh my God, Zoey... Oberon had done it! She was alive!

"Oh, and I'm also supposed to give you this," he added and handed me a brown envelope. I peeked inside. A large stash of money, a new ID, and one plane ticket to New York were in there.

"Okay, I'll go pack a bag."

"The blonde chick said to tell you not to pack anything. The money in the envelope is yours. You can buy whatever you need later."

"Fine, but I gotta write a note to someone. I'll be quick," I said and stepped inside the house to look for a pen and paper, then scribbled down a note for Gideon.

Hey,

I won't be here when you return. Now that our deal is over, it's time for me to leave. I wish you good luck with finding Edwin's vial and pray that you find it before Damon does. For everyone's sake.

Thank you for everything.

Sydney.

As I put the piece of paper on the coffee table, something tugged at my heart. I ignored it as I strode out of his house and out of his life. I climbed into the man's cab, and we drove off.

After I landed in New York, I met another cab driver at the airport. He held a sign with my name on it, and he too seemed under the influence of magic. When we reached my parents' house, he parked three houses down.

"Before you get out, take this." The driver handed me a baseball cap. "I'm waiting here until you finish with your business."

I put the hat on and stepped out of the car, walking in the direction of my parents' house. I stopped across the street from it, standing under a broken streetlamp emitting a weak flicker of light. My peripheral vision caught a movement. I turned and saw a beautiful blonde girl approaching me. Although it was cold outside she was clad in a thin jacket and a short black dress revealing long legs. She smiled at me, her eyes bright blue, the color of the morning sky, her long wavy hair touching her waist, her white skin glowing.

When she reached my side, she said, "My king wanted you to witness the safe return of your sister. He's swamped, so I'm here on his behalf. I apologize for the long ride, but since I'm not a royal fae, I don't have the ability of teleportation. On the plus side, you can look at me without any danger to your well-being." Her gaze moved to my parents' house. There was a long pause before she continued. "Right about now, not far away from here, a police officer, a friend of your father's, is noticing a disoriented girl walking inside the station.

"He recognizes her. 'Jesus, it's Newbern's daughter,' he says and calls your father. He's answering his phone at this instant." She tossed her hair over her shoulder, and a happy scream came from my parents' living room. "Your mother has just received the good news about Zoey. The officer is taking her to his car. In a few moments, she'll be on her way over here."

The front door of my parents' house opened, and they stepped outside, waiting for her on the sidewalk.

I took a step back and pushed the baseball cap down farther to shield my face from them. "What does Zoey think happened to her?"

"She thinks an obsessive admirer kidnapped her, forced her to drop out of school, and after a while, let her go without harming her. The memories of Ice Prison and everything related to it, like Brad and Kelly, have been erased from her mind. Her friend Izzy, who died, will not be in her memories as well," she answered.

"Zoey will still put herself in danger to look for me, as I don't plan on returning to my home soon. I can't. Not until I figure out who kidnapped me, and get rid of this dark magic inside me."

"My king assumed you wouldn't wish to contact your family in your current situation, hence the baseball cap. He ensured that Zoey will no longer feel the need to investigate your disappearance. To your family, you're missing, but they'll leave the search to the cops."

Good. Zoey would be safe and away from the supernatural world.

We waited about twenty minutes before a police car pulled up to the curb, and my sister got out.

My mother shouted, "My baby! My baby girl!" She ran to her. Zoey, in a coat and beaten jeans, hugged her. They cried with excitement and joy. Even my father, the tough detective, had tears in his eyes. He gathered both of them into his arms. They looked elated, and I smiled. Zoey was alive. Emotion clogged my throat as I wiped my own tears away.

"I've booked you a room in a hotel," the fae said. "It's under your name. The taxi driver will take you there when you're ready to leave. The money in the envelope is yours. Use it wisely, and remember: you will stay away from Gideon, the vampire."

I nodded, and she walked away. My parents and Zoey went inside the house and closed the door behind them. I took a deep breath. My heart ached that I couldn't join them.

I glanced around. Were they being watched at the moment? As I asked myself this question, I knew what my next plan had to be. *Find the man who destroyed my life. And get answers to questions like why he put dark magic in me, why it was counting down, and why it gave me martial art skills and physical strength.* Then I'd force him to de-spell the tattoo.

Until then, I couldn't come back here. In my search for that man, I'd be dealing with dangerous creatures that I did not want anywhere near my parents and Zoey. Not ever again. My family was safe now, and I intended to keep it that way.

I turned and walked back to the cab. When I slipped into the back seat, I stared down at the number on my palm. 700. I brought the image of my kidnapper to my mind. *Whoever you are, whatever you are, I am coming for you, and I swear to God I'll make you pay.*

"Miss, you ready to go?" the driver asked, looking in the rearview mirror.

"Yes, I am ready."

He stepped on the gas, and I looked outside the window. My house became smaller and smaller as we drove farther down the street. I placed my hand on the window glass. *I'll return someday. I promise.*

www.ingramcontent.com/pod-product-compliance
Lightning Source LLC
Chambersburg PA
CBHW021945120726
47992CB00001B/159